Changeling Press, LLC

ChangelingPress.com

Lady Troubles

Emily Carrington

Lady Troubles
Emily Carrington

ISBN: 978-1-60521-819-9

Publisher:
Changeling Press LLC
315 N. Centre St.
Martinsburg, WV 25404
ChangelingPress.com

Printed in the U.S.A.

Editor: Crystal Easu
Cover Artist: Angela Knight

The individual stories in this anthology have been previously released in E-Book format.

Table of Contents

Technical Difficulties (Lady Troubles 1) 4
    Chapter One...5
    Chapter Two 18
    Chapter Three...27
    Chapter Four...41
    Chapter Five 59
    Chapter Six...77
    Chapter Seven 97
    Chapter Eight...111
    Chapter Nine 123
Practical Difficulties (Lady Troubles 2).....................139
    Chapter One...140
    Chapter Two 152
    Chapter Three...165
    Chapter Four...180
    Chapter Five 192
    Chapter Six...199
    Chapter Seven 208
    Chapter Eight...223
    Chapter Nine 236
Tactical Difficulties (Lady Troubles 3) 243
    Chapter One...244
    Chapter Two 253
    Chapter Three...260
    Chapter Four...268
    Chapter Five 276
    Chapter Six...285
    Chapter Seven 292
    Chapter Eight...299
    Chapter Nine 306
Dedication 315
Emily Carrington...316
Changeling Press E-Books 317

Technical Difficulties (Lady Troubles 1)
Emily Carrington

Sonya is straight. She's also terrified of werewolves. So, when she's forced to work with a male-to-female transgender wolf, the last thing she expects is to fall in love. But, hey, not so fast. Falling in love with a werewolf means living in her pack, where first-time sex equals mating. For life.

Chapter One

The dragon had been brutalized. As Medical Technician Sonya Johnson worked over the corpse, she couldn't miss the signs. The poor dragon-in-human-guise was female. She'd given birth recently. Her distended stomach, open cervix, and other signs all bore witness to this.

Sonya whispered, "I think you were dead when most of these were inflicted." She'd quickly discovered the cause of death: a crushed skull that had occurred while the dragon was in human form. Now all she wanted was to be done chronicling the postmortem atrocities and see to it that the poor soul had a decent burial.

Sonya smiled just a little. Thinking of any dragon as a "poor soul" was a little like calling a lion a kitty cat. Dragons, like werewolves, she thought with a shudder, were known for taking care of themselves. Both apex predators of the magical world, for slightly different reasons, they were treated with respect and almost obsessive politeness by other magical beings and the few humans unlucky enough to know about their existence.

"Humans like me." Her smile was gone as she finished cataloging the last injury. Shaking her head, Sonya covered the body with a sheet and left the autopsy room. She locked the door before heading into her office.

All right, so it wasn't technically "her" office any more than the autopsy room belonged to her. But she thought of both as her property because she spent more time in them than anyone else. That was thanks to the doctoral-level degree she was seeking from SearchLight Academy in Reptilian Magical Creatures:

Treatment and Dissection. Unlike those who studied humans, magical creature experts were expected to have a wider knowledge base. The closest comparison Sonya could make was a general-practice physician. And even they weren't responsible for both the living and the dead.

She had just finished her second year of postgraduate work. It was May. She had a blissful ten weeks off for the summer. Of course, she was still expected to work on her dissertation, so "rest" wasn't in her vocabulary. But she wouldn't be attending biweekly meetings with this or that professor to discuss her research. She might even have considered a week away from the city of Tampa, where she worked, and its lesser cousin, the city of St. Petersburg, where she lived. But she hadn't scheduled any time off because she'd been too fixated on her dissertation to think beyond the next few days.

Someone knocked on the office door. Not closed completely and made of a light pressboard, the door opened a little more. Sonya caught sight of a skirt in a bold print and a tapered shoe. She called, "Come in."

A woman stepped inside, saying simply "Sorry to disturb you" -- and Sonya's mind went sideways. Not because there was anything particularly wrong with the voice. It was just that she wasn't used to hearing a slightly male-sounding voice coming out of a woman's body.

Transgender. That's what they call themselves. And, on the heels of that, *I hate it when someone says "they" about my people so I will not start out by thinking of this person as a part of "they." She's dressed as a woman. I'll call her "her."*

"Um," she said uncomfortably, "you're not. Please sit down."

The transgender person -- the woman, Sonya scolded herself -- didn't sit. Neither did she shut the door. "Thanks, but..." She looked briefly discomfited. "I'm Agent Brown. Maxine."

That surely wasn't the name you were born with. Oh, shut the fuck up! She doesn't want you staring, and you will get over yourself.

Sonya realized Maxine was waiting for a response. Her small, delicate and frankly attractive nose was turning slightly red, just like Sonya's did when she was embarrassed. "I'm sorry," she said, rising and extending her hand. "I'm Sonya Johnson, one of the medical techs."

The moment their hands touched, the hair on the back of Sonya's neck stood up. She pulled back rather quickly. "Um... um..." She looked away from the hand she'd shaken and into eyes that were startling in their beauty. Honey-brown and shadowed by long, thick lashes, they took Sonya's breath away. She forgot for a moment that her neck was prickling and smiled. "How may I help you?"

Maxine, who had taken a step forward to grip Sonya's hand, retreated at least that far. "Agent Wellington wants to see you when it's convenient." She hesitated before adding, "He's the head of Werewolf Watch."

Sonya shivered. She couldn't help herself. She hated werewolves. They were the craziest, most terrifying -- *Oh, get ahold of yourself. If you're being called, you specifically...* She met Maxine's eyes. "You *are* looking for me, right? Because Jenny Davis could --"

"I'm sorry. He wants you personally." She really did look empathetic. "If it helps, it will just be him, you, and me in a large conference room."

Sonya's particular skills were needed. She

specialized in dragons and basilisks. What could she possibly do for a werewolf? Because Wellington had to be a werewolf. Unlike in the Department of Dragons, with which Sonya worked on a regular basis, Werewolf Watch was stuffed to capacity with, well, what else? Werewolves.

Shit. That probably means this woman is a werewolf. She looked directly into Maxine's eyes, needing to know. "You're a werewolf too?"

Maxine nodded. "Agent Wellington said to tell you he understands your circumstances, whatever those are, and that he wouldn't call for you unless it was absolutely necessary. He also promises you can have a large conference room and it will only be the three of us; Agent Wellington, you, and me. We want to make you as comfortable as possible."

Whatever those are. She doesn't know. Sonya felt a little better. "Can he give me fifteen minutes to... to..." She glanced down at her report. *To finish my work* flashed across her mind, but it would take at least two hours to do that.

"I'll tell him you'll be up in thirty," Maxine said gently.

Feeling a little more comforted, Sonya said, "Thank you. I'll be up soon."

Maxine left, closing the door behind her. *Black, like me. But transgender and werewolf.* The three modifiers to the name Agent Maxine Brown hit one right after the other. Sonya sank into her chair and covered her face with her hands. If she was going to have a prayer of working with werewolves...

Her mind insisted on calling them monsters.

If she was going to have any hope in hell of working with those... people... she needed to calm down. So, instead of focusing on her report, Sonya began the deep breathing exercises a SearchLight therapist had taught her shortly after a werewolf nearly ripped her arm off.

* * *

Maxine was just leaving the frightened human's office when she heard the distant *ching* of elevator doors closing. She ignored it and started, slowly, away from the site of confrontation. It wasn't that she hated near-arguments, but the stench of MedTech Johnson's fear had shortened Maxine's breath and made her heart speed up.

The only things that had saved the encounter from becoming a meltdown were Sonya Johnson's refusal to dwell on her terror and the woman's distraction (bordering on obsession) about Maxine being trans. Mild telepathy could be more than a little helpful.

The sound of rubber wheels on tile caught Maxine's attention. Putting her thoughts about Sonya Johnson aside, she walked around a corner -- and saw a genie approaching.

To be fair, he wasn't dressed like a cartoon genie and, so far as she knew, there wasn't a stereotypical way for a wish-giver to walk or talk. In this case, Maxine wasn't even relying on her telepathy. Her nose told her what kind of magical creature was pushing the sheeted gurney. "Agent Morrison."

Blond-haired and blue-eyed, he flashed a stellar smile. "Luke, please. You have me at a disadvantage."

"Maxine Brown, field agent in Werewolf Watch."

The genie nodded. "Mark, er, Agent Tavery, found another pair. A dragon and a werewolf. They were discovered in Ybor City about an hour ago. I'm taking the dragon half to Sonya."

Obviously, Luke had worked with Sonya before,

to call her by her first name, and with such respect in his voice. "She's been summoned up to WW. Do my bosses know about the latest bodies?"

"Absolutely." Luke frowned. "Does Sonya know she's expected to go into the wolf's den, if you'll excuse the expression?"

"She does. I promised her a large conference room so she'll have distance from Agent Wellington and me."

Luke nodded and his frown smoothed out. "I'll leave them in the autopsy room."

Maxine looked down at the sheet-covered form and felt her gut tighten. If this turned out to be murder, as the first two killings had been... No one, not even a dragon, deserved to die before his or her time.

Luke said, "The werewolf half isn't a member of the Fehrna pack."

Not from Maxine's pack. Fehrna Susan, the only alpha in Tampa, had come here from Montana after the slaughter of '78.

"Michaela, your mate's beta, confirmed that the second wolf isn't from your pack either."

"What's the dragon's gender?"

"Female."

Like the first pair. A female dragon and a male werewolf.

Luke shook his head. "I don't understand why they're being killed in twos."

"Probably they killed each other. Either out of self-defense or hatred."

"They came all the way to Florida to do that?"

"Maybe they were both here for separate reasons and met by chance." Maxine frowned. "Although finding a second similar pair, female dragon, male werewolf, makes that less likely." She started past

Luke, heading for the stairs since traveling in an elevator was too confining.

But she stopped and turned. A question appeared like a floating neon sign in her head. "Agent Morrison, Luke, aren't you in the MMCD? Why are you delivering dead bodies?"

Luke chuckled. "The head of Miscellaneous Magical Creatures let me run this errand since he had nothing else for me to do."

This thought flitted from Luke's mind to hers. She didn't often get complete sentences. He must have been feeling his gratitude, or his love for his husband, intensely. *I'd do anything for my Mark but getting out of that cramped office… he was doing me a favor.*

Maxine felt a pang of sorrow. She missed having a mate who filled her with a sense of strong devotion.

Luke had reached one of the autopsy rooms. He raised his hand and waved it in front of the door. There was the sound of an invisible hand knocking and then the door opened even though the room, Maxine saw, was empty.

"MedTech Johnson is in her office," she told Luke.

He glanced over his shoulder. "I guessed as much." He touched his ear. "I can hear her breathing. Have a good day." He wheeled the gurney in.

As Maxine opened the door to the stairwell, her thoughts went back to Sonya Johnson and the fear rolling off her in waves. *Except for one instant. When our eyes met. Then she seemed… interested? Aroused?* Maxine shook her head. *I can't read humans very well. Just werewolves or half-wolves. Whatever she was feeling, she wasn't scared for a moment.* Did that mean Sonya Johnson had hope to be not afraid some day?

Maxine wished for it to be so. Both for Sonya's

sake and because, under the fear, the woman was attractive. *And probably straight. And at least somewhat intimidated by trans people.*

She reached the first landing. *In other words, she's not attainable.*

* * *

Sonya emerged from the stairwell. She was in the main building of the Tampa SearchLight campus. Her heart thundered and her breath was short. Sweat was nestled at her temples. *Any werewolf within a mile will be able to smell how panicked I feel.* She winced and tried to muffle her terror under a memory of the first-ever dolphin she'd touched. The remembered feeling of the mildly rubbery skin soothed her, and she looked around the foyer in which she found herself. It was decorated more like a human office building than she'd expected. There were vases on little tables in the corners, potted plants in other places, and pictures -- bright oils -- on the walls. Everything she saw made her feel better.

"Hi," said a soft, husky voice. "Welcome to the WW."

Sonya blinked in surprise. Was that the same voice that had spoken to her in her office? She looked into Maxine Brown's eyes and smiled. She sounded so much calmer than before. "Hi."

"I'm glad you're here. Please follow me." She, definitely she, even though her hips didn't sway, led the way out of the foyer and down a broad corridor with offices on both sides. Most of the doors were closed and that made Sonya feel better.

Sonya found herself studying the line of Maxine's shoulders. They were narrow, more like a woman's than a man's. The brightness of her blouse, a solid white like a cloud, contrasted with the cocoa of her skin, and her long skirt brushed gracefully just above delicate ankles. If Maxine hadn't possessed an Adam's apple and a male-sounding voice, she could have passed flawlessly into a group of women and disappeared.

And I'm looking at a woman *like that why?* Sonya felt herself blush. She hoped her nose hadn't turned red, that it was only a mild flush.

Maxine guided her into a generously appointed conference room. The technology quotient alone made Sonya jealous. She often had to deal with no more than a projector when presenting her findings to a group. This place had computer keyboards half hidden in wall openings and an LCD. "Such a big room for three."

"Like I said, we wanted to make you comfortable if we could." She paused. "I'll be your partner in this investigation." Maxine held up a hand. "But I'm dumping too much on your head. Let's wait for Agent Wellington."

The conference room door opened. A tall man in a suit -- presumably Agent Wellington, which meant he was also a werewolf, walked in. He smiled a little when he said, "No need to wait."

Standing, Sonya held out her hand. She was still scared, but the werewolf male's lack of growl or bite so far urged her to be polite.

He shook with her. "Thank you for coming up here, Ms. Johnson. All of our pictures of the deceased are here as well as all the data we've collected." He rounded the table, drew a wireless keyboard down into his lap, and began typing. "Maxine, if you would close the door? We should get started."

* * *

Maxine watched Wellington manipulate the computer. She didn't care much for what she thought of as "modern" technology. She didn't even own a car, preferring to walk -- although she sometimes regretted the six-block walk from her house to SearchLight's Tampa campus in August. Hell, from about mid-May until early October.

As images appeared on the screen, Maxine took over the briefing. It was Wellington's right, but he'd given it over before Sonya arrived, saying Maxine had a more soothing voice. Getting such a compliment from a high-ranking SearchLight agent *and* a fellow beta was flattering. Wellington, called Ashley John by his packmates in the local straight werewolf pack, shared her beta rank, although the Fehrna eros pack was much smaller than the straight pack to which Wellington belonged.

Maxine stood and walked to the far end of the conference room, both to give Sonya space and so she could pick up a pointer. The first thing to appear on the screen was an image of the United States, specifically north of the Mason-Dixon line. "There have been rumors circulating for the last year that werewolves in the northern half of the United States are disappearing. They're also vanishing from the southernmost parts of Canada, although there are fewer werewolf packs in Canada as a rule because of the high dragon population."

The map changed, showing all of Canada. "The last two or three months have seen rumors about dragon disappearances. They may have gone missing a year ago, like the werewolves, but we don't have as many friendly channels open with the dragons as we do with the werewolves."

"It's not for lack of trying," Sonya said. Then, smiling a little self-consciously, she added, "At least that's what Agent Tavery says."

Maxine caught the name *Mark* from Sonya's mind before she said Agent Tavery, and Maxine was left to marvel that the head of the Department of Dragons was on a first-name basis with a technician. Not that there was anything inherently "lower" about a tech's position. It was just that, in Maxine's experience, higher-ups didn't take the time to make friends with their subordinates.

The map changed to a street in Ybor City, which was a section of Tampa. "This is Junction Avenue," Maxine told Sonya. "It's a poverty-level street in a similar neighborhood. "Eleven days ago, a dead female dragon and a dead male werewolf were found together behind an abandoned house. They were both in human form.

"The second pair, also female dragon, male werewolf, were found this morning. They were also in human guise."

"Now I know why you wanted me," Sonya said.

Maxine blinked.

Sonya smiled a little. "It's because of my fear of werewolves. When dealing with any werewolf pack we might have to question, I'll come across as an outsider with less knowledge than I actually possess about werewolf physiology. Werewolves, like dragons, are secretive by nature." She paused, seemed to remember she was talking to two werewolves, and added, "Because you have good reason. But my apparent lack of knowledge may encourage those we question to reveal more than they would otherwise."

Sonya was right about werewolves hiding themselves, both from humans, who didn't know about any magical creatures by and large, and from other magical beings. Their lack of cooperation was one of the reasons they were so far behind in science.

Like being unable to give me hormones to begin my change from male to female. To Sonya, she said, "I thought your specialty was dragons."

"And basilisks, but I'm in the middle of my second year of doctoral studies, and that includes a required second concentration. I figured I could work on dead wolves without triggering my fear." She snorted again, lightly. "It's not quite that simple."

Maxine was impressed. "You're working to challenge your panic. That's courageous."

Sonya straightened a little in her chair. "I refuse to be ruled by my past." She looked embarrassed. But she shrugged it away, tossing her head a little, and asked, "How can I help?"

Wellington said, "It's mostly a matter of questioning, at least to start with. You're supposed to present, at least to other magical creatures, just as you are: SearchLight agents looking for answers. To humans, of course, you'll present as police or FBI, whatever the situation calls for, seeking the same."

Maxine took over. "We'll probably start with the people who found the second pair of bodies."

Sonya was silent for a moment. "Are you a tracker, Agent Brown?"

"No. I've led a few investigations. There's a lot of crossover in most departments."

"Not in the medical field." But then Sonya added, "Although we're trained as nurses and coroners, so that's similar."

Agent Wellington said, "Maxine will give you a copy of all of our notes."

Sonya nodded and looked at Maxine. "I'll send you my medical reports also. We should probably meet to discuss them. Tomorrow?"

"Sure," Maxine answered, admiring the guts it

must have taken Sonya to make that suggestion. "Are you a morning person?"

"Definitely. As long as there's coffee involved." Sonya smiled a little and some of the tension so obvious in her shoulders released. "Eight?"

That was a full hour before work. Maxine shuddered. "Eight-thirty?"

Sonya actually laughed. "It's a date."

Chapter Two

At seven-thirty the next morning, Wednesday, Maxine stood in front of her full-length bedroom mirror and grinned at her nude body. Her penis, which was often as much a source of annoyance as it was of pleasure, was half erect. *You're getting tucked, mister, so you'd better behave yourself.* She grinned even more broadly. It amused her to call different parts of her body "mister" or "miss," especially her nipples and dick.

Maxine's cock had a reason for being awake; she'd had a strangely erotic dream. Strange because it took place in a generic doctor's examining room, a place Maxine couldn't imagine as being arousing. But in the dream, Sonya Johnson had been there. Dressed in nothing more than a white lab coat -- like the one she'd been wearing yesterday over red scrubs -- and a pair of half-inch heels that made her feet look delicate. Her breasts had been hidden by the scrubs. In her sleep, Maxine saw the round and welcoming melons only half sheltered by the lab coat. They were the same rich brown as her face, and the nipples were larger than Maxine's, firm little pebbles that Maxine longed to take between her lips.

In the dream, Sonya had bent over the examining table, slipped her hand between her legs, and started masturbating. It was a glorious image. The shifting of the lab coat was a sensual counterpoint to the movement of Sonya's cocoa-dark fingers. Her short cap of black hair stirred a little as she bobbed up and down on her hand. Then she looked up and smiled directly into Maxine's eyes. "I want you to touch me."

Maxine couldn't move at first.

Sonya laughed. "Your ears still work, don't they,

werewolf? Come over here and pleasure me."

Maxine yanked her body into motion. She crossed on wobbly knees to Sonya's side. "Do you…" Her voice failed her. Damn it! She coughed. "Do you like penetration?"

"Not yet. Just caress my nub." She caught Maxine's hand and brought it down to the juncture between her legs. "Touch me."

The room was full of the smell of sex, heady and wild. Maxine stared into Sonya's light brown eyes and bit her lip uncertainly. "Sonya, are you sure?" She knew full well that Sonya would answer however Maxine wanted her to answer, because this was a dream. But if it was a dream, why was the aroma so intense and the contrast between lab coat and skin so fetching and sharp?

"Touch me."

That was when Maxine had woken, hard and needy. She'd put on a condom, refusing to mess the sheets she'd changed only on Monday, and stroked herself to completion, imagining that her fist was Sonya's hand. She'd played a long time with the slit in her glans, the closest thing she had to a clit.

Now, standing before the mirror, Maxine ran her hands up her legs, testing for hair growth. She could go another day without shaving. She tucked her penis and then pulled up her panties. It was an uncomfortable endeavor that nevertheless made her feel more female each time she did it. With her penis-bulge largely disguised, she smiled at herself. Even with her flat chest, the lack of hormones, and arms naturally muscled because of her werewolf nature, she still looked female.

Maxine dressed more quickly after this prolonged beginning. She wanted to be at Sonya's office, if at all possible, before the human. She wanted to fight her way past her own distaste of early mornings with something that would make them both smile. Coffee would probably do that all on its own, but Maxine wanted to bring her a treat.

Because a tiny part of my heart is already crushing on her. She felt her skin grow hot and laughed a little.

She was dressed by five minutes to eight. She left her apartment and met her alpha, Fehrna Susan, at the stairs. "Good morning, alpha."

Susan flashed her a tired smile. "I thought you usually didn't leave until quarter to nine."

Maxine felt her cheeks heat up. "I have an early meeting."

"That you're looking forward to," Susan said as she started down the stairs ahead of Maxine.

"She's… attractive."

"Wolf?"

"Human."

Susan made a disapproving noise. "Playing with poison there."

"She's straight," Maxine admitted.

"Does she know you're trans?"

"She does."

"At least she's a perceptive human." Susan chuckled. "It could be worse. Just watch yourself. And remember: just because she might like what's under your skirt, she might not like the idea of being with someone who thinks of herself as a female first."

They'd reached the outside door. Susan made for her car. She worked at the hospital near the airport. There, they didn't call her Fehrna. That was a werewolf honorific, given to only the alpha of a pack and by which all the wolves under that leader were known. To the people at the hospital, patients and staff alike, she was Dr. Susan Roberts.

Before Maxine could head toward the front of the building, her alpha called, "Be careful."

Maxine smiled a little and waved. "I'll be fine," she murmured. "Sonya's not even interested in me." Nevertheless, a flutter of wings settled in her stomach.

At the coffee shop -- a free trade, locally owned place that had coffee beans sent straight from the source -- there were four people in line ahead of her. Maxine had time to choose the treats she would bring.

Humans -- especially human women -- are supposedly obsessed with counting calories. That probably means I shouldn't get anything too sugary. She eyed the menu and spied breakfast sandwiches. *Those will do.* But then she saw raspberry-chocolate scones and flaky, French croissants. *A few of those are going to come along.*

Reaching the front of the line a few minutes later, she ordered four large coffees -- three for Sonya, just in case -- with a cup of half and half on the side. With permission, she loaded her pockets with sugar packets. Then she bought two breakfast sandwiches, two scones, two croissants, and a miniature apple pie that caught her attention.

Loaded down and wondering if she'd gone slightly overboard, Maxine walked the rest of the way to work. Halfway across campus, passing the garage exit, she saw Agent Luke Morrison and the genie's lover. Maxine inhaled, smelled dragon, and knew it was Agent Mark Tavery, the only dragon working at this campus.

"Do you want some help?" Luke took the flimsy drink carrier from her. "Where are you headed with enough breakfast for five?"

"Five genies, maybe," Mark said as he helped Maxine with one of the bags. "One lone dragon." He smiled. "Or werewolf. Would have it gone in moments."

"It's for Sonya. MedTech Johnson."

Luke's golden eyebrows shot up. "How romantic."

Maxine's cheeks heated. "Go away." She made to grab for her drinks.

"We'll escort you to the elevator and then get out of your hair," Mark said.

His discretion relieved her mind. The rumor mill probably wouldn't be started by *him*. She darted a look at Luke and muttered, "She's afraid of werewolves. Please don't tease."

Luke stopped grinning. "I would never. Sonya's a good friend."

Convinced, Maxine thanked him.

* * *

It was eight thirty-five. Maxine was five minutes late. Even though this meant Sonya had been given extra time to meditate, she was irritated. And she was honest enough with herself to admit that her frustration had very little to do with the clock.

I don't know what to call Maxine. I mean, I can't just say "Maxine, Maxine" instead of "she" or "Maxine's" instead of her or hers. That's going to get annoying. Granted, Sonya had thought of Maxine as "she" the day before, but now she'd had a night to think about it. She was grateful she hadn't been asked to assign Maxine a gender. True, she *looked* female, but she sounded male. What did she want to be called? Sonya had the nagging feeling that Maxine had referred to gender in some way, but she couldn't remember what pronoun had been used.

Why was it Sonya's responsibility to ask? *Because it's polite. Wouldn't I want someone to call me by my proper title?* She thought of her coming doctorate and how she was looking forward to everyone calling her Dr. Johnson.

At eight thirty-seven, there was a soft knock on her partially closed door. Maxine stood out in the hallway. She was carrying what looked like half a coffee shop.

Sonya was unsure if she could bring herself to reprimand Maxine for being late. Before she could gather either her anger or her wits, Maxine spoke.

"I brought a bunch of breakfast-y things."

Sonya took one of the bags, feeling it was her responsibility to at least act gracious. "Thank you." Then she caught the smell of raspberries and chocolate and she took in the second bag with full awareness and the *four* cups. "How much coffee does a werewolf need?"

"Just a cup. But I wasn't sure how much you could use." Maxine smiled tentatively. "There are croissants and scones and a little apple pie as well as some breakfast sandwiches." She proffered the tray. "Take as many as you want. I brought a sealed container of creamer and a lot of sugar because I didn't know what you like."

Anyone who is so thoughtful deserves the truth out of me. She walked around Maxine and closed the door. "Thank you." She noticed how uncertain Maxine looked and said, "I really do appreciate it." Still, the werewolf appeared nervous. Probably Sonya's question wasn't going to make her feel any better, but, what the Hell. They were both disconcerted. "May I ask you a question about your, um... gender preference?"

Maxine blinked and her mouth opened. She coughed a little. "Oh, I like women."

Sonya blushed. "That's, um, nice, but that's not what I meant. What do I, um, call you?"

"Maxine." Then the trans wolf laughed. "All right, I'll take it easier on you. Please use 'she' and 'her.' And, before you have to figure out a way to ask, yes, I still have all my male parts, but I feel and act female. I just don't want to go through the surgery, not when my people's medical knowledge is so far behind humans and humans themselves haven't perfected the procedure." She winked. "I'd rather still feel pleasure rather than end up like *Hedwig and The Angry Inch*."

Sonya blushed again, or maybe she had never stopped, but she found that she liked Maxine's frank delivery. She set down the bag with the treats in it and held up her coffee cup. "Cheers to being a woman."

Maxine grinned and they touched cups.

"Since we *are* being so honest," Sonya went on, "can you tell me why you're so nervous?"

"I don't know much about humans," Maxine admitted. "But even if I did, I'm so worried about scaring you because of, well, whatever happened to you."

Sonya retreated behind her desk, her favorite bit of furniture in the office. "I was mauled when I was a kid. Well, about twelve, if you can still call that a kid. My mama didn't. They considered me an adult at about four." She waved a hand. "I'm not saying that to make you feel sorry for me. It's just that my parents, well…"

"It must have been hard on them, not knowing anything about werewolves, to find out you were almost killed by one." Maxine remained by the door.

"Please sit down." She added, smiling, "I won't bite."

"That's not the problem," Maxine answered, but

she did as Sonya asked, setting the second bag on the desk.

Sonya tried for levity. "You won't be biting me either, so we're both safe." In spite of her brave words, she still felt better with the desk between them. "They didn't believe me, that I was attacked, until SearchLight agents arrived at their door to offer me counseling. After I got over my initial nightmares, about three years after the event, I started becoming really interested in other magical creatures." She shrugged, feeling uncomfortable. "I guess dragons caught my fancy because they're the natural enemies of werewolves."

"They didn't believe you?" Maxine looked confused. "But... you'd been badly injured. What did they think happened?"

"Mama thought it was a big dog. I grew up in a rough neighborhood where people kept attack dogs." She shivered a little. "They still do. I'm glad I moved away."

"What did your dad think happened?"

"Well, he's not my real dad, but he took care of me for years. He never said one way or the other, but until he died, he was always there to gentle me out of a bad dream. He died about six months after I was mauled. Heart disease."

"I'm sorry."

Not knowing why she was saying it except that Maxine was easier to talk to than she'd expected, Sonya said, "Considering how drunk or out of it my mama was all the years I was growing up, having Papa Vern around was a huge comfort."

Maxine reached for Sonya's hand, but then she froze. "I'm sorry. I just --"

Sonya caught Maxine's fingers and squeezed.

The werewolf's skin was soft, the opposite of what Sonya had expected. Even though they'd shaken hands before, she hadn't taken any notice. Maxine had short but strong fingers. Sonya held on for probably longer than she should have, but she was fascinated. And that interest comforted her. "Thank you," she said as she finally let go.

Maxine smiled and left her hand on the desk. "You're overcoming your fear by leaps and bounds."

Sonya laughed a little. "Only with you, I think." She picked up one of the large cups of coffee. "You said there was creamer?"

Maxine handed it over. "I'm sorry your whole family wasn't there for you. That's one good thing about SearchLight. We're a family, especially within each department."

"Does that mean I can call you my sister?"

"Definitely."

Sonya smiled broadly. She felt warm inside. "I've got the notes you sent me. And I have a few questions based on the dragon dissection I did."

Maxine took a sip from her cup. "Coffee first. Then work."

Sonya chuckled. "I won't argue with that."

Chapter Three

Two months later, in the terrible heat of July, Maxine followed Sonya into the gardens on SearchLight Tampa campus. These were a collection of five distinctly themed plots: a rock garden (complete with fountains), an herb garden, a flower garden, and one comprised completely of decorative shrubbery. The fifth was where they sat now: a sort of "wild" patch of earth with tall trees and tangles of weeds and bushes between. There were three benches, widely spaced apart, and it was to one of these that Sonya went, Maxine following. She carried her lunch tray while Sonya bore a lunch bag.

Being assigned to compare notes every few days during the last eight weeks, they'd quickly become friends. They took turns bringing the coffee in the morning and they ate lunch together every noon. Sonya wasn't comfortable with werewolves in general, but she made it obvious that she liked Maxine.

Sonya unpacked a fried chicken breast and a large salad. She set the covered salad to her right on the long bench and smiled up at Maxine, indicating a seat for her.

Maxine settled down, the tray on her knees. They began to eat in silence.

Sneaking a glance at Sonya about ten minutes in, Maxine saw she had finished the chicken and was digging into the salad with gusto.

Sonya caught her looking and smiled. "I guess werewolves don't eat vegetables." She winked. "Just kidding, I know they do but more meat is essential for their bodies to run efficiently." She dug in her lunch bag and produced another fried chicken breast. "Do you want this?"

Maxine blinked. She liked chicken, although fresh-killed rabbit was her favorite. "You don't want it?"

"I'm almost full."

"Werewolves can hear and smell lies," she reminded her friend.

"I'm confused. I wasn't lying."

Maxine heard the truth in that statement. "Say it again."

"I'm almost full." Sonya paused. "I have a little snack cake in my pouch. That's what I'm hungry for."

Maxine took the chicken. "Even lie detectors can be wrong."

"For the record, I'm a Christian, so I try not to lie."

Maxine felt her hackles rise. Her shoulders stiffened and she'd drawn back a little before she could stop herself.

Sonya looked confused but then she smiled. "I guess you feel about Christians sort of the way I feel about werewolves, huh?"

"I was never attacked by a Christian, at least not more than verbally," Maxine answered evasively.

"Not all Christians *act* like the loving people Jesus wanted us to be." Sonya frowned a little.

"I didn't mean to be judgmental."

Sonya touched Maxine's knee. "If I'm allowed to be afraid of werewolves but I like you, can you dislike Christians but still like me?"

The hand on her knee sent shivers up Maxine's spine. Without thinking, she leaned over and planted a soft kiss on Sonya's cheek. Feeling herself blush even as a pleasant knot of enjoyment settled in her stomach, Maxine said, "I'm sorry."

Sonya, her nose red but her eyes full of laughter,

answered, "You're lying." She giggled. "Don't take this the wrong way, but that kiss didn't bother me. It doesn't mean I want another one." She began eating the snack cake. "Will we go out this afternoon to knock on doors and ask for witnesses to the body disposal?"

Maxine, who could feel a tingle of sensation on her lips, struggled to get her wits back. There had been another dragon/werewolf pair murdered last week, bringing the total up to three duos. This one had also been found in Ybor City, comprised of a male werewolf and a female dragon. She and Sonya were being sent to do questioning. "Yes, let's go out after lunch."

"Shouldn't I finish the autopsy on the dragon so we know what questions to ask?"

Maxine smiled. "Another medtech, Jenny, did them. They're on your desk. I thought it would save time since we were talking over the other deaths all morning. According to Jenny, they're very similar."

"You're a step ahead of me."

Unable to read Sonya's expression or voice, Maxine tried a joke. "Only because I have longer legs."

Sonya chuckled. She lifted her hand, let it hang in the air for a moment, and placed it on Maxine's knee as she had before. "Come on, Long Legs. Let's see what the differences between the reports are."

* * *

Sonya drove them from the center of Tampa's business district to Ybor City. She immediately liked the architecture, but she could also see that this part of the lightning capital of the world wasn't as well looked-after as others. She'd been in Ybor City before and felt protective of the place because it reminded her of the neighborhood where she'd grown up. How must Maxine, who made Sonya think of a high-class sort of person, see all this disrepair?

Maybe Maxine was reading her mind because she said, "Seeing how humans are forced to live in some places makes me glad I'm a werewolf. Our alphas take care of us, make sure we get into good jobs, and shelter those who just can't find work no matter how hard they try."

Maxine's reaction was one of empathy rather than condemnation. Sonya liked the wolf for that. "We're almost there," she said when the silence had stretched out. "I don't know if we'll find anyone home in the middle of the day."

"Maybe night-shift workers. Of course, then we'll be waking them up." Maxine paused before adding, "I'd like to lead the questioning, if that's all right with you."

Sonya nodded. "Definitely." She found a place to park. According to the pictures of the crime scene, they were about half a block from where the bodies had been dropped. "Will we canvass the entire block?"

"At least that far." Maxine got out, checked the holster Sonya hadn't noticed until now, and then closed the car door.

Sonya got out quickly and rounded the car. "You're packing?"

Maxine blinked. "It's standard procedure. I'm not expecting to need it."

"But you're a" -- she lowered her voice -- "werewolf. You don't need a weapon."

"If I can avoid making my species common knowledge, it'll be better for everyone."

They were walking toward the first dilapidated house. The stairs creaked when they climbed. Sonya hung back, watching Maxine. The wolf approached the door and knocked, at the same time pulling a badge out of her pocket.

Remembering that they'd both been given badges, Sonya followed suit. Looking at it, she saw that it identified her as MedTech Johnson, SearchLight, but she knew that most humans would see it as belonging to Tampa's police.

The door opened and an old man, probably on the cusp of retirement if he hadn't reached it already, looked at them. His eyes were sharp; no squinting or glasses. He limped, using a cane. "Wha'choo want?"

Maxine held up her badge and said pleasantly, "There was a disturbance on your block last night. I was wondering if you saw or heard anything."

The elderly man scowled. "You're talking about them co'pses. A guy and gal. Yeah, I saw the truck dropped 'em off. Big panel job. I didn't approach no co'pses, though." He hesitated, and then added, "I didn't call no police. None of my business. They's dead already. I *did* go out to check. Just to make sure they'uz beyond help."

"Do you know what color the panel truck was?" Maxine asked. She'd produced a notebook and was writing very fast.

"Light colored. They ain't many workin' streetlamps down here."

"Do you know what time it was when you saw the bodies?"

"Still dark."

"Thank you so much for your time."

The man closed the door without responding.

As they made their way back down the walk, Maxine said, "I didn't expect to get so much so soon."

There was no one home at the next three houses, but Maxine still looked confident that they'd find someone. "One of those places" -- she cocked a thumb over her shoulder --"had at least three people at home. But I could smell meth. They definitely didn't want to talk to the cops."

Sonya smiled a little. "People can't get away with much around you, can they?"

Maxine smirked. "It's a hazard, having a wolf sniffing up your trail."

At the next house, this one a duplex, the house on the right was empty. But a woman came to the door of the left side. She just looked at them without saying anything for a moment. But then she grunted, "Abe called. Says you're trying to find out about those poor people in the middle of the street. I didn't see much, but I did go out with Abe to see if they were dead. He called me, you see, so's he could have a witness and he wouldn't be accused of anything. The truck was gone by the time I got outside, but it had a big diesel engine. Woke me up."

"Thank you, ma'am," Maxine said. "Do you know about what time this was?"

"Two thirty-six according to my clock."

After saying goodbye, they kept going down the street. "You're really good at this," Sonya said. "You barely have to say anything."

"In my experience, most people want to talk about something horrible they've seen. I think it's a comfort to them."

Sonya frowned. She had never wanted to talk to the police when one of her family members was injured or in trouble.

"Family's different, of course," Maxine went on as if she'd picked up on the thought. "We always want to protect our family and we often think that involves using our silence to keep them safe."

"You're not reading my mind, are you?" Sonya

asked.

"Well, sort of." Maxine spoke quietly. "My telepathy isn't very sharp or strong, but I can pick up the occasional stray thought. I don't even read emotions like a psychic vampire. I just get things as if you'd spoken them." She paused and then added, "That bit about family, in case you're wondering, didn't come from me spying on your brain. I just know how protective most people are of their kin. Or their pack. Plus, well… I saw the look on your face and took a guess."

"I *do* have a really expressive face. I could never keep anything from my mother when I was a child." As if confiding a secret, she murmured, "By the time I was ten, I'd lost two siblings to drugs. My mama is now so drunk most of the time that she doesn't bother to notice me."

"I think one of the sayings in AA is that users don't need a reason to use. But if anyone had a reason, it sounds like your mother did."

Touched because this was exactly how she thought of her mother's addiction in her kinder moments, Sonya caught Maxine's hand briefly and squeezed. "Thank you."

They walked up the next walk to a single-family home. Maxine knocked on the door and Sonya settled back to watch her work.

The woman who opened the door was younger than those they'd met so far. And she had the added distinction of being the first to wear sunglasses. It was strange, Sonya thought, considering how dim her house looked through the sheet curtains. Then again, maybe the woman's eyes were just extremely sensitive. Sonya had read about certain eye conditions that made seeing in specific kinds of light difficult.

"Go away," the woman snapped.

Maxine began, "Ma'am, we're with --"

"I don't care if you're with the president himself, nigger dyke bitch. Get off my porch." And she slammed the door in Maxine's face.

Sonya stared, unbelieving. But then she saw Maxine's shoulders shaking and she pulled herself together. She rested a hand on Maxine's arm. "Come on."

Maxine turned blank eyes above a frozen-in-place polite smile on her.

Sonya grasped Maxine's shoulders. "Don't," she said firmly. "Don't go there." She tugged Maxine down off the porch.

"Go to hell!" the woman screamed from an upper window.

Sonya did something rather unwise, considering that anyone, anywhere, could be armed in this day and age. She showed the woman her middle finger.

Then, pulling herself back from the brink where she wanted to start shouting at the rude ass, she took Maxine's hand and guided her away.

Maxine tried to pull free. "She'll think you're a d-d…"

"I don't care what she thinks," Sonya told her. "We're done for the day. Someone else can come and finish this street, or else we can come back tomorrow." She reached across her body so she was holding Maxine's left hand with her own left. Then she put her right arm about the werewolf's shoulders. "Let's take the scenic route back to work."

* * *

Two Mondays later, after a stormy weekend, sleep-wise, Sonya dragged her butt out of her car. She locked her vehicle, an eight-year-old four-door in excellent shape, and headed across the parking garage.

She'd been carefully not thinking about the reason for her restlessness when her mind produced a simple, powerful image: Maxine, standing shirtless and beautifully black against a white-walled background. She wasn't wearing the fake boobs that she did at work, but neither was her chest hairy. Sonya had never liked men with a lot of hair.

In one of her dreams over the weekend, Sonya had walked in on Maxine while she was in the process of taking her shirt off. All the buttons were undone and the clothing lay open. It was a peacock blue, that shirt, and it complemented the soft and close-to-ebony color of Maxine's skin. Her coloring put Sonya in mind of the 90 percent cocoa candy bars she enjoyed from time to time. She longed to put her tongue to that skin because she might be able to make Maxine shiver with delight.

She leaned against a pillar with her eyes closed and relived the feel of the soft, peacock blue shirt under her fingers. She'd touched that blouse once. The day Maxine had kissed her cheek, Sonya had felt the silkiness of what she wore over her fake boobs.

There was a bra, full in the cups, under the shirt, but when Maxine shrugged out of the blouse, the bra and, presumably, the false breasts, disappeared. Sonya was left gazing at a hairless, well-muscled chest. She had dropped her gaze and seen a flat belly.

Beyond this point, unfortunately, her mind seemed unwilling to go, at least while Sonya slept. She'd woken from several similar dreams aroused. She'd masturbated to the thought of Maxine's chest and nothing more. She occasionally thought of Maxine's penis, and though this excited her a little, it was the play of peacock blue against elegant dark brown that made her come.

Shaking her head, Sonya came out of her reverie and started walking again. In truth, it wasn't just hairy men she didn't like. She didn't like most men. They seemed designed for nothing more than lounging around, getting high, and screwing others behind your back. She *knew* all men weren't like that, but for the most part she'd only found gay men measured up to her idea of what a real man should be. When she fantasized -- not masturbated -- she tended not to think of anything specific then except for the smooth glide of her finger over her clit -- she pictured a man like Mark Tavery, only black.

And if that makes me racist, so be it.

She knew Mark was gay and very happy with his husband, Luke. But he was kind, sweet, thoughtful, and intellectual. All the things she wanted in a life partner.

All things, her mind whispered, that Maxine had in spades.

"But I am *not...*" She realized she was speaking aloud and shut her mouth. *I am not going to be attracted to a woman. Female werewolf. Whatever. Even if she does have a penis, she's female first. Female in her thoughts and actions, female in her reactions.*

Wasn't that what she liked about Mark's husband, Luke? Mark was an alpha, Type A personality, but Luke was sensitive. Gentle.

Maxine considers herself a woman. And I will not be a lesbian. I don't like pussy.

Maxine has a penis, her mind whispered.

But she's a she. End of discussion.

Dreams about Maxine's well-toned chest aside, she refused to fantasize about the wolf. She opened the door at the bottom of the stairs and saw Maxine waiting for her by "her" office door. "Good morning." Sonya felt herself blush and tried to walk briskly past the feelings that prompted the reaction. "How are you?"

Maxine held up the two large cups of coffee. Sonya knew one cup was laced with cream. She offered Maxine a real smile. "Thank you." Taking the cup, she asked, "How was your weekend?"

Maxine didn't look directly at her. "Eventful."

"In a good way or --"

"A very private way. I shouldn't have even mentioned it."

Sonya teased, "Busy with a lady friend?"

"Busy with my own hand."

Sonya gaped a moment, but then laughed. "Me too, girl. Me too."

* * *

Later that morning, Maxine and Sonya climbed the stairs out of the basement hallways that comprised the medical section of the Tampa campus. There were two other medical stations in the organization, but they held little more than a first aid kit. Even the doctors and nurses had to be called for.

Walking behind Sonya, Maxine appreciated the swing of Sonya's hips clad in beautifully tailored red slacks. At some point over the last week, she'd dumped her scrubs. The short jacket she wore fitted her exquisitely and matched her pants perfectly. Her full dimensions -- hips, butt, not-too-narrow waist -- all suited her broad and lovely face.

By contrast, Maxine was built like a dude: square. She often found it difficult to find attractive, feminine clothes that fit her masculine frame. Luckily, there was a seamstress in her pack who didn't mind altering things as long as Maxine gave her plenty of notice.

They emerged from the stairwell and walked, side-by-side, toward the first floor exit. Maxine glanced at Sonya and saw she was smiling slightly. "Want to share?"

Sonya smirked. "I don't know you well enough to share my nighttime fantasies."

I wonder what you'd do if you knew my *fantasies were about you.* Maxine pulled her mind out of the gutter. "Will you be all right in the conference room again?"

"We're meeting with Agents Wellington" -- her smirk increased --"and Mark Tavery, right?"

Maxine nodded.

"I'll feel a little safer with Mark there. That whole he's-a-dragon thing." She darted a look at Maxine. "It'll help that you're there too."

Maxine knew she was glowing as they entered the main campus building, heading toward the stairs that led up to the second floor. She walked ahead of Sonya to act as a barrier and guard.

"You really need to muffle your terror, little rabbit," was the first thing that greeted them when they emerged on the second floor. "You make me want to hunt."

Maxine glared at Daryl Hendricks. "Back off." She sensed Sonya retreating to have her back against the stairwell door.

Daryl licked his lips. "Her fear tastes absolutely *mahvelous.*"

His mate, Carol, stepped around the nearest corner and showed both Maxine and Sonya her eyeteeth. "Positively delectable."

"Back the fuck off," Maxine snarled. She widened her stance and bent her knees, setting herself up as an impenetrable wall. But she was fully aware that she could do nothing about their words.

Sonya said in a shaking voice, "Aren't you ashamed of yourselves? This is the sort of behavior SearchLight works against."

Carol laughed and Daryl said, "First, you stop smelling like a scared rabbit. Then I'll --"

"Shut the fuck up," Maxine ordered. She had little authority over members of other packs and despite the edict by the alpha above all alphas that all packs were now equal, she had even less with members of straight, what were still called traditional packs. But, she *was* a beta. "Get on with your idiotic lives and leave her alone."

"Well, *we* got told off," Carol said to her mate.

Sonya said, "Hi, Agent Wellington," and both Daryl and Carol jumped.

Wellington wasn't there of course and both wolves glared at Sonya, obviously furious at being fooled.

But before either of them could start in on her again, an office door opened and Agent Tavery walked out. "The threats stop now, Hendricks." He stepped between the mated pair and Maxine. "Get about your business before I *do* involve your beta. I'm sure Wellington would love a chance to sanction you considering you're both already on his shit list."

After the two wolves had retreated, both Maxine and Tavery turned to Sonya. She looked like she was going to faint.

"Come on," Maxine said, her voice not quite steady. "Ladies' room for a minute."

Sonya was leaning against the door. She seemed unable to get her feet moving. Gently, Maxine took her hand and urged, "Come on."

Sonya suddenly came to life. She ripped her hand from Maxine's grip, shoved away from the door, and dashed forward. The bathroom sign was right across the foyer; she rushed to it, yanked open the door, and flung herself inside. The click of the lock into the single-person little room came a moment later.

"Well," Agent Tavery muttered, "that went well." He sighed. "I'll tell Wellington we need to postpone the briefing."

Maxine shook her head. "I'll talk her down. Can you give me twenty minutes?"

Tavery nodded, looking relieved. "More if you need it." He strode back to the office he'd vacated, tapped once, and reentered.

Maxine approached the bathroom door and knocked lightly. "Sonya? Please let me in."

Chapter Four

Sonya didn't open the door immediately. What finally persuaded her was the realization that everyone on the entire floor could hear Maxine talking. She flicked the lock and let Maxine in. "It won't do any good," she muttered, gesturing at the closed door. "They'll hear everything we say anyway."

Maxine pulled out her phone.

"What are you doing?"

"Putting on the radio. That way, anyone listening will be mostly blocked by the music. Especially if we keep our voices down."

"You're a cockeyed optimist," Sonya grumbled.

"Nope. I'm a lesbian." She shrugged. "Sort of."

Unable to help herself, Sonya smiled. "How *does* that work?" she half whispered. "You're still a, well..."

"I still have male genitalia." Maxine sounded amused. "But since I think of myself as a woman first, that means I'm a lesbian." She laughed. "I am the real meaning of a lesbian trapped in a man's body."

"I always thought that was a stupid claim," Sonya admitted. Then she happened to glance in the mirror and she saw how terrible her makeup looked. Groaning, she muttered, "I look like a raccoon."

"I have makeup remover in my office," Maxine offered. "If you'll lock the door till I come back, I'll get it."

Sonya considered. Then she dug her own kit out of her purse. Maxine's presence alone was comforting. "I think I can survive." She reached out and touched Maxine's hand. "Thank you for defending me."

"I'm just sorry the assholes didn't listen," Maxine snarled. Her sharper-than-human eyeteeth flashed.

Sonya looked for the expected fear... and found

it, although it was mixed with appreciation. Maxine was angry on her behalf. "I just need a few more minutes. Then I'll be ready to go back out there." She used the tools in her bag to take away the signs of her panic and distress. Then, she took paper towels from the dispenser and began mopping up the counter with the single sink in the middle. This done, she settled herself on the counter, crossed her legs, closed her eyes, and began to pray.

Only to be interrupted. "What are you doing?"

Sonya patted the counter. "Come sit with me. I'm praying." She added, thinking of Maxine's reaction to hearing about her faith, "Not that you have to pray too."

"I can, though. Just to my goddess instead of your god."

"Werewolves believe in the spiritual world?" Sonya asked, opening her eyes. Maxine was settling beside her, on the other side of the sink, her long legs dangling. Today she wore a shorter skirt that left her shapely calves bare. Sonya was reminded of a Regency romance novel she'd read once, that talked about footmen stuffing their clad calves to make them appear more muscular. Maxine needed no such cheat. Her legs were a dream.

Sonya looked hastily away as Maxine answered her question.

"We pray to the moon goddess. Some of us are more devout than others of course, just like Christians. I usually meditate rather than pray, but the peace I find is just the same."

Sonya held out her hand. "I believe that when two or more are gathered together, their combined peaceful thoughts feed off each other."

Maxine took her hand, kissed it, and then laid it

on her thigh. Sonya's gut tightened pleasantly. She looked away, feeling her nose burn. She tried to pray.

It was an abysmal failure. She found herself watching Maxine instead. She had never been granted such an uninterrupted opportunity to gaze at the werewolf. That word -- werewolf -- didn't hold the same terror it had out in the hallway. Probably because it was Maxine sitting next to her. Maxine, who had been unfailingly gentle from the first.

Her gaze wandered to Maxine's long hair. It was plaited and wrapped around her head like a crown. Sonya found herself wondering if it was all Maxine's or if she had extensions. Depending on how old she was, it could go either way. She *looked* approximately Sonya's own age, but all werewolves stopped aging at a certain point, retaining their youth for centuries.

She looked into Maxine's composed face, admiring unashamedly the squareness of her jaw. It was one of the only features that gave a clue as to her true gender. *No, that's wrong. I mean her birth gender.* She was privately glad that Maxine couldn't read her mind.

Then she remembered that Maxine was an occasional telepath. Blushing furiously, she bowed her head and tried to concentrate on prayer.

Only to feel Maxine squeeze her hand. She looked up, straight into the honey brown eyes of her dreams.

"If you want to kiss me, I won't mind."

"But I'm not interested in women," Sonya said automatically.

"No? Maybe I'm the exception that proves the rule." Maxine leaned over the sink, offering her cheek.

Sonya's gut tightened pleasantly again. She reached up, touched Maxine's cheek, and turned her head. "If I'm going to be hung, I might as well be hung for a ton instead of a pound."

"I don't think that's quite how the phrase goes."

"Who cares?" And Sonya kissed her.

It was soft. Tentative. It was short too, but only because Sonya couldn't figure out how long she should do it. She pulled back, tasting both Maxine's lipstick and her own. Neither was a particularly enjoyable taste, but the taste of coffee on Maxine's breath was heavenly. "I liked that," Sonya told her hands, which she had knotted together in her lap.

"I did too." Maxine stroked the side of Sonya's face with one finger and then let her hand drop. "Shall we go to the briefing?" She slid off the counter.

Sonya gathered her courage, glanced at Maxine, and smiled. "Yes." Standing, she hesitated before heading for the door. She couldn't decide if she wanted Maxine at her back to guard her from that direction or if she wanted her to lead.

"I'll play rearguard," Maxine said softly. "That way no one can sneak up on you."

Leaving Sonya to step out first. She swallowed, pulled herself together as best she could, and unlocked the door. Stepping out into the foyer, she didn't see anyone waiting. "To the conference room?" she asked without looking around.

"Yes. We'll stop at Wellington's office on the way to let him know we're ready to start."

That was exactly what they did, notifying, it turned out, Agent Tavery along with Agent Wellington. The four of them trooped down to the conference room, Wellington leading the way, and Sonya felt safer with three powerful people guarding her.

It wasn't as if she couldn't defend herself, it was

only she'd never done so against more than mere humans. The thought of trying to use her self-defense training against a magical creature who could both move faster than she could and hit harder than she would ever be able to imagine... It filled her with mind-numbing terror.

Once they were all seated around the table, Sonya seeking out a place beside Maxine, Wellington opened his small laptop and began typing. "All right," he said after a few moments, "let's get all the cards out. Bring Agent Tavery up to speed since his computer ate my e-mail."

Sonya glanced at Mark and saw him smile slightly at Wellington but not as though he was pleased.

Maxine began. "According to the witnesses we met" -- there had been more after the rude bitch once Maxine had regained her composure --"a large, diesel-powered panel truck with a pizza logo on its side arrived in the neighborhood sometime between one and three a.m. The local pizza shop stops delivering at eleven, and even the chain stores quit after twelve. The corpses were still in human form and yet appeared to have fought or at least used their fingernails before they died. Both of them had cement dust and metal shavings under their nails. The dragon blew fire sometime in the last twelve hours before her death."

"It doesn't sound like they were fighting," Mark Tavery said. "It sounds like they were trying to escape some prison."

Wellington nodded. "That's what I think as well."

Sonya said, "Dragons can't blow fire in human form."

"Yes, we can," Mark said. "Although we have to

partially shift to do it."

Well, and that was what Sonya had meant. They weren't wholly in human form. But she didn't contradict Mark.

"What does 'partially shift' mean?" Wellington asked.

"We, at least water dragons, have to will our insides to change. Usually, this means our mouths grow wider too. But that's the extent of the shifting." He frowned. "I'm missing some information, though. I think land dragons have to shift all the way. Was the female dragon a land, water, or ice dragon, Sonya?"

"Land."

Mark smiled ruefully. "There goes the protest I was about to make. Ice dragons are like those who love water, right? They have to partially change?"

Sonya nodded. "That's what I was thinking of when I mentioned that she was in human guise when she was found. She must have either regained her human form or been forced into it using curare." She saw the question on Maxine's face and answered it. "Dragons can be forced into their dragon or human forms by the use of hemlock or curare respectively. How much it takes depends on the dragon's age and exposure to the specific plant in the past."

"It also depends on how motivated the dragon is," Mark put in. "If he or she is being held in human guise but is given the right stimulus, he or she can still shift. Although they'll be weak afterward and unable to keep the other appearance for long."

"Full-blooded werewolves can't be forced into a guise except by the full moon, and then only up until a certain age. It varies depending on the strength, probably the will, of the pup or wolfling, but the oldest age I know of when speaking of forced transformation is seventeen," Maxine said. "Not just the actual night of the full moon, though. It includes the night on either side of that one."

"What about during those days?" Mark asked.

"Most pups and wolflings can control themselves by the time they're seven or eight, while the sun is in the sky," Agent Wellington said. "Think of it as delayed potty training."

"So," Sonya murmured, "the dragon might or might not have been forced into human form, but the werewolf chose his guise." She glanced nervously at Mark but decided to say what was on her mind anyway. "Dragons are usually more ruled by their heads than nature, at least that's the experience I've had. Agent Tavery was born a dragon, obviously, but he didn't shift for the first time until he was around thirty."

"Female dragons are born in dragon form," Mark told her. "My birth mother told me I was born human. If I ever showed signs of shifting, or even starting to shift when I was very young, my father, who had the raising of me after the first couple of days, dosed me with curare. I was raised in such a way that I never knew a magical form lived inside me. What I don't get is why all three of the dragons we found were female. They're notoriously harder to capture, almost impossible to control even with heavy uses of curare, and their families are much more likely to look for them."

"Maybe that's why they were dumped so far from their home," Sonya said.

All three agents looked at her.

Her cheeks flushed. "Between Jenny and I, we managed to do the autopsies completely." She *would not* tell them that Jenny had forgotten to check the contents of the dragons' stomachs. Jenny was usually incredibly thorough. "Most of what the three dragons ate were things not found around here. Moose. Larger deer. Black bear. So, we were right in our assumptions, and based on the soil samples in their clothing et cetera, that they were not from this area."

"They're all land dragons, then," Mark said, scowling. "I should have asked that straight away."

"The werewolves were similarly from the northern parts of the United States and/or Canada," Maxine put in. "Similar contents were found in their stomachs."

Sonya knew this already but she didn't object to Maxine putting it out there. "So they were either brought here to avoid detection or because there's something here that isn't anywhere else."

Maxine said, "I agree, but I wanted to bring one more piece of information out. Near where the bodies were discovered, I smelled a great stench of snake."

Sonya bristled at the slur. "A *dragon* was killed there. And they're not called *snakes*."

"I did smell dragon," Maxine said, her voice quiet. "But I also smelled a great serpent. I can't be more specific than that. Maybe it was someone's pet boa constrictor, although finding the scent right near the corpses' last location... that seems a little odd to me."

It did to Sonya too. "I'm sorry I jumped down your throat. I just... Werewolves don't like dragons, generally, and I, well..." She glanced at Mark...

He smiled. "Luke will be relieved to know he's not the only one looking out for my honor. Thank you, Sonya." He turned to Wellington. "Next step? I think we should start contacting werewolf packs and the more powerful female dragons to find out if any of them have lost people over the last year."

Wellington nodded. "Maxine, will you start with the packs native to Canada?"

"Yes."

"Sonya," Mark said, "I'll give you a list of the more dominant female dragons. There aren't too many, so probably you'll be going on to the less-dominant ones if you don't get results."

Five minutes later, Sonya was leading the way down the stairs.

"I hope Mark wasn't uncomfortable with me exposing his secret about not having shifted until he was much older than most," Sonya murmured.

"He wasn't."

Sonya glanced at her. "Telepathy?"

"More the expression on his face. Agent Tavery's a much stronger telepath than I am. I wouldn't dare to glean anything he didn't want me to."

Sonya chewed on the inside of her cheek. This was probably the wrong time, but when exactly would she have another chance for them to be alone? "I dreamed about you."

Grinning, Maxine tugged Sonya lightly to a halt. Then she kissed her cheek. "I'm flattered. I'll see you at lunch?"

Sonya nodded, dry-mouthed.

"And maybe this Friday we can go out for drinks?"

"Yeah… I don't drink, but going to dance or something at a bar would be…" She swallowed. "Great."

Maxine squeezed Sonya's hand and then rushed back up to the second floor. Sonya all but floated down the remaining steps and positively flew across campus to her own building.

* * *

Sonya sat in her car, wondering why Maxine hadn't wanted to meet until six. If they'd even met at eight, she would have had time, barely, to get back across the bridge to St. Pete and then return to Tampa. This way, she was stuck in --

Her thought broke off cleanly. Maxine stood about half a block down. It was obviously Maxine despite the distance. Her curves and face were unmistakable. She was dressed in what Sonya called, meaning no insult, "gay boy" jeans: ones that looked as if they'd been sprayed onto the individual. Not only was Maxine's ass obvious in the denim but so was the slight bulge of her cock.

Her cock. Such a strange phrase. But it fit Maxine perfectly.

Sonya started up the sidewalk. Her eye traveled up from the tight jeans to the half shirt Maxine wore. It showed off a muscular midriff. Above it, stretching the cloth taut, were her breasts. They *were* hers, even if not by nature or surgery. The image on the half shirt wasn't obvious from where Sonya was, but as she drew closer and Maxine turned fully toward her, she saw it was a happily panting wolf.

Maxine grinned. There was no evidence of eyeteeth. "I'm glad you found Tobias's."

"The neon palm tree is a dead giveaway."

Maxine offered Sonya her arm.

Sonya hesitated. Not because Maxine was a werewolf. That fear seemed to have taken a hike, at least where this particular agent was concerned, but because they might not be walking into a lesbian-friendly establishment. *Oh, fuck it. I can deal with being on a woman's arm. As long as that woman is Maxine.*

The bar they entered was for straight people.

Sonya saw this immediately. Still, Maxine looked completely comfortable. "You've got guts."

Maxine shrugged. "Because I'm a trans woman in a straight bar?"

"No, because you're obviously dressed up for me and you brought me to a straight bar where I might see something... Not more attractive. You've, um, got that covered. More to my taste? I think that's what I mean." She was glad her possible blush wouldn't show in the dim room.

"I believe in playing the field. And while I *did* dress up for you, I brought you some clothes to change into if you want and I figured you'd feel more comfortable here." She dropped her voice and whispered in Sonya's ear, "They're all human, by the way."

Sonya laughed, but not about the idea of a nonhuman hangout. "You brought me clothes?"

"And makeup remover and makeup. I want everyone to watch you tonight."

They were at a table now, but Sonya didn't sit. "You're not the jealous type?"

"I have nothing to be jealous of. Yet. It turns me on to watch someone I'm with having a good time. Do you want to get dolled-up?" She gestured toward the bathroom.

Sonya grimaced. "I bet it's filthy in there."

"Nope. Not until about nine or ten. This is one of the cleanest bars in Florida."

* * *

Maxine sat on a barstool drinking a white sangria. It was a low-alcohol drink, but she wasn't worried about the alcohol content. Werewolves could hold their liquor. She just liked the taste. It had been her lover, Carrie's, favorite drink.

Before she killed herself. Maxine scowled and began drinking in earnest just to get the wine gone. She resolved to order a slippery nipple or a fuzzy navel next. Anything to take her mind off Carrie, who had refused to order spirits with "screwball" names.

Maxine glanced toward the bathroom door. Sonya had disappeared behind it almost thirty minutes ago. Whatever she was doing in there, it would probably be worth it. Unless she kept Maxine waiting out here for hours, a small corner of Maxine's mind whispered. *Unless she's decided to stay hidden until you give up and leave.*

Just then, the door opened and Sonya stepped out. It was Sonya, wasn't it?

Her makeup was different. That was the first thing Maxine noticed. The second thing she saw was that she'd been right about Sonya's body type; the clothing she'd picked fit perfectly, leaving some things to the imagination while highlighting Sonya's best characteristics.

The short, dark green skirt clung to her muscular thighs and beautifully curved ass. Below it, her legs all but shone through the dimness. The little shoes Sonya had worn to work looked ten times sexier with those long thighs and curvy calves.

The blouse was a green three shades lighter than the skirt. With a plunging neckline and capped sleeves, it showed off even more of Sonya's beautiful skin.

There was only one problem. Everyone, or so it seemed, was staring at Sonya. The men with hunger, the women with mixed emotions. Some looked ready to kill her. Others looked as though they might not be completely straight after all.

And just like that, Maxine was jealous. It was quite funny, actually. She'd never been jealous of

Carrie. The two of them used to pick up a third woman for a little play every once in a while, although no actual penetration had taken place. Not even with toys. The statutes of the pack were firm.

Sonya started toward Maxine, her hips swinging and her eyes shining. She looked so much more comfortable in the clothes Maxine had chosen for her. Not that she didn't seem at ease at work but she appeared to be in her element now.

Maxine's was the only available stool; she slid off it and offered Sonya a seat. Once Sonya had smilingly taken it, Maxine stood behind her with a hand on the small of her back. Claiming her.

It soon became obvious that Sonya was a lightweight when it came to alcohol. She had half a drink -- wine -- and began to loosen up. If she'd been in her element before, now she was on fire.

Slipping off the stool, she waved at Maxine not to follow her. Striding over to a small group, she queued up by the DJ.

Was she requesting a special song? Sonya was shunted to the front of the group, many of the people laughing. She spoke to the DJ.

Maxine bent her hearing in that direction and, listening intently, caught the DJ saying, "I think everyone wants you to go first, darling. What song?"

Sonya named it. Maxine had never heard of this particular song. She couldn't even guess what genre it was based on the title. Sonya walked to the middle of the dance floor -- empty yet -- and the DJ announced, "Karaoke time."

Sonya began to sing. Maxine immediately learned the song was about bad relationships. It was upbeat nonetheless. Then one line made Maxine laugh out loud.

"The more boys I meet, the more I love my dog."

Or your wolf?

It was a country song; she was amazed to hear a black woman sing a genre dominated by white men.

After Sonya left the dance floor to great applause and cheerful whistles Maxine stood and went to meet her. She caught the woman by the shoulders and grinned. "That was *great*. Where did you hear that song?"

"An ex-boyfriend," Sonya answered. "I'd never dated a black man who liked country before, but Jim did. He had it going all the time in his truck. Not that this song was ever on the radio, just the artist. I own all of her CDs." She laughed and added, "I don't really listen to all of her songs religiously. Just the ones about killing people. Like cheating husbands, abusive fathers, and the like."

Maxine laughed and whispered in Sonya's ear, "She sounds like a werewolf after my own heart."

They returned to the bar. Unable to find seats, they simply ordered, Sonya a drink to replace the one Maxine had left sitting there, and Maxine some good, hard whiskey. Then they retreated out back to a collection of tables where the music wasn't quite as loud.

Sonya said, "Mama hates that side of me, the country side."

"Why?" Maxine nudged Sonya's drink toward her.

Sonya sipped. "Mostly because she's a racist." She sighed.

Maxine took her hand.

Sonya confessed, "My mama's a drunken lump who used to be abusive to me until I told her to fuck off. I wonder sometimes if she earned the right to be so awful after everything she went through."

After everything she went through… How that reminded Maxine of Carrie, who had said many times how she deserved the peace of death after "everything she went through." When Maxine insisted they had to keep living, that life was what their dead son would want, Carrie responded, *"Sometimes I don't think you even loved James."* James had died, after an arduous labor and two weeks of life, at his first full moon.

Carrie had committed suicide less than eight weeks later. And those nearly two months had been stuffed with accusations of Maxine's lack of grief, Maxine's spending too much time with the pack, and Carrie's own depression.

Unable to think in that vein any longer, Maxine stood up, took their empty glasses, pinching the tops together in one hand, and then caught Sonya's hand and pulled her to her feet. "Come on. Dance with me."

To her vast relief, Sonya grinned. "Definitely. And leave the glasses. We can't get to the bar right now anyway, I bet."

They walked in on a slow song. Maxine hesitated at the edge of the dance floor. She didn't want to make Sonya uncomfortable by holding her too close. To her surprise, and renewed relief, Sonya pulled her forward. When they were on the floor, Sonya wrapped her arms around Maxine's neck and leaned against her.

At first, Maxine was completely taken up with the feeling of warm, compliant, gracefully dancing human in her arms. She inhaled the fragrance of Sonya's cap of black and kinky hair and the aroma of shea butter on her smooth and kissable skin. She luxuriated in the warmth and gentle movements of Sonya's body.

Then, glancing casually beyond Sonya for a

moment, she caught the narrowed eye of a burly human male. He made a gesture Maxine didn't immediately recognize. Then she remembered how some humans made the finger-lifting move when they were mad at each other. "Flipping the bird" they called it and although Maxine couldn't see anything remotely connected to the aviary, she realized she was being judged. Judged and found lacking.

It was hard for Maxine to repress a growl.

Sonya, meanwhile, was still dancing with unconscious grace. She was a little wobbly on her feet, probably because of the alcohol, but she still managed a duchess's carriage most of the time. She'd drawn back a little, settling a hand on Maxine's shoulder and the other in Maxine's free right hand. Their fingers entwined, she started leading the dance, which Maxine didn't mind in the slightest.

The song ended and a fast one began. Sonya let go of Maxine at once but she didn't step back. Instead, she began undulating her hips in a very suggestive manner. Hands in the air, she looked like she hadn't a care in the world.

"Oh, dance with me," she said, laughing at Maxine's stillness. "Don't your people dance to fast songs too?"

Maxine considered the idea that Sonya wasn't as drunk as she'd first thought if she could remember to say "your people" rather than "werewolves." Then her hands were seized and Sonya was guiding her firmly.

"Loosen up," Sonya commanded as she tossed her head and wriggled her hips. "Here," she added when Maxine apparently didn't loosen up enough. Sonya, still dancing, backed into her and began rubbing her ass over the bulge in Maxine's jeans.

Maxine was briefly lost again. Her hands fit well,

one over the other, on Sonya's slightly rounded belly. A fire had started in her groin and her nose was full of Sonya's light and flowery scent.

She glanced up, just to make sure they weren't going to run into anyone else, and saw that the floor had been mostly cleared, that the few couples still dancing were doing so on the edges of the floor. She scowled. Were they afraid? No. There was no smell of terror coming from them. It was, instead, disgust and anger Maxine saw in their eyes and smelled in their sweat.

"Sonya," she murmured, "maybe we should stop."

"Why?" Sonya ground extra hard against Maxine. "Are you afraid you'll come?"

Maxine flushed. "No," she whispered, glad no one probably heard Sonya over the music. "They don't want us here."

"This is *your* bar, though," Sonya argued, still dancing. "You said it was a good place."

"I've never brought anyone except friends here," Maxine admitted.

"Oh fuck 'em," Sonya said. "We're having fun. There's no law against that. It's not like you couldn't take 'em."

Maxine considered that. It was true but she didn't necessarily want to get into trouble with SearchLight for taking on a group of inebriated humans.

"Besides, gay bashing..." Sonya stumbled, straightened, and then turned and met Maxine's gaze. "Do you even call it gay bashing when you're trans?"

"It comes out to the same," Maxine answered, amazed that Sonya wanted to talk semantics.

"Well, whatever it's called, we're fine. If you

don't want to fight them off, I will." She turned around and resumed dancing.

Pondering that, Maxine moved with Sonya. *I cared when that woman called me a nigger dyke, but somehow, with Sonya, I'm not as worried about what they'll call me.* In a strange way, she thought she shouldn't be bothered by either the "n word" or by the antigay slur. She was a werewolf, after all, and neither term actually applied to her.

It wasn't the words. It was her tone. Her stench of hate. Those are the things that bothered me.

Another slow song started and Sonya whirled around to catch Maxine's hand and place her fingers delicately on Maxine's shoulder. "We're perfectly safe," Sonya said. "Just let go of your fear and dance with me."

Tempted and not really wanting to resist, Maxine danced with her until after midnight. She was falling in love with Sonya's movements as the night drew down.

Chapter Five

Maxine had taken Sonya's keys at around ten. Sonya hadn't imbibed more than that glass and a half. She seemed quite sober. Still, Maxine didn't know much about humans and alcohol and refused to take any chances.

Now it was just after midnight and Maxine had succeeded in persuading Sonya to come home with her. "Not to do anything," she said, interpreting the sudden tension in the woman's shoulders. "Just to sleep it off. You'll have a chance to shower off the day and sleep comfortably. I have a really luxurious couch." She *did* want something more to happen; she had a serious case of blue balls. But she wouldn't change anything that had happened tonight. Not even, she realized, the glares and scowls. Because Sonya hadn't noticed them at all.

Round about twelve-fifteen, the two of them headed for the exit. They didn't walk hand in hand, but with Sonya first and Maxine acting as rearguard again. She might have chosen to not care about the stares but that didn't mean she didn't neglect to keep an eye on the people. Even though the dance floor had filled up after a while, people still hadn't brushed against them.

Stepping outside, Maxine asked, "Where are you parked?"

Sonya gestured. "This way." Then she dropped a step back and took Maxine's hand.

Maxine had never seen Sonya's car, so she had a little fun trying to guess which it was. "This one?" she asked about a topless job.

"Never." Sonya laughed. "I'm not into my hair blowing all over the place."

"You don't have enough hair to do that."

"It gets static-y. I don't like having a mushroom helmet."

"What about this one?" She pointed at a Lexus.

"On a medtech's paycheck? You've *got* to be kidding me. Mine is several years old. That thing's brand-new."

"Maybe that --"

"Hey, dykes. Where are your bikes?"

Maxine stiffened. She hated dealing with drunken humans. Well, that wasn't exactly fair. Or accurate. She hated dealing with drunken *males* and it didn't matter either that she was born male herself or that most of the drunks she'd met were human because magical creatures had to consume an awful lot to be even mildly tipsy.

Sonya dropped Maxine's hand but she didn't turn to flee back toward the bar. Instead, she took a curious stance: feet apart and both hands above her waist. She looked as though she was ready to fight.

The three men approaching them from the direction of the bar weren't visibly weaving but the stench of alcohol wafted from them. They were still laughing over the dykes comment and didn't strike Maxine as remotely dangerous. That being said, she did not quite dare turn her back on them.

They stalked forward and tried to surround Maxine and Sonya. Sonya, however, blocked her half of the sidewalk and Maxine took the hint. "What do you want?" Sonya demanded.

"Cheeky bitch."

Sonya smiled and if she hadn't been human, the smile would have been predatory. "Back off, friend. I'm a brown belt." She said this rather more loudly than Maxine thought was necessary.

"A what?" one of the other men asked.

"One step below black belt," Sonya answered calmly, although still at a higher volume. "Now go away."

The guy on the left -- torn jeans and a T-shirt that smelled of booze -- launched a bottle. But as it was thrown from a half-assed position and without any real oomph, it would have simply smacked Sonya on the stomach and fallen to the ground.

Instead, Sonya blocked the projectile with her right forearm. A moment later, as the bottle fell, she stepped forward, raised both hands, and did something interesting with the palm of her left hand and the forearm of her right.

The man who'd thrown the bottle staggered backward, arms pinwheeling, and fell, sitting down hard on the pavement. He screamed and blood poured from his mouth.

Sonya turned toward the others. "Do you want to have your jaw dislocated too?"

They fled, leaving their howling companion on the sidewalk.

Maxine caught Sonya's arm. "Let's get out of here." She wasn't sure Sonya would come with her. When some werewolves had their hackles up, it was all but impossible to call them off.

Sonya led the way to her car, a nondescript but well-kept anonymous four-door in dark blue.

Once they were in the car and the car itself was away from the curb with Maxine behind the wheel, Maxine had to ask. "Why were you being so loud about your brown belt?"

Sonya raised an eyebrow. "Because I wanted anyone nearby to know I gave the asshole fair warning. I'm technically a deadly weapon."

Maxine found that her hands were shaking on the steering wheel. "I've never seen a human move that fast." She paused before adding, "You're coming home with me for a shower and a hangover cure."

* * *

The large main room of Maxine's apartment was painted white on three walls. The fourth was burnt umber. It faced the large broad windows behind a low, long couch. Sonya's gaze was next drawn to a bright and energetic painting on one of the walls adjacent to the windows. It was full of jags and spirals. It was unsigned.

"Do you want a drink?" Maxine called from the kitchen.

Assuming she meant more alcohol, Sonya hesitated. Another half a glass was bound to put her flat on her back and snoring. "Sure." Why the hell not? She was in no condition to drive as it was. The icy calm that had flooded her when she found herself in danger had departed and now she only felt headachy and tired.

Retreating to the couch, she sat, still surveying the eye-popping modern art. "Who painted the picture out here?"

There was the sound of liquid pouring into a glass. "Carrie painted all the artwork hanging in my apartment. She was the pack's official *artiste*." She sounded amused.

Sonya wasn't. "You miss her a lot, don't you?"

"Only on certain nights. I really miss running with her during a full moon." More pouring. "But most of the time, I'm left with the happy memories."

Relieved, and refusing to analyze why, Sonya kicked off her shoes and stretched out on the couch. Pillowing her head on one arm, she closed her eyes.

She drifted.

Someone was singing. It was a slow song conveyed in a low-pitched alto voice.

When she came back to herself a little, the singing seemed to be coming from right over her head. A firm pillow had been placed beneath her cheek and she snuggled into it.

"Swing low, sweet chariot. Coming for to carry me home…"

Sonya blinked and rubbed her eyes with one hand. "Maxine?"

"Right here, dear."

Smiling a little, Sonya asked, "Do you mean the animal deer when you say that? Coming from a werewolf, that's a little spooky."

"I do *not* mean the animal." Maxine sounded amused. "I must admit, I never thought of it that way. Sit up now. Drink some water. It will help prevent a hangover." And she helped Sonya to an upright posture.

Sonya took careful sips. "And here I thought you were mixing more alcohol."

"You look as though another inch would knock you flat." Maxine laughed. "And while I admit I'd like to see that someday, this is not that day." Her tone grew serious. "Although we do have to have a conversation about sex at some point."

"Not tonight, okay? My head's spinning."

"No, not tonight. Keep downing that water."

Sonya took deeper swallows this time. "This is going to sound rude, but where did a werewolf learn our spirituals?"

"We picked them up out of books," Maxine murmured, sounding like this might be a terrible crime. "For the psychic wolves, before we were allowed equal standing, we were oppressed as badly as American slaves."

Sonya's gut twisted. "You weren't forced into sex like my ancestors were."

"I wasn't aware you were so familiar with the psychic wolves' plight," Maxine said, and although her tone was mild, her eyes flashed. "We were often forced into sex, both with each other and with straight wolves. Sometimes for their amusement, sometimes for the higher birth rate psychic wolves usually have."

A little guiltily, Sonya asked, "Usually?"

Maxine sighed. "Yes, well... My son is dead because I couldn't ease his transformation at the first full moon of his life. I don't have the telekinetic power that would have made it easier on him. And Carrie, who did have that ability, thought herself too weak to help him."

Sonya heard the bitterness in the wolf's voice. "Do you blame her?"

"Not often, but my hackles are already up and I tend to blame the whole world when I'm feeling cornered."

Sonya said, as gently as she could, "Singing our songs as if they were your own *is* cultural misappropriation."

"No. It's not. It's cultural diaspora. Maybe that's not the right term, but as people migrate, they bring their culture with them and share it. If the military is allowed to take on bagpipes and drums from the Scottish to conduct their ceremonies, beaten-down werewolves who aren't even permitted to sing in Werewelsh can certainly borrow from a people similarly deprived in their past."

Sonya considered this. "You're right. I'm sorry I jumped all over you."

"You're protective of your culture. There's no shame or apology needed for that."

Sonya drained the water glass. "Thank you for being so tolerant." She paused before adding, "Maybe if everyone was like you, there would be less unjustified hatred in the world." She touched Maxine's shoulder. "If you'll forgive me, I want to kiss you."

Maxine leaned close and they kissed. The interplay of tongues was sweetly sensual. Sonya felt tingles up into her hair and down her spine. She mumbled against Maxine's mouth.

Maxine took the water glass and set it somewhere out of reach. Then she cupped Sonya's face and began kissing her more deeply.

Sonya's hands rose of their own accord to rest on Maxine's chest. But the strange feeling of breasts stopped her. She drew back. "Can you take off your, um, boobs?" She added quickly, "I'll take off my shirt too."

Maxine stood, opened her bra in the back, and the two boobs slid down her front inside her shirt. She then pulled off shirt and bra as one.

Sonya gazed upon the most feminine-looking male chest she'd ever seen. It wasn't overly muscled. Nor was it hairy. It looked like a woman's chest without tits. She bit her lip and then said, "Your body seemed to know you were transgender."

"It's mostly, maybe all, chemistry-driven, my transgenderism," Maxine answered. "My penis is smaller than the norm, my hips are broader, and my torso is, well, as you see it."

Sonya hastily removed her own shirt. She hesitated over her bra, saw Maxine looking understandingly at her, and took it off. Maxine giving her mute permission to take it off or leave it on gave her courage. "I, um, I haven't been with a woman before, and I haven't been with a guy since I was taking first-year classes at SearchLight Academy." She moistened her lips. "That song about the more guys I meet, the more I love my dog? That's true. Or would be, if I had a real dog. I have a stuffed one from my childhood." She was babbling; making herself shut up, she gazed at Maxine: face, chest, and belly.

But she couldn't keep silent for long. "I thought werewolves were really muscular."

"Almost every one I've ever met has been," Maxine agreed. "But it's part of that transgenderism. Our females have more curves than our males and I've sort of got a little of each."

"I'm too shy to touch you." Sonya added quickly, "Or to let you touch me. Can I just look and appreciate?"

"You like the way I look? Without all the rippling pectorals and six-pack?"

Sonya nodded.

"Then looking is enough. I like how you look too. Your breasts are full, but more like small cantaloupes than watermelons. They look like the right size for my smaller-than-masculine hands."

My nose is turning red. I know it is. "I have a little extra belly," she said self-consciously.

"Extra according to whom? Society? I like that you're all soft curves. And you're quite healthy, in body and mind. I like that too."

Sonya yawned. "I'm sorry. I'm a little, well…"

"Intoxicated and exhausted." Maxine stood. "I'll be right back with some more water. After you drink it, you should sleep." She also yawned, although Sonya thought maybe it was a fake one. "We can both use some sleep."

Sonya didn't put her shirt back on. Instead, she pulled the afghan off the back of the couch and wrapped herself up in its colorful yarn. "Who made you this afghan?"

"I made it."

"For Carrie?" Sonya asked cautiously. "Or your son?"

"Nope. It's the first thing I'd ever made for myself." She returned with the water.

"Everything else you crocheted was for Carrie?"

"No. For the straight wolves. When I ran away from my birth pack and joined Fehrna Susan's, I made it as a celebration of freedom."

Sonya drank down the water. "Thank you."

"Welcome." Maxine sat beside her and urged Sonya to lay her head on the available thigh. "Do you mind if I sing a few more songs? I know some lullabies."

Sonya snuggled in. Facing in with her face toward Maxine's stomach, she became aware of a small bulge in the denim-covered crotch. She smiled at it but didn't touch despite a longing that rose inside her. Smaller than average Maxine had said, or something like that. "I'd love that."

* * *

Sonya awoke with her mouth tasting of cotton but the delicious smell of frying bacon on the air. She pried open her glued-shut right eyelid with her fingers and saw it was morning. The couch on which she still lay faced away from the windows but the walls were illuminated.

Gingerly, she lifted her head, expecting it to split open at any moment. When it didn't, she sat up fully and looked around. There was a full glass of water on the floor by where her head had been, and a note was under the glass.

Good morning, dear D-E-E-R.

Sonya snorted.

I've left you some water. Feel free to go in and use the GREEN toothbrush. It's new.

Sonya downed the water, grateful for the way it unstuck her throat. Then she looked toward the kitchen and saw Maxine at the stove, her back to the living room. There was no way she hadn't heard Sonya's abortive laughter. Still, she seemed thoroughly absorbed in what she was doing. So, Sonya decided to take advantage of the new green toothbrush.

When she emerged from the bathroom, all of her body more comfortable after her visit, she moved toward the kitchen. Only to see a note on the couch next to a pile of folded clothes.

Hi, deer. Feel free to take a shower. I've already showered. These are clothes you can borrow.

Feeling positively like a queen, Sonya went off to the bathroom again. She luxuriated in the hot spray. Then she thought of what had, and hadn't, happened last night. Desire and embarrassment washed through her in equal measure. She'd dreamed about Maxine's bare chest but her first thought hadn't been jumping the werewolf, it had been, well, less romantic things.

Emerging from the shower, she hesitated. Should she dress or should she try to bed Maxine now? Granted, she wasn't exactly sure she wanted to sleep with the werewolf, but she wanted to do something sexual with her. At the very least, she wanted to kiss her again.

Confused and unsure, she dressed slowly. By the time she emerged from the bathroom, she was aware of the scent of hot coffee, toast, and maybe even eggs, ready in the kitchen. She went to the breakfast bar and gazed directly into Maxine's eyes. "You're so beautiful," she murmured.

Maxine bit her lip. "I'm flattered. Especially coming from a straight woman." She added quickly, "I did not mean that as harshly as it sounded."

Feeling sad, Sonya said, "I'm sorry I couldn't give you what you wanted last night."

"I didn't really expect anything," Maxine answered. "It's just…" She laughed. "It was hard watching you sleep. Your lips are so lovely and…"

Sonya got up, rounded the little breakfast bar, and walked to Maxine. She took the werewolf's hands. "I dreamed about kissing you. I loved it, both the dream and when it actually happened."

Maxine smiled. "I sort of wish we hadn't started this. I'm afraid of what comes after kissing."

"I wouldn't be your first," Sonya said, confused. Then she added, "But your first since Carrie." She squeezed Maxine's fingers gently. "If you want to stop, I'll be disappointed, but I don't want to hurt you."

"It's not that." Maxine drew Sonya close against her, hugging her. "I want you. It's too soon to want you to be part of my life forever, but that's what I crave."

Sonya turned her head and kissed Maxine's jaw. "Don't be afraid of a kiss. Please don't." She laughed softly, a sound that barely passed her lips. "That should be your line, I think. I should be the one hesitating. But, oh what the hell." She touched the side of Maxine's face and kissed her full on the lips.

Maxine melted against her. "You're so beautiful," she mumbled against Sonya's mouth. "I just want to bed you right here, right now." She began kissing down Sonya's jaw to her neck and then, moving the edge of her shirt, on to her shoulder.

Her lips left a wet and steamy trail over Sonya's skin. Each kiss was a promise. Sonya closed her eyes and flattened her hands against Maxine's back, feeling the muscles there. She inhaled a perfume that she doubted came from any bottle.

Maxine kissed down Sonya's arm, the heat of her mouth evident even through the shirt.

"That can't taste very good."

"Does it *feel* good?"

Sonya grinned. "Yes."

"Then hush up and let me keep going." She'd reached Sonya's wrist and she lingered at the place where the fabric ended.

A prickling sensation raced up Sonya's arm. She shivered a little and felt herself glowing. She wanted those soft lips somewhere else.

Oh, stop being coy. You want them on your clit.

And she trembled, pressing her thighs together to increase the tingle between her legs. "Maxine, do you think we could skip breakfast and…?"

"Not on your life." Maxine drew back after one final kiss to Sonya's palm. "Werewolves cannot pursue pleasure on an empty stomach. And it's not too good for humans either."

The tingle between Sonya's legs increased and diminished and increased again in an endless cycle as they ate. She continually shot glances at Maxine and felt like a teenager. Maxine seemed to be feeling along the same lines because she ate quickly and, while Sonya was still mopping up the last of her egg with toast, got up to wash the dishes.

"I can help if you'll just wait a minute."

Maxine glanced over her shoulder and grinned. "You finish. I don't mind. I'm just a little obsessive when it comes to cleanliness." She added quietly,

"Where I grew up, things were kept pretty slovenly and it was the psychic LGBTQ wolves' job to hunt the mice and rats that came out to investigate."

"Werewolves hunt animals, don't they?"

"Yup. But there's a big difference between being treated like an overly large cat and being allowed to hunt out under the full moon."

Sonya finished her toast, thinking hard. "You weren't allowed to hunt with the pack?" she asked as she brought the plate and silverware to the sink. "Isn't hunting essential to who you are?"

"It is." Maxine immersed Sonya's plate in sudsy water. "That's one of the major reasons I left. Well, that and... After hearing about the way female wolves were treated, even in eros packs, I didn't want to go into one of those either unless it was run by a female."

"I thought eros packs were golden," Sonya admitted. "I've never heard a bad word spoken about them."

"They're largely better than straight packs. But females are treated like fragile creatures, and that was brought over into the eros packs. I wanted to be treated like the equal of any male, not like my ability to have pups was the most important thing about me."

Maxine's shoulders were slumped.

Sonya put her arms around the werewolf from behind. "I'm sorry your son died."

Maxine wiped her hands on a towel and turned in the circle of Sonya's arms.

Sonya hugged her tighter. "What stopped you from following Carrie into oblivion?"

"I couldn't. Fehrna Susan, my alpha, and her mate needed me. I don't know if I ever told you, but I'm the beta of the Fehrna pack."

"What does Fehrna mean?"

"Fierce."

"In what language?"

"A strange hybrid between the were-Spanish *feroz* and were-Latin *ferox*. I think there's a little Greek thrown in too." She snickered. "The only ones that aren't in constant flux are Werewelsh and Wererussian."

"Professor McLaughlin used to say English is" -- she dropped her voice to a gravelly growl, the best she could do --"the 'bitch-kitty of all tongues.'"

Maxine laughed and hugged Sonya still nearer. She bent her head and whispered in Sonya's ear, "You're even sexy imitating a man."

Sonya felt herself blush. "Thank you. I think."

"It was definitely meant as a compliment." Maxine kissed her cheek.

Sonya turned her head so their mouths met. She grabbed the back of Maxine's head with both hands to keep her from pulling away and then she ground her crotch against Maxine's. *Enough talk.*

She smiled into the kiss when Maxine moaned and pressed both hands against the small of her back. Then she gasped as Maxine bent her backward a little. There was no fear of falling, not the way Maxine held her.

They resumed the kiss. Sonya gazed directly into Maxine's eyes. The sweetness of Maxine's tongue in her mouth made her dizzy and she whimpered when Maxine pulled away.

Maxine looked miserable. This was probably the only reason Sonya forgave her. "I need to stop."

"All right," she said as patiently as she could. "Why?"

"Because of the pack rules."

Sonya scowled, pulled out of Maxine's arms, and

retreated until she bumped the breakfast bar. "This is about not being with a human, right?"

"No." Maxine looked surprised. "We don't have any policies against that, unless the human in question doesn't know anything about werewolves."

"So-o-o?"

Maxine bit her lip. The uncertain gesture was adorable. "It's not about being with you. It's about *being with you.*"

Hearing the emphasis but not understanding, Sonya raised her eyebrows and waited.

"Sexually. Beyond kissing. Um, beyond oral sex. The actual, um…"

"Penetration?" Sonya's eyebrows were still raised. "So, how do lesbians do it in a wolf pack? They *have* to penetrate the vagina for the pack to consider them together?"

"It's a little different for straight-up lesbians. They can declare themselves together or not, as long as no penetration of vag or ass has taken place. But once they declare themselves, they can't undeclare."

"This seems a little arbitrary," Sonya hedged.

"Yeah. It is. But even though Tilthos Charles, the alpha above all alphas, has made it so sex doesn't automatically equal marriage, the packs are still allowed to keep the tradition if at least sixty percent of the wolves involved want to keep it."

"What are the rules for a human woman and a transgender wolf?"

"Male-to-female trans specific, it means you and I can do anything we want outside the bounds of the pack except penetration. Once that last step happens, you're officially a member of the pack and you can never leave."

Floored, Sonya stared. "No wonder you said you

need to stop. We were headed straight for the bedroom." She felt stunned but at the same time she had to laugh. "You're definitely a female first, no matter your penis. Most guys would have just bedded me before declaring their intentions." She crossed the small kitchen and put her hands on Maxine's shoulders. "We can still kiss?"

Maxine smirked. "If you want to live dangerously."

"I do."

They retreated to the couch and pulled off their shirts. Maxine took off her bra with its fake boobs and dropped the cloth unceremoniously on the floor. She smiled into Sonya's eyes. "When I say stop, we have to stop."

"Don't worry. *I'll* help us stop too." Sonya grinned. "That's the advantage to dating a woman."

"Well, that and I'm not attracted to men."

Sonya considered following that train of thought because she had so many questions about being transgender. But her body's needs were stronger than her curiosity so she took off her bra. "I guess that means you like nipples."

Maxine smirked again. "I do. Although I'm more a mind or leg or butt lady. How do you like your chest touched?"

I love having a woman for a bedmate. Sonya felt herself blush. "I like them licked. The nipples. And I like my breasts gently kneaded."

Maxine set to work.

She was talented. Her lips and tongue were moist velvet. Her talents extended to her dexterous fingers. Caressing, stroking, and, yes, kneading softly, she made Sonya's breasts feel like warm melons. Arousal trickled down, seemingly a drop at a time, from her chest to her pussy.

Sonya was decidedly wet by the time her thoughts caught up with her racing heart and she realized she hadn't laid a hand on Maxine's mildly sculpted body. Voice slightly unsteady and the sound of blood rushing in her ears, she asked, "Where do you like to be touched?"

"I enjoy having my neck kissed."

Sonya scooted closer immediately, nudging her left breast against Maxine's flat and hairless chest. She stroked Maxine's hair lightly and then licked her way up the expanse of neck offered. Gently, she nibbled at Maxine's jaw.

Maxine moaned and put her hand between Sonya's legs. She didn't move more than that but Sonya was very aware of her fingers.

Sonya rested her right hand over Maxine's covered erection. It seemed to burn her with sacred fire. She moaned and went back to laving Maxine's marble pillar of a neck.

"You're so beautiful," Maxine murmured. She cupped the back of Sonya's head with her free palm.

A shock of pleasure shot from the base of Sonya's skull to the base of her spine. She felt like a live wire. "Oh fuck. I *want* you."

"I know. I want you too."

"You know?" Sonya laughed against Maxine's throat. "That's a little egotistical."

"I can smell your arousal and hear your heart racing. It turns me on."

Sonya began baptizing the other side of Maxine's throat. "If it meant only marriage, I might take you right now and damn the consequences. But I refuse to make your pack uncomfortable."

"They wouldn't mind you."

"They'd mind my fear."

Maxine didn't answer, and Sonya knew this was only because she spoke the truth.

Chapter Six

Maxine floated down the stairs toward the medtech department. She opened the door to the basement corridor… and Sonya fell into her arms.

Not in joy. Maxine saw this at once even as her mind tried to catch up with the sudden feel of the woman in her arms.

"Pu -- pu -- puppy!" Sonya wailed, burying her face against Maxine's chest. *Hiding* her face in the fabric of Maxine's blouse.

Maxine let the door close. She leaned her back against it and hugged Sonya. She didn't try to speak or to get any sense out of the sobbed words. She knew Sonya would need to calm down before she would be able to explain.

"Dead…" Sonya hiccupped. "Pu -- puppy…"

Maxine's stomach clenched even as she reminded herself that "puppy" didn't mean "werewolf child" to Sonya. More than likely, she'd seen a small dog dead on the side of the road on her way to work. *Which is still upsetting.* Not for the first time, Maxine wondered how humans could be so cruel to animals.

"In my office," Sonya wept.

Making her voice as gentle as possible, she asked, "Do you mean there's a dead dog in your office?"

Sonya hiccupped again. "Y-yes." She stepped back a little and wiped her face.

Why would someone kill an animal and leave it to be found? Maxine's mind flashed to the *Godfather* movies and the horse's head the guy found in his bed. *Oh, calm down. We're not dealing with the mob here.* "Is your office unlocked?"

Sonya shook her head. "I didn't want anyone to

see it. And if it's a crime scene…"

Smart. Maxine hugged Sonya against her once more. "Let's get security." She got an arm around Sonya's shoulders and led her down the hall. "Don't worry," she whispered when Sonya balked. "We're going to another office."

Sonya slipped out from under Maxine's arm but caught her hand. "Come on. In here. It's got good cell reception."

They were in the morgue. Maxine shivered a little. She wasn't afraid of the dead, exactly, but all those unmoving bodies gave her the creeps.

Sonya, on the other hand, seemed more at ease, especially when the door closed. "I'll, um…" She cursed. "My cell's in my purse."

"In the office?"

Sonya nodded.

"And mine is in my cubicle. I dropped my purse off early." Maxine moved toward the door. "I'll get your purse. What color is it?"

Sonya gestured at her pink skirt. "Pink." She sat on the corner of a gurney. "I'm not going back in there until the… body… has been removed." She trembled all over.

Maxine crossed to her, kissed her temple, and then headed for the door. "I'll be right back."

"Don't touch the knob with your hand. There's no need for more fingerprints clouding up the situation." She fished in the pocket of the pink skirt that so lovingly clung to her hips and came out with a tissue. "It's clean," she said as she shook the wrinkles out. Then she handed Maxine her keys. "Be careful. I'm pretty sure whoever left the poor animal there is long gone, but…"

Maxine nodded. "It'll be all right." She left the

morgue gratefully and strode down the hall toward Sonya's office. The coast seemed clear. She used the key and turned the knob with the tissue. She could smell death through the door and her heart tightened.

There *was* something dead in the office, laid across Sonya's usually immaculate desk. But it wasn't a small dog or what humans called "puppies." It was a werewolf pup, barely old enough to have seen its first full moon. By process of elimination, and assuming it had come from one of the dragon/werewolf pairings they'd found, this little one would have died quite some time ago. Yet it was preserved. Had its little body been kept on ice?

Maxine stifled a scream, screwed up her courage, and moved farther into the office. She saw the note Sonya had probably missed and bent closer to the deceased. The note said: "*Stop meddling, or this will be your Partner.*" Complete with a capital letter and a period and a warning tone suitable for an old-timey mystery. Who the hell wrote notes like this anymore?

And what exactly was Sonya meddling in? So far as Maxine knew, she was making calls to powerful female dragons and trying to find out if they'd lost a relative. There wasn't anything serious about that, was there?

"I've seen enough," she whispered. She found Sonya's purse and left the office, relocking the door. Then she was hurrying back along the corridor, actually glad to be returning to the morgue.

When she entered, Sonya was pacing. She'd been worrying at her hair because it was puffed up in random places. She looked at Maxine. She smiled tremulously. "You found it."

Maxine handed her the purse and when Sonya had pulled out her phone, Maxine asked, "Can you thumbprint that thing?"

Sonya nodded. "Better you talk than I do." She unlocked her phone and handed it back. "Who are you calling?"

"Wellington." Maxine dialed. She listened. And cursed when her boss's recorded voice began to speak. She left a brief message and hung up.

Sonya's hand wasn't quite steady when she took the phone. "I'll call Mark. He's part of this too."

As she did so, Maxine wondered if they should have been calling the head of the tracker office. She wasn't sure why Sonya hadn't suggested that, but her own reason was because the trackers gave her the creeps. The few crossovers who worked nominally in Werewolf Watch and Tracker Central froze her blood.

"Mark? Thank God. There's a dead puppy in my office. Someone left it there, right on my desk."

Maxine didn't contradict her. She listened to Mark Tavery say he'd send someone right away and for Sonya to stay away from the office. About ten seconds after Sonya ended the call, there was the sound of doors slamming closed and locking all over the place. Probably not just in this building either.

Maxine hugged herself convulsively. She *hated* feeling caged in. Sonya closed the distance between them and wrapped her arms around Maxine's back. Maxine quit hugging herself and embraced Sonya. They were still that way when a tracker poked her head in to make sure the whole floor was clear.

* * *

The herb garden had a single bench near its center. Mostly, this plot of land was used for growing some of what was used in the kitchens and some of what was used by the witches on staff for their spells.

Sonya   sat   with   her   hands   in   her   lap,

contemplating the nail polish she'd taken such pains to apply this morning. Normally she wore a clear coat, but she'd decided to dress up for Maxine. She'd wished for longer hair so she could do something fun with it. She'd even considered dyeing her hair.

Now, though, she wasn't pleased by the job she'd done on her nails or the bright pink skirt she'd chosen. All she saw when she closed her eyes... well, it was best to keep staring at her hands. Sonya was fully aware that she needed to calm down. She'd been given time in which to do so.

That warning... Maxine said it was overly dramatic and cheesy, but it had cut right to Sonya's heart. Especially when she learned the "puppy" was a "pup," a werewolf child. And despite the fact that it had probably died of natural causes, someone had still taken the time to leave it in her sacred place.

How long would her office smell like decomposition without formaldehyde? Probably not long as far as her nose could tell but that didn't mean Maxine wouldn't be able to smell it for weeks. Sonya shuddered.

"Hey, dear."

Sonya jumped.

Maxine stood a few feet away, her expression tense. "I didn't mean to scare you."

"It's not your fault. Everything's making me jumpy." She patted the bench beside her, moving over to give Maxine room. "Did someone send you to find me?"

"Sort of." She settled beside Sonya and took both of her hands, holding them lightly. "Agent Tavery told me if I wanted to take a walk, he'd appreciate me looking in on you."

Sonya frowned. "Isn't it Agent Wellington who

gives you permission to skip out on work?" She stared at their joined hands.

"It is normally. But they're sort of working together on this case. I'm sure Agent Tavery had Wellington's permission." She too appeared to look at their joined hands. "How are you doing?"

"Not so hot."

"Yeah, death is never easy." Maxine grunted; it might have been a laugh. "Cliché warning. What I meant to say is that death sucks."

Sonya nodded. "I'm sorry I thought it was a dog," she told their connected hands.

"It's all right. I only knew by the smell."

"How long will it smell like dead pup to you?"

"Only a day or two. SearchLight cleaners are used to working within the constraints of a shapeshifter's nose."

That made Sonya a little easier in her mind. She glanced up into Maxine's face. "They threatened you. And I think I'm more scared than you are."

"The cheesiness of the threat --"

"It doesn't sound cheesy to me."

Maxine nodded. "My boss agrees with you. Security around the compound has been increased until we find out who killed those dragons and werewolves and who left the little one." She leaned forward and kissed Sonya's cheek.

Her lips were warm. Soft. Inviting. Sonya turned her head and their mouths met. Slipping her tongue out to play, Sonya tasted the salt on Maxine's upper lip.

"I have a little more to tell and then I want to show you a place. Afterward, you need to see the surveillance video. It caught just a little before the cameras were burned out."

"By what?"

"We're not sure. There wasn't anything electronic used. What I wanted to tell you is that Wellington and Tavery want us to go forward with the phone calls but not with anything else."

"I was going to check Jenny's work on the autopsy of the latest dragon one more time. I trust her." She shrugged. "But I'm a double-checker by nature.

"I think that would be okay. But you might want to check with your boss."

Sonya smiled. "Mark lets me get away with murder." She sobered. "I didn't mean that."

Maxine kissed her on the lips again, gently and briefly. "I know, dear."

"I still think of the animal when you say that." She chuckled. "But I have the feeling you're the wolf who will protect me from all the rest of the scary stuff out there."

"You took care of those gay bashers pretty well."

"Yeah, but they were just human. I'm not foolish enough to try and take on magical creatures."

Maxine scooted closer and hugged her. "I'll keep you safe. Deer. Now. Come and see my secret place."

Hand in hand, they rose and left the herb garden. Sonya allowed Maxine to guide her toward a huge statue of a phoenix. She'd never seen a real phoenix but she'd learned some of the mystical bird's medical stats at SearchLight Academy. She giggled when she saw the way its stony tail feathers were obscured by a large bush. "You know, I think this is the only statue of a magical creature -- or human -- on campus. There are photographs all over the place but mostly of those who look human. I wouldn't know most of them are magical creatures if there weren't little legends under each picture like 'Chinese dragon matriarch.'"

Maxine dropped her hand and crouched. "Come under here for a minute." She crouch-walked beneath the bush.

Sonya gaped. "What…"

Hidden now, Maxine called, "Come on."

I must be crazy. Sonya checked to make sure no one was looking and then hiked her skirt to her waist. Now fearing exposure, she crawled rapidly forward until she was… inside the statue? Not quite; she saw the statue's tail feathers arched above her. The earth on her hands was soft and deep brown, very unlike the sandy soil that seemed to be everywhere else in this part of Florida. She saw Maxine waiting for her, apparently not caring if she got dirt on her slacks.

"What do you think, dear?"

Sonya looked around again, marveling at the coolness of the enclosed space. "This place shouldn't be so cool," she murmured.

"Probably not. That's why I think it's magical. Well, that, and I'm pretty sure the SearchLight equivalent of bomb shelters are directly under this thing. It feels like a safe place, a healing place."

"It feels that way to me too." Sonya moved a little closer and touched Maxine's arm. "Kiss me?"

Maxine did and Sonya closed her eyes, absorbing the sense of safety the other provided. She stroked the werewolf's long hair, made up in tiny braids today, and drank in the kiss. *If I could just remain this way forever, I'd be happy.* She laid her hand over the bulge in Maxine's crotch -- or where there should have been a bulge. "You're not aroused?" she asked, pulling away and looking nervously at Maxine.

"I am. I'm just tucked."

Sonya raised her eyebrows. "Huh?"

Maxine unzipped her trousers. Then she pulled down her underwear a little.

Sonya gazed at the strangely bent penis. "Doesn't that *hurt*?"

"Honestly? No more than the high heels. I've heard it's more difficult for some than others." She adjusted herself. "Although it is uncomfortable when I'm starting to get hard."

Sonya's mouth had flooded with saliva. She was aware of her racing heart and was even more excited by the idea that Maxine could hear it. "Maybe I can take care of that for you." She *knew* her nose was scarlet.

"I'd love that."

Sonya bent forward, planting her hands on the ground on either side of Maxine's thighs.

Maxine's cell phone rang.

Sonya laughed as she drew back. "Well, that was sweet while it lasted."

"Tonight?" Maxine asked, not answering her phone.

"Yes. No." Sonya sighed. "When I don't have to get up early in the morning. Or at least when I've brought work clothes. Let's get out of here."

Maxine caught her arm. "Friday night?" Her eyes were full of need.

Unable to refuse, Sonya nodded.

Maxine relaxed her grip. "I'll go out first to make sure no one's watching."

* * *

By Friday, Sonya had enjoyed so many dreams about Maxine that she was used to waking up wet. She didn't always have time to masturbate and so she came to work horny. Her favorite dream was short but intense: the moment when Maxine had untucked herself. The cock was small despite being half erect. Sonya liked that. It was narrow and short and didn't have a huge head.

But penetration meant joining the werewolf pack, and she was still afraid of werewolves. Wasn't she?

It was ten o'clock on Friday morning. The third week of July was almost gone. And she wanted to see Maxine, not just to talk to her over the phone. Sonya got up, locked her door behind her, and started down the hall. She had news, nothing important enough to walk halfway across the SearchLight campus for, but she definitely, as the country song said, had a girl crush.

As she walked, she forced her thoughts into a productive channel just in case she met someone who wasn't Maxine. *I've seen the footage of the woman who put the cameras on the fritz and she looks familiar.* That fact annoyed her to no end. She hadn't told anyone besides Maxine that she *knew* the woman's face. *I have an especially good memory for faces.* Hell, she could still remember the human face of the werewolf who'd attacked her when she was a kid.

She paused at the bottom of the stairs in the main campus building, gathering her courage. When she could no longer see the monster's features in her mind's eye, she opened the door and climbed the stairs. Slowly.

Emerging on the second floor, there seemed to be no one around. She liked that and left the foyer.

"Hey, *dear.* You going to run from me?"

Sonya froze as the male werewolf's voice lanced into her.

"Isn't that what Maxi calls you? Deer? Like the animal? It's pretty obvious she wants prey and you're just too stupid to get it."

Rage shot through Sonya's head like a bolt of lightning. Without pausing to think, she spun on her heel. "How *dare* you use her pet name for me against me?" She stalked forward, not quite close enough to poke a finger into the werewolf's chest.

"Your boyfriend's no lady."

"Let's get two things straight, buster. Maxine is more of a man than you'll ever be and more of a woman than you'll ever get." It was a quote from *Rent* and would probably lose some of its power if the asshole realized that, but Sonya was too fired up to care.

Daring greatly, she turned her back on the werewolf. The moment she did, terror assailed her. Knowing he could smell this, however, pissed her off all over again. She stalked down toward Maxine's office.

Maxine wasn't there. The door stood open and she wasn't inside.

Feeling suddenly cornered, Sonya bit her lip and glanced over her shoulder. The werewolf who'd insulted both her and Maxine was prowling toward her. He smiled when their eyes met.

"The problem with bravado, little deer, is that it doesn't work on werewolves."

He can't eat me. Not here. These words did nothing for her racing heart. Sonya pressed herself against the wall and stared at death in an off-the-rack suit.

"*Daryl.* My office. Now."

Agent Wellington had appeared like a miracle. And Maxine was with him.

She brushed past Daryl without looking at him, demonstrating an unconcern that filled Sonya with pride. "Are you all right?"

Sonya glanced over Maxine's shoulder.

"Don't look at him, dear. Just at me."

Deer. Sonya shivered.

Maxine snarled as she spun to face Daryl, who was just turning toward Agent Wellington. "If you've ruined my pet name for my girlfriend, I'll use your balls for earrings."

Agent Wellington escorted Daryl away. He flashed Maxine a grin that the other male werewolf didn't see. Then they were gone.

"Come on." Maxine guided Sonya into her office with her hand on the small of Sonya's back. "He can't stand it that I'm getting some, or he thinks I am, and he's not." She shut the door.

"Isn't he with Carol?"

"Except the scuttlebutt is that she's been refusing him for at least two weeks."

Sonya laughed. A bit. "That's why he's acting like a jerk?"

"It's just why he's acting like a jerk without Carol as backup." Maxine gently helped Sonya sit. She crouched beside her, holding her hands. "Are you all right?"

"Better now."

"We would have come out sooner, but it sounded like you had it well in hand."

"I did. At first." Sonya took a breath. "I'm glad you stepped in when you did. I came to see you," she admitted. "I mean, I have news, but I mostly just wanted to be with you."

Maxine lifted Sonya's right hand and kissed the palm. "Tell me. Then I'll walk you back to your office."

"I finally heard from a female dragon who says she's the head of the Ontario Territory. Her name is Nicole. No last name. But that's normal. She says that by the description I left on the phone, she thinks the first dragon we found is her daughter. She'll be here this afternoon by plane."

Maxine nodded. "I have a little news too. The pup we found was half werewolf and half dragon." She blushed. "Wellington and I spoke with such certainty, but apparently, according to Fehrna Susan, if you apply curare to their outside, you can force them, even after death, to take their magical form. Jenny said it's that way for dragons too."

Sonya nodded. "The pup was kept on ice; there were burst cell membranes to prove it. And Jenny told me about the pup's dual parentage. I checked the latest female dragon for fluids in her uterus and found semen. I think artificial insemination happened. Although how a dragon could be subdued enough to be impregnated is an open question. And we don't even know if she was in human form, which would mean fewer offspring but a better chance of holding her in one place. If she was in dragon guise, and unless she was drugged insensible, which I guess is possible but would cause problems for the fetus, she would have fought. Have you ever heard of the red-tailed boa constrictor?"

"No."

"It's the only reptile that gives birth to live young. It's called ovoviviparous birth, which basically means live babies from eggs." She waved her hand. "It's complicated. Dragons are like that, except with magic thrown in to really confuse things."

Maxine seemed to grasp the basic concept. "What danger would the fetus be in?"

"The drug mixture needed to keep a dragon unconscious and in dragon form is hard to come by. It's a blending of at least a dozen poisonous plants aided by the addition of silver. It would kill an unborn pup."

"I thought silver only affected werewolves." Maxine frowned. "Although if they *are* related to dragons, as legend suggests…"

"It's more than myth, at least in the minds of the basilisk community. Basilisks maintain that both dragons and werewolves are descended from them."

"Can they say how?"

"They can't even say when." Sonya sighed. "But there are too many similarities between all three species to completely discount the basilisks' assertion. As far as silver goes, it only works on dragons when mixed with the plants I mentioned. Otherwise, dragons can be poisoned by an overabundance of metals, like humans can, but that kind of death is extremely rare."

"What do you get when you inject werewolf sperm into a dragon's egg?" Maxine wondered.

"According to legend, a basilisk." Sonya blinked. "I didn't think to check for that possibility. I just assumed she was pregnant when she was captured."

"But wouldn't the differences be obvious in any form?"

"That's the screwy thing about magic in shapeshifters. It only shows up when the person is in their quote-unquote animal guise."

Maxine caught her arm. "Hold on a second. If the baby's half dragon and half werewolf, who will take the remains?"

Sonya frowned and settled back into her seat. "I hadn't thought of that. Mark had me calling all the female dragons, but this is the first one to respond."

"The alpha who called me has heard rumors about another missing wolf, but he's still chasing that down. He definitely lost a werewolf of the description I gave for the third body." She stood and offered Sonya her hand. "Please let me know if it's a basilisk. I don't know if that will solve anything…"

"You suspect something," Sonya said.

"Not really. I just have a feeling."

"Feelings are usually based on facts your conscious mind has forgotten."

"Really?" Maxine was smiling. "Who taught you that?"

"Professor Boyle, the parapsychology teacher."

"I sort of remember him saying something like that. Do you have any feelings about this?"

"Just about that woman on the video."

"Keep that feeling then. And I'll try to figure out what I've forgotten." Maxine kissed Sonya's hand. "See you tonight still?"

Sonya was reminded of what the offensive Daryl had said. "You're not my boyfriend. But… are you my girlfriend?"

"Do you want me to be?"

"If you're not, I'm having erotic dreams about a friend. And kissing a friend. And wanting to suck a friend off." She grimaced. "Okay, maybe not that last so much. I've spent too long giving head. But I *do* want to taste you a little."

Maxine smiled. "I love your honesty. And I'd love to be your girlfriend."

When they started back to Sonya's office, Sonya glowed.

* * *

That afternoon was hot, sticky, and uncomfortably close. There wasn't a cloud in the sky, but the humidity was thick enough to hack with a saw. Sonya was aware of the weather as she seldom was because she'd been standing outside waiting for the arrival of the dragon matriarch for almost twenty minutes.

It was one o'clock and her lunch was a brick in her stomach. Her feet ached and she wished she hadn't worn heels today no matter how good they made her calves look through her stockings and below the hem of her knee-length skirt. She'd dressed up with Maxine in mind, instead of a matriarch who could be as late as she wanted.

That's unfair. She can't control when her plane arrives. Or how bad traffic is.

She glanced at Maxine and saw that her girlfriend was sweating lightly. She looked as uncomfortable as Sonya felt.

Turning her head to the right, she observed Mark Tavery sweating freely; it streaked down his skin. *At least Maxine and I are only in blouses. He's in a suit coat and tie.*

She stood in between the two of them because she, as the official dragon coroner, was supposed to give SearchLight's condolences and escort the matriarch to see her daughter. Despite the uncomfortable circumstances, she felt prepared. The keys when dealing with dragons were respect followed by courage.

"Here we go," Mark said and he straightened. "Ready, Johnson?"

She nodded even though his use of her surname made her stomach twist. She knew it was his way of reminding her that this was a formal situation. He would refer to her as "Johnson" or "Medical Technician Johnson" during the rest of this event. "Yes, sir."

A Lincoln Town Car pulled up to the curb. Mark bowed toward the passenger door before stepping forward to open it. "Madame Nicole, welcome to SearchLight."

The stately woman who stepped out looked to be no older than Sonya or the magical creatures who flanked her. Nicole was several centuries old, according to Mark, making her one of the longest-lived dragons in the world. Dragons tended to die in fights or as a result of negative run-ins with SearchLight agents.

Nicole had been alive when her species hunted humans.

That wasn't a helpful thing to be thinking.

The dragon matriarch was the same height as Mark. All dragons stood at five-ten in human guise and eight feet in dragon form. Unlike most species, there wasn't a size difference between the males and females.

Basilisks aren't different heights either. They all come at about nine feet long from head to tail. The giant serpents were rare nowadays, and tended to be reclusive. Sonya had only ever met one, a female professor at SearchLight Academy in Washington, DC.

Nicole extended her hand and Mark bowed over it. Then she glanced at Sonya.

Dropping into a deep curtsy, Sonya wished for a longer skirt. "Madame, you honor us with your presence."

Nicole offered her a nod. Then her gaze fell on Maxine and she scowled. "Why, precisely, is a dog present?"

Maxine snarled, her upper lip rising and her eyeteeth showing. Werewolves, like dragons, had eyeteeth longer than a human's that would grow or shrink in appearance depending how close they were to changing into their true form.

Sonya took half a step as Nicole's eyes narrowed and her lip curled. "Please, Madame --"

"How dare you?" Maxine demanded.

"I dare, little dog, because you are nothing more than a four-legged beast."

Rage shot through Sonya, shocking her with its intensity. She took a full step this time. "Really, you shouldn't insult my --"

Mark seized her by the upper arm and forced her back to her original position. The strength in his hand startled her enough to cut off her speech.

"My dear lady," Mark said, "you are here because your daughter was killed. A werewolf died beside her. That is the reason for Agent Brown's presence."

"Are you insinuating that my daughter killed this dog?"

"The wolf and your daughter were both killed by an unknown enemy. If you can provide any information that may lead to the killer's whereabouts or reason for kidnapping your daughter, that would be greatly appreciated."

The female dragon hesitated for the first time. "They weren't fighting?"

Sonya took over. "No, Madame. We believe your daughter was impregnated, through in vitro fertilization, with the werewolf's sperm."

"Why?" She sounded shocked.

"That remains unclear as of yet. We are seeking the answer with all due diligence."

"Was there a... thing... born from this forced union?"

"She gave birth, Madame. It was half dragon and half werewolf. The baby boy is dead as well, of natural causes."

"What causes?"

"When he shifted for the first time, during the first full moon of his life, the change was too dramatic for him."

The matriarch scowled. "Such a disgusting half breed should never have been allowed to live in the first place. Let the dog's pack take care of it."

"You would allow a werewolf pack to bury your grandson?" Mark asked softly.

Nicole hesitated for the second time. "I suppose," she said slowly, "that the werewolves may have the honor of burying a… grandson… of mine."

Maxine, who had stopped snarling, replied, "I am sure the alpha of the deceased wolf's pack will accept that honor with good grace. Thank you."

Sonya's nerves were still jumping. Abruptly, she ceased to care. Because her anger had cross-patched with the anger she'd felt over a week ago while standing on a woman's porch with Maxine.

I know who the woman is that burned out the cameras and presumably left that poor hybrid on my desk.

Mark was saying something; Sonya struggled to bring her mind back to the present.

"-- follow Medical Technician Johnson, she will lead the way to the morgue."

Sonya curtsied before turning her back on the matriarch. She led the way into the mercifully cool building.

About an hour later, she stood outside again with Mark and Maxine. They were watching the hearse, followed by another Lincoln Town Car, leave the parking lot.

As soon as Mark went back inside, Sonya turned to Maxine. "I know who that woman in the video is. Not by name, but she's the one who cussed you out when we went looking for witnesses."

"Do you know how she burned out the cameras?"

"No. She looked basically the same both times…" Sonya frowned. "Hell, I think she was wearing identical clothes, though I can't be sure. But I *think* she was wearing jeans and a flannel shirt, which I thought at the time was really warm for Florida. And she was definitely wearing at least a flannel-like shirt in the surveillance video." She chased the idea, puzzling it out as she talked. "The only real differences were her expression and… something else. An accessory difference."

"Like a necklace?" Maxine asked.

"She wasn't wearing *sunglasses* when she was caught on tape," Maxine marveled. "But why would she? It was the middle of the night."

"Why would she wear sunglasses inside her house?" Sonya countered.

"Maybe she only put those on to answer the door. People can be photosensitive. Or maybe she was high and didn't want it to show in her eyes."

Sonya said, "What do you say we skip the bar tonight and seek out this woman after hours? Then we wouldn't be technically breaking any rules."

"Rules?"

"I'm pretty sure this should technically be a tracker case now."

Maxine smirked. "You're wicked."

"Is that a no?"

"It's a definite yes."

Chapter Seven

By five-thirty, when Sonya found a parking spot one street over from where the bodies had been dumped, all the flirtation had gone out of the day. Maxine was sure there had been daring and romance in Sonya's suggestion that they sneak a little intel. But now that they were here Maxine, at least, was worried about her girlfriend's safety.

Sonya made a move to open her door.

Maxine caught her by the wrist. "Maybe you should stay here."

That bald pronouncement earned her a narrow-eyed expression. "Why?"

It was a little embarrassing to admit how worried she was, but nothing ventured, nothing gained. "If this *is* the woman who left a dead body on your desk, she's almost certainly dangerous."

"My karate skills served me fine with those bastards."

"Yes, but…" Maxine shook her head when Sonya's eyes narrowed even more. "You're human, dear. I'm a werewolf. I can resist more than you."

"Even werewolves can't fight everything."

"And you think you can?"

Sonya flared. "No, but rule one of investigation is to have backup. For verification and for… well, just for common sense." She tugged her wrist out of Maxine's grip.

Maxine got out of the car after Sonya. "All right, but let me do the talking."

"You *are* the more experienced when it comes to asking questions. But what are you going to do if she insults you again?"

"This time, I'm ready for her." She'd hardened

her heart against the pain. It was strange but she'd fought against the prejudice of other werewolves all her life until it scarcely bothered her. But either she'd grown soft after her long years in a pack that loved and accepted her, or unexpected sources of vitriol affected her more.

They were about halfway down the block toward the woman's dwelling. Maxine noticed Sonya checking all the windows they passed. "What are you looking for?"

"Just making sure, in case this does turn dangerous, that there aren't any civilians nearby."

A prickle of anxiety spiraled up Maxine's spine. *Maybe this wasn't a good idea.* "Maybe --"

"This was my idea and you're not my supervisor." Sonya winked as she said this and dropped her voice to a whisper. "Hell, we haven't even gotten into the sack yet to see who's dominant."

Maxine gaped at her. "You're like a light switch, up and down, on and off."

"Nope. I'm just aware that life's short and I haven't flirted with you in something like six hours."

Maxine flushed. "You're making it hard to --"

"Am I? That must be uncomfortable. Maybe, if there's no swallowing involved..." She grinned, probably at the look of utter shock on Maxine's face. "Let's get this done." And she led the way up the concrete steps.

Maxine hurried to be the one closest to the door. Flirting aside -- although, shit, it was difficult to think past her body's reaction -- this woman had probably broken into a very secure facility. She nudged Sonya half a step back and rapped on the door.

There was silence from within but then the door opened. The woman they'd met before appeared with her sunglasses firmly in place. "Whadda you want?"

Maxine flashed her badge. "Hello, ma'am. We just want to --"

"I ain't got nothing to do with SsearchLight."

Maxine swallowed her surprise. If this woman knew about SearchLight, if the badge showed her SearchLight instead of, say, Tampa police, she was more than likely a magical creature. There were very few humans who knew about SearchLight except when they'd been exposed to magical creatures.

Sonya asked, "Ma'am, how do you know about SearchLight?"

"Get out of here, SsearchLight."

Sonya suddenly gripped Maxine's shoulder. "We should go."

Maxine didn't glance at her. "Ma'am, the dragon and werewolf who died here --"

"*Now.*" Sonya pulled on her arm.

Maxine moved away from her, closer to the magical creature. She inhaled deeply but didn't recognize the other's scent. Whatever she was, she wasn't human, but she also wasn't any of the magical creatures Maxine had met. Although she did smell like a big snake. She must own a python. "Ma'am, we're not here to bother you. But we need to know about the dragon and werewolf whose bodies were dropped on your street."

"It'ss none of your conssern."

"Maxine, we need to go." Sonya was, oddly, shielding her eyes. "Come *on.*" Then: "Excuse us, ma'am. We have the wrong address."

"You go. I'll follow when I'm done questioning --"

"Your partner hass the right of it, SsearchLight. Go away." And she started to close the door.

Maxine blocked her from doing so. "We need information, ma'am. You can't just --"

"Watch me." The woman ducked her head and let out a long hiss.

Sonya seized Maxine's shoulders and shoved her, face first, against the side of the building.

Maxine cried out as her nose connected. Shit, that *hurt*. She had a feeling her nose was broken. The good news was that her werewolf healing abilities would take care of it.

There was the sound of a great, long, *large* something passing Maxine, shoving her, and Sonya also, against the building.

Maxine struggled to see what was going on but Sonya grunted, "Hold the fuck *still*."

All right, so maybe Sonya had a reason for pushing her. And for trying to get her out of the area. So, Maxine waited. Although she couldn't imagine how Sonya would know when it was safe. She started counting seconds silently.

She got to seventy-two before Sonya stepped back.

"Okay, it's clear." Sonya sounded winded.

Maxine stepped back from the wall and wiped her nose. Yup, there was blood. She felt her nose carefully, found it wasn't broken, and stopped prodding. "What --"

"That bitch was a basilisk."

Maxine gaped. "No way," she whispered.

Sonya put her hands on her hips. "A huge snake just slithered out of here. And even if she hadn't just turned into a three-meter -long magical creature, she hissed her words, she was wearing sunglasses, and they're special sunglasses."

"How do you figure that?"

"Because a standard pair of sunglasses won't protect you from a basilisk's gaze."

"But…" Maxine struggled to catch up. "I thought all basilisks…" She shook her head. "I'm lost."

"The basilisk doctors haven't been able to figure out why only some can do it. They think it's tied to the basilisks' inability to reproduce."

"But didn't you say a basilisk can be made by a dragon and a werewolf? Why did that pup show up as half and half and not a basilisk?"

"I'd guess because we don't know as much about basilisk physiology. I mean, we know their basic similarities to werewolves and dragons, but there are a lot of unanswered questions. I do want to try one more test on the child's body. Come on." She held up a pair of sunglasses, probably the ones the basilisk had been wearing. "We can test these to see if they're the kind that deflect the killing sight." She went down the steps and started away from the house.

Maxine could understand why Sonya had sounded winded; it was how she felt now.

When they reached Sonya's car, Sonya said, "I don't want to call Mark while I'm driving." She laughed weakly. "Do you mind going back to your place? We need to call SearchLight."

"Why?" Maxine winced at the way her voice went up in both pitch and volume. "Can't we wait until Monday? We're going to get our asses handed to us."

"I learned the hard way not to delay calling this kind of shit in."

Mostly to distract Sonya, who was looking nervous and tense, Maxine asked, "What happened?"

Sonya's hand returned to the steering wheel. "It's pretty simple. I was working under Mark Tavery when he was just an agent and not head of the DoD. I'd been sent a dead dragon from his latest investigation. I discovered the female dragon was pregnant and I forgot to tell him. Boy, did Dr. Zabreki -- the head of the DoD back then -- lay into me."

"That was a case of forgetting, not disobeying orders."

"I'm guessing the result would be the same."

Maxine nodded glumly. "Probably. Let's go to my place to make the call and await the inevitable."

Fifteen minutes later, they arrived at Maxine's building and she directed Sonya to her personal parking space. "I don't have a car, but I have to pay for the thing."

Upstairs, they decided to eat something light, mostly because it was after six and not because they were hungry. While Maxine began putting together a salad, Sonya sat at the breakfast bar and dialed.

Then she sighed. "Hi, Mark. This is Sonya. Please call me when you get this, no matter the hour. We have a basilisk running around Tampa possibly killing people." She hung up.

Maxine said, "I doubt either of us wants to eat much, but maybe a salad will satisfy."

Sonya crossed the kitchen and put her arms around Maxine from behind. She leaned her cheek against Maxine's shoulder. "I couldn't have stood it if you'd died."

Maxine turned and hugged Sonya against her. "I should have listened."

Sonya snorted. "Damn right." She snuggled against Maxine. "Please understand what I'm about to say isn't meant as a rejection, but I'm just not ready to belong to a pack."

Maxine's gut tightened. Was this a good-bye

speech?

"Can you give me a little more time? Let me kiss you and hold you and maybe try oral sex at some point?"

Every tightened muscle let go and Maxine laughed her relief. "Of course, dear."

* * *

"Oral sex at some point" turned out to be forty-five minutes later. First...

Sonya and Maxine ate their light meal, or rather, Sonya ate and Maxine picked at her food. So. After Sonya had eaten all she could with plans to play with Maxine later in the mix, she took their dishes into the kitchen.

Maxine followed. "I'll wash."

"You won't." Sonya took Maxine's bowl and set it on the counter. "We're going to ignore our chores and play instead." She wrapped her arms around the slightly taller woman's neck.

"I'm not in the mood, I guess."

"I understand."

Maxine raised her eyebrows. "She forgets I'm a lie detector."

Sonya flushed. "I guess I forgot you're a werewolf. Okay, so I don't understand. But I want you to be comfortable." She frowned. "What's wrong?"

Maxine stepped back. "You're not worried about the trouble we're going to get into for letting a potential murderer escape? For tipping off said murderer?"

"I am, but I care more about the fact that we could have died today and I would have never found out what sex with you is like." She touched her nose, sure it was red. "I know we can't go all the way, but..." She pushed past her hesitation. "I'm nervous about oral sex, but mostly because I don't like really huge dicks."

Maxine smiled a little. "Well, I'm only four and a half inches. I know that sounds really tiny but…"

"That actually sounds like the ideal size."

Maxine laughed a little. "You're probably the first person to ever say that."

"What about your former lover?" Sonya bit her lip. "I mean, you don't have to answer if you don't want to."

"She liked fingering only."

"Did you, um, get your needs fulfilled?"

Maxine hesitated. "I don't want to think about the past."

Sonya nodded. "Will you sing to me? It will raise your spirits, and I just love your voice."

They settled on the couch, Maxine offering her lap for Sonya's head.

When Sonya was comfortable with her eyes closed and her fingers intertwined with Maxine's, the werewolf began to sing. It was a Paul Simon song this time.

Sonya thought she would drift but she was very aware of the slight bulge under her ear. On the pretext of adjusting her position, she put her right hand, palm down, under her cheek. She cupped Maxine's crotch gently.

Maxine laughed, her belly moving against the back of Sonya's head. "You didn't want me to sing. You just wanted me in a vulnerable position."

"I do too want you to sing. I just need to touch you at the same time." Sonya closed her hand a little and grinned when Maxine gasped.

"If you keep doing that, I won't be able to sing."

Sonya repeated the gesture. "This won't be our

last night together. I think I can wait to hear you sing again. Maybe even until tomorrow morning."

"What if Agent Tavery calls while we're…"

"I'll let it go to voicemail." Light squeeze. Slightly harder squeeze.

"I hope you're going to follow that up with something else, or you're going to give me the worst case of blue balls I've had in decades."

Sonya rolled off the couch and began to strip. "Do you like having your balls played with?"

Maxine smirked. She was obviously enjoying watching Sonya take off her clothes. Sonya was already topless. "I like them handled but not licked."

"Do you like anal play?"

"Do *you*?"

"No, but I don't mind putting something up your ass."

"I don't like it. I'm more about watching my partner get herself off."

Sonya grinned. "Really?" She unzipped her skirt and dropped it, loving the way Maxine's gaze followed the fall of the fabric. She rubbed her fingers along the waistband of her pink panties. She wished they were silk, but she had to settle for cotton. Fully and comfortably aware that Maxine was avidly watching, she slipped two fingers between her legs and caressed her clitoris through the underwear.

Maxine groaned. "You're a tease. I love it."

Sonya pulled her damp-crotched panties down until they joined her skirt. She stepped out of her shoes and removed her knee highs.

Now starkers -- a word she'd picked up from Jenny, who was English-born -- she walked slowly toward Maxine. "Your turn."

The gorgeous werewolf scrambled to her feet

and all but tore off her blouse. Then the bra, complete with its fake boobs, was gone. She hesitated with her hand on the zipper of her dress slacks.

"Go on. If you do, I'll do this again." She dipped her finger between the labia and stroked her vulva with a single digit. She then quit touching herself and waited.

Maxine shed the rest of her clothes with alacrity.

Smiling, Sonya crossed to Maxine and palmed her sparsely-haired testicles. "You're lovely," she said as she gazed into her partner's eyes. "Absolutely lovely." Crouching, she licked the tip of Maxine's sex before straightening again and retreating a few steps. "You want to watch me?"

Maxine nodded. Her lips slightly parted, she resembled a statue titled simply "Wonder" that Sonya had glimpsed once.

Sonya wetted the pads of both index fingers and traced these around her nipples. Her body responded at once and she arched against her hands. Laving her fingers again, she trailed the damp digits down her breasts and over her slightly rounded stomach. She paused just above the juncture between her legs. "Do you want to see me stroke myself?"

"Please." Maxine's penis wore a single drop of pre-ejaculate. It was pearly, catching the light.

Sonya's mouth watered and she only hesitated a moment. She'd never liked the taste of semen but her tongue seemed to leap in her mouth. She approached on the balls of her feet, took the pearl, and put it between her lips.

It wasn't sweet.

But it wasn't heavy with stench or musky flavor either. When another pearl appeared, she took this one on her pointer finger and slipped it between her labia to be smoothed on her clit.

Maxine grabbed Sonya by the shoulders and pulled her close with shaking hands. She kissed Sonya, thrusting her tongue between Sonya's lips but just as quickly retreating.

Sonya gave chase. She traced the other's teeth with her tongue tip and then pulled out. "Shall I continue?" she purred. Then she spoiled it, at least in her own mind, by laughing. "I'm not used to being seductive."

"You're great."

Encouraged, Sonya retreated a few steps to give herself room and began to rub her clit in earnest. She watched Maxine's pupils dilate and grinned mentally, although she couldn't be sure a tiny smile didn't escape her seductress's mask.

When she was on the edge, she left off petting herself and approached Maxine.

The werewolf caught her damp fingers and brought them to her mouth.

Sonya blushed.

Maxine said, "You're going to taste me, aren't you? It's only fair. And pleasurable."

Never had she been "tasted" by another. The idea made her dewy and she laughed a little. "Being with you is like being in a wonderfully equal relationship. I've never been able to share these parts of myself before."

Maxine smirked. "This means one of three things. You should have tried werewolves sooner, you should have tried a transgender m2f earlier, or we were meant to be and the moon goddess was just waiting for us to be ready."

Amused, and yet moved by the words, Sonya dropped to her knees. "I'd like to taste you. But I can't deep-throat."

"Ask me if I care."

Sonya grinned and parted her lips, accepting the narrow and only faintly scented cock into her mouth. She wondered why Maxine didn't stink there as most men did and her mind replied at once. *She's a woman in all the ways that matter.*

Yes, but sometimes even I smell there.

Then she's taking good care of herself. Listen to her moan.

Maxine was indeed moaning, and though she didn't thrust her hips, her thighs trembled.

Sonya experienced the first drop of Maxine's precum like a mildly salty drop of slightly viscous fluid. She swallowed.

Mmm.

"Okay," Maxine panted. "Stop."

Sonya drew back, confused. "What did I do wrong?"

"Nothing. I just don't want to come in your mouth or all over my floor."

Unable to repress a giggle, Sonya said, "You are a neat freak."

"Guilty as charged." Maxine helped Sonya to her feet. "Please, follow me to my bedroom where I have condoms and I can masturbate while I watch you do anything you please."

The bedroom was decorated with an accent wall of a mild yellow-gold-orange. Sonya arranged herself against this wall, fully aware that it complemented her skin, and alternated between toying with her nipples and dipping her fingers between her legs. She watched Maxine expertly roll on a condom and face her. They stood less than three feet apart.

"Before I come, may I taste you?" Maxine asked.

Sonya nodded.

"Spread your legs." Maxine dropped to the floor gracefully and crawled forward until her face disappeared against Sonya's thatch.

Sonya moaned just from the contact of a soft face against her pubic hair. She cried out softly when Maxine breathed on her. Then she was shuddering all over and struggling to keep her feet as Maxine licked her clit.

Lights flashed behind her eyes and the world seemed to shift under her feet. Groaning, straining not to shove herself against Maxine's mouth, she squeezed her eyelids shut and prayed the sensation would never stop.

Abruptly, her orgasm washed over her and her cry was of mingled relief and regret. Even before she was done trembling, she was apologizing. "I didn't mean to. I'm sorry. You can, um, come in my mouth. I didn't mean --"

Maxine looked up at her and she wasn't angry. At least there was no anger on her face or in her lovely eyes. "I would never do anything you didn't want. At least, not on purpose. There may come a day when I, well, come without meaning to, but I'm older than you." She grinned and there was no more doubt that she was pleased. "Besides, I like that I undid you."

Maxine got to her feet. "And now, will you kindly play with yourself while I jack off?"

Sonya's legs were still shaking; she leaned back against the wall and slipped her hand between her legs. She moaned softly when Maxine began stroking herself. By the time Maxine had found her orgasm, Sonya had come twice more.

"And now," Maxine said, "we're going to lie down and rest." She chuckled. "After I shower. I hate smelling my sweat." She made a show of scenting the air. "Although *you* smell divine."

Blushing, Sonya said, "I'll join you in the shower."

Chapter Eight

Sonya needed to pee, but it wasn't urgent. Why was she awake?

The moment she swung her legs over the side of the bed, she saw her phone was lit up. She heard it buzzing.

Scooping it up, she hurried out of the bedroom, closing the door soundlessly in an attempt to let Maxine sleep. Then she crossed the living room and moved into the kitchen, putting herself as far from her sleeping lover as possible.

Lover... She grinned and answered the phone. "Hello?"

Mark Tavery answered. "Blue fuck, Johnson, what were you thinking?"

Sonya, wincing, responded softly, hoping he would lower his voice in return. "I was thinking that if I was wrong, I didn't want to waste company time."

Mark did indeed drop his volume to match hers, though he sounded just as furious. "You didn't stop to think what would happen if you were right."

Annoyed by his big-brother attitude, and remembering how she'd protected Maxine efficiently, Sonya responded, "I can take care of myself, *Mark*."

He sighed. "I've seen you take people twice your size. But these are magical creatures."

"Don't you even want to know where she lives?"

He sighed again. "Give."

After she gave him the address, he said, "All right, initiative is why you're the top medical technician in Florida."

She glowed to hear that. Mark's compliments were rare.

"But you leave it to others from now on. If

there's some reason basilisks are involved, this is out of your hands. And mine. This is a matter for our top negotiators. Besides, I have a feeling the only reason this basilisk didn't roast you both is because you're human and she stops at that. If Maxine had been there alone, she'd probably be dead now."

"You're just saying that to scare me."

"Nope." He sounded very tired. "Just... try to figure out why a dragon and a werewolf didn't make a basilisk baby, okay? That might give us some more information." He seemed to be talking to himself when he added, "I wonder what brought them so far south? The werewolf was from the Catskills and the dragon was from Ontario. We haven't figured out where the other wolves were from, but the other dragons were definitely Canadian born." He paused. "Sonya? I'm sorry I called you Johnson. I didn't mean to come down on you so hard. I just don't want anyone dying on my watch. Especially not when you've just come out of your box."

Sonya grinned at her reflection in the microwave. Thinking of her "box" she blushed. "Is there anyone who doesn't know I'm dating Maxine?"

"Maybe a couple of junior agents. In Tallahassee."

Sonya snorted. "Thanks a pant load."

"Promise me you'll stay out of this."

"Unless someone involves me."

Mark laughed without humor. "All right. That sounds like something I'd say. Especially if Luke got into trouble."

"Give my best to Luke."

"He's sleeping, lucky bastard. Good morning, Sonya."

Sonya hung up and turned around. She jumped

back when she saw Maxine standing in the shadows between the kitchen and the living room. "Oh, hell," she muttered, and then she laughed. "I didn't want to wake you."

Maxine approached and touched Sonya's free hand. "At least he didn't rip you a new one. Come back to bed."

"It wasn't anywhere near as bad as I expected."

"Same here." She leaned forward and kissed Sonya's cheek. "Come on. Bed."

Five minutes later, after they'd made themselves comfortable between the sheets and under the light comforter, Sonya nuzzled Maxine's neck until the werewolf laughed.

"What are you doing?"

"Acting like a deer, of course."

Maxine laughed harder. "You're a goose as well as a deer. Good night, you silly animal."

"Good night, beautiful."

* * *

After Sonya left to go home to work on her housecleaning and ready herself for the next week, Maxine headed back up toward her apartment, her heart light. She met Fehrna Susan and her mate, Michaela, on the first floor.

Both looked sober.

Maxine stood with her back to the stairwell door. "What is it?"

Fehrna Susan answered, "The pack stayed out of your way. But we won't do that forever. Stick with your own kind."

A punch in the stomach would have been kinder.

Michaela tried to gentle it; concern lived in her dark eyes. "She's terrified of werewolves."

"She's less frightened than she used to be."

Fehrna Susan said, slightly quieter, "How will she feel, surrounded by werewolves 24/7? And I will not confine our people within their own home."

Maxine winced. She'd been ignoring those facts, hadn't she? Sonya still couldn't handle Werewolf Watch and although that was mostly because of two assholes, there *were* jerks in the Fehrna pack. Worse, Maxine couldn't be everywhere at once. "Fuck."

* * *

Sonya's stomach was in knots when she arrived at work Monday morning. Not because she'd heard anything more from Mark, or from Public Relations, which would have been much worse, but because of the way she'd been summarily dumped. Via text.

Without looking at her phone, she could quote it. "My alpha made it brutally apparent that a relationship with you will lead nowhere. I'm sorry, but we have to end this."

As she'd driven to work that morning, dreading and yet longing to see Maxine, she'd meditated on the state of her stomach and how well it reflected the state of her thoughts.

Now that she was parked, she decided not to seek Maxine out while she herself was in so much pain. Sonya headed directly for the autopsy room. She found a list of questions on a clipboard in Jenny's handwriting and parked one hip on the corner of an autopsy table to read. As was her habit, Jenny had starred each item with a little doodle that wasn't quite an asterisk. She was also one of the few people Sonya had ever met who used semicolons in her printing.

- **The baby's werewolf form has quite a lot of hair over its spine; how can it be that it died during the full moon transformation?**
- **There's a form between dragon and werewolf,**

picked up by the X-ray when I decided to have the corpse transformed right on the table instead of removing it like we've been doing; unsure what the form is; ask Sonya to take a look at the readings

- All forms have membranous shell remains; just thought this worth noting since it doesn't appear in any of the other notes
- Also, how many were actually born? Not knowing the dragon's guise when she gave birth makes a mystery

Sonya cursed herself over the second-to-last. She'd noticed the shell, but she'd failed to write it down. She'd been making assumptions. The central-most of those seemed to be that she'd decided, somewhere in the back of her mind, that the dragon form wasn't as crucial as the werewolf guise. Probably because the pup had died while in furry form.

Playing a hunch, she went into her office, found Jenny there ahead of her, and smiled wanly. "Sorry about the umbilicus."

"You never miss anything," Jenny answered without looking up from whatever she was doing on her computer. "It was nice to get one up on you." She flashed a smile at her screen that was surely meant for Sonya.

Sonya sat behind her desk. "Do you have a second? I need to bounce some ideas off you."

"Sure." Jenny turned toward her after saving whatever she'd been working on. "Are you going to discuss the furry spine business? Because that's what's bugging me the most."

"The current statistics for werewolf pup survival rates are a little over half live past their first month. Werewolves who want to mate often don't do so until they're sure they're at least third cousins. Inter-pack arranged matings are still common, although LGBTQ, psychic wolves don't hold with that tradition because conception is rarely involved." She frowned, thinking of Maxine. "Werewolves have been mating more with humans during the last century because half werewolves have a higher viability rate, as much as seventy-five percent."

Her throat went dry and she coughed, blinking away the image of Maxine and the idea that they were never going to get a chance to try for pups of any kind because she couldn't bear to live under the same roof with two dozen werewolves. Of course, that probably wasn't Maxine's reason for cutting their relationship short.

Jenny helped. "So far as we know, since the werewolves don't like SearchLight doing experiments on their dead, and no living, full-blooded wolf will submit to endless tests, pups with thick fur down their spine tend to survive the full moon change better than those without thick fur. Hell, since werewolves are born human, at least in every case they cared to share with SearchLight, that thick fur has been reported as a birth defect by at least a dozen human doctors who helped deliver the babies."

"We assumed the pup, dragonlet, or basilisk baby died during the full moon transformation because it was in wolf guise on my desk. But it also had a human form."

"Maybe it was born as a dragon."

"No. It's male. Only females are born as dragonlets. It has something to do, we think, with the depth at which the eggs are buried. Something like alligator eggs, which come out male or female depending on how deep they're buried."

"But," Jenny said, "dragons do a weird live birth-egg combination. In a sandy nest?"

Sonya shrugged. "Our best guess is that the eggs are closer to sea turtle eggs in terms of thickness but still allow for live births. The dragonlets just depend on the yolk instead of a placenta."

"So…" Jenny frowned. "Maybe the fact that it had four forms actually killed it. That's a hell of a lot of shifting. Though maybe not. Certain parts of the human brain develop for years after a baby is born, so maybe it's like that." She passed Sonya a file folder. "Here's a printout of the report."

"Thank you." Jenny knew she liked things in tangible format. Half knowing what she was looking for already, Sonya accessed the electronic archives, looking for everything SearchLight knew about basilisks. She was unsurprised to find that the new, third form shared most of these characteristics.

"It was developing into a basilisk when it died," she announced. "If that's what the basilisk Maxine and I met wanted, she was about to get it when the baby died. Now, the only question is, what killed him?"

Jenny frowned. "What keeps dragonlets from dying as often as werewolf pups?"

"A minimal amount of hemlock mixed with blood prevents them from shifting to human too soon. Their mothers tend to give it to them during their first full year. Maybe four forms, dragon, werewolf, human, and basilisk, were too much for this little one." Sonya began typing away on her computer. "And, hey, look at this," she said about a minute later. "Basilisks have approached SearchLight to help them figure out how to perpetuate their dying species."

"The lady you confronted wasn't going through any official channels."

"Agreed." Sonya stood after logging out of the SearchLight archives. "I'm going to talk to Agent Tavery. Probably it's been moved on to Public Relations or maybe to the trackers but he'll still have his hand in. Thanks for digging deeper and thanks for listening."

Jenny waved as she turned back to her computer.

Sonya was up the stairs and headed across the sun-bright courtyard between her building and the one that housed the Department of Dragons when she spotted Maxine running, shoeless, across the hot pavement. Picking up speed and thanking her stars that she'd decided to wear flats today, Sonya called, "Maxine? What's wrong?"

"Fehrna Susan's missing." Maxine halted before Sonya. "She disappeared during her morning run. My pack's in an uproar."

Sonya touched Maxine's arm to calm her. "Breathe. Are you sure she didn't just take a longer run than usual?"

"She didn't show up for work."

"Your pack calls her at work?"

Maxine gave her a disdainful look. "Her hospital called us."

Sonya digested that. Did Fehrna Susan really have her own human hospital? Then she dismissed it. "Where were you headed?"

"To get that damn basilisk's address from you. I didn't write it down."

"She isn't there anymore," Sonya pointed out even as her stomach turned to ice at the thought of Maxine confronting the basilisk on her own. What Mark had said came back to her. *"If Maxine had been there alone, she'd probably be dead now."*

"Maybe she left a clue behind. Besides, it's got to

be her that took my alpha. I stopped at Tavery's office and I overheard him telling someone that a local water dragon's disappeared." She shifted her weight. "So. Can you give me the address?"

Sonya considered telling Maxine to let trackers handle this. Knowing this would do no good, and refusing to let Maxine face the danger alone, she said, "We need to make one stop before we head over there."

"We?" Maxine's voice was loaded with skepticism.

"Yes." Sonya started back toward her office, trusting Maxine to follow. "We need to buy the sunglasses that can block a basilisk's killing stare. I looked up the ones she let fall and I have the make and manufacturer. There's a place we can buy them only a mile from the basilisk's lair."

"You get me the sunglasses and I'll handle --"

"I'm coming. That's nonnegotiable." And, reaching the inside of her building, she took the stairs down as quickly as possible. Before Maxine could decide to try and find the basilisk on her own.

* * *

Sonya had worked hard to persuade Maxine to wait until after work, pointing out that if they needed to call for backup while "working" they would be in trouble. But if they just "happened" to be in the neighborhood after hours, it would at least look like they'd been following orders. And, she kept this to herself, the trackers who had been dispatched to follow up on the leads wouldn't leave much to follow at the apartment if they left anything and surely they'd find Fehrna Susan. Safe and sound, Sonya prayed.

She and Maxine parked a block from the apartment. Maxine climbed into the back and began...

taking her clothes off?

"What are you doing?"

Grunt. Grunt. Dropped shirt. Unclasped bra.

"Maxine…"

"I'm going to shift into my werewolf form."

Sonya broke out in a cold sweat.

"I won't come after you," Maxine said, sounding exasperated. "I need to be able to sniff around. We don't currently have any werewolf trackers working for this branch of SearchLight."

Sonya hadn't looked into this, but supposed it was true. "The others aren't human, though. They should be able to use their noses just as well."

Maxine had her shoes off and she was going to work on her trousers. "I know my alpha's scent better than anyone else. Even if they got a piece of her clothing to run under their noses, I'll know her better."

She sounded desperate. Probably to be doing something. Sonya shut up and watched her in the rearview mirror. She didn't quite have the guts to face a transforming werewolf head-on.

Naked, Maxine opened the back door a crack. Then she changed.

It occurred in less than three seconds, but it was horrible. Maxine's beautiful face and flat, hairless chest were replaced by a muzzle ringed with sharp teeth and a deep, furry barrel. Her lovely hands grew fur and claws and she drew into herself even as she gained weight in that magical, completely nonscientific way most magical creatures had of obtaining or shedding pounds.

When the eyes of the predator looked at her in the mirror, Sonya shrank into her seat and hugged herself.

Maxine bolted out of the car and, dropping her

nose to the ground, began sniffing her way down the nearest sidewalk.

On trembling legs, and after closing and locking the doors with shaking hands, Sonya followed. She put on her special sunglasses and wished, in spite of her fear, that there had been a way to make sure Maxine wore hers. Because despite her terror, her heart still cried, "There goes my lover! Without protection!"

She hurried after Maxine, catching up with her at the corner because even though her ex-girlfriend --

Who's a werewolf. A fucking werewolf!

-- was stopping to check out smells along the way. Which made sense because what if they didn't find the alpha wolf at the apartment? Surely they wouldn't. The trackers must have searched the area.

Sonya reached the apartment steps first and hesitated at the bottom, waiting for Maxine. "Let me go in first," she said, her ex's safety paramount.

Maxine charged up the stairs past her and slammed her huge paws halfway up the door. Then she turned her monster's head and barked at Sonya. Probably she only wanted Sonya to open the door, but that sound turned Sonya to jelly. She stumbled back, tripped, and fell on her ass in the street. Staring up at the creature who had taken her lover's place, she shook all over. Maxine backed off from the door. She came slowly down the steps and sat facing Sonya. She lowered her head and licked one of Sonya's hands as if to say, "It's all right."

That she cared enough to do that even with her alpha missing got through to Sonya. She lifted her trembling hand and stroked the side of Maxine's head. "Just give me a second. I'll get the door."

But when she'd gotten up and tried it, she found it locked. She turned to explain but Maxine rushed up the stairs and slammed her meaty shoulder into the door. It creaked. She hit it again. This time it flew open and she disappeared inside.

Chapter Nine

Maxine entered the apartment with her eyes squinted almost shut just in case the monster -- or so she thought of the basilisk -- was there. It wasn't impossible.

Her nose told her Sonya had entered. The stench of her terror was acrid and awful. Distracting too. Maxine left the front room to get away from her and found a small, quarter-sized scrap of cloth with her alpha's scent all over it. Probably the trackers who'd been here had removed the rest.

She wondered if the basilisk was keeping her alpha anywhere nearby.

"Hey, look at this," Sonya called from the front room.

Maxine came back into the living room and the upswing in Sonya's terror assaulted her nose. Shifting in order to talk, she stood, naked, in front of the human and glared. "When you're so scared, it's -- hey. What's that?"

"An address. In my neighborhood. Well, nearly. It's in the 'hood in St. Petersburg. I know this street. It's crowded with houses that are falling apart either from termite damage or simple neglect. Like here, the neighbors would be reluctant to call the police if they saw something suspicious."

Maxine started forward to grab the paper but Sonya held it away.

"You're naked."

"It's a shifter thing." She noted that Sonya's fear was a little more manageable now. That didn't change what she had to say. "When you're so scared, it's really hard to smell anything else. When we get where we're going, you're staying in the car."

"Excuse me?" Sonya put her hands on her hips. "Ms. I-can't-wear-protective-glasses, do you hear yourself? If the basilisk is at this place, one of us has to be able to look her straight in the eye."

Maxine sighed. "Okay. You're right. Take us to St. Petersburg. By way of a fast food place. I need about a dozen hamburgers."

Sonya stared. "Why?"

So I don't eat you. Maxine quashed this unkind lie and spoke the truth. She blamed Sonya's fear for the thought, even though she was honest enough with herself to admit she knew where it really came from. "So I won't get weak. Shifting too many times is exhausting." She transformed into her lupine guise. To her surprise, Sonya's fear didn't spike as high. Was it possible Sonya had really been afraid of finding the basilisk at home?

Maxine left the apartment. When she was outside, she heard sirens. Maybe the police were headed here, maybe they were headed someplace else. In either case, Maxine wanted to be long gone.

* * *

When they were on the road bound for St. Petersburg, Sonya felt the cloying silence. She'd stopped at a fast food drive through after Maxine got dressed again and now Maxine was eating the greasy hamburgers.

Really wolfing them down.

Stopped at a red light, Sonya closed her eyes for a couple of seconds to better picture the werewolf who'd been briefly sharing her car and then sharing her personal space inside the apartment. She recalled first the sharp, absolutely huge, teeth. But then her mental eye roved to the very human expression of worry in the brown eyes. This image gave way to that of the luxurious fur.

Someone honked behind her and Sonya refocused. "Sorry."

"It was green for less than a second," Maxine answered from the back seat. "I'm sort of glad I don't drive on a regular basis."

Relieved to have anything to talk about, Sonya asked, "Why not? What about groceries?"

Maxine tore into a new hamburger. "I either walk with an empty backpack to the nearest store -- there's a great butcher near us, run by one of the pack -- or I snag a ride with one of my packmates when they're heading out."

It sounded great to Sonya. She admitted, "I like the way you share and work together. I never realized wolf pack members took care of each other."

"If you weren't so afraid of us, maybe you'd know more."

Sonya ignored the sting in those words and said, "Maybe you can teach me not to be afraid."

"No offense, but I would only take the time to teach that to a girlfriend, not a coworker."

Well, ouch. Sonya felt her eyes fill with tears. "Maxine --"

"Let's listen to the radio."

Sonya was silent but she didn't turn on the radio either. After she'd had a little time to think -- they were finally on the Howard Franklin Bridge -- she whispered, trusting Maxine's sharp ears to pick up her words, "I miss you."

Maxine didn't answer.

"You aren't giving me a chance." Sonya winced at the whine in her voice. She blew out a breath. "Didn't we agree to take some time? What happened to that?"

"My alpha helped me realize you'll never be over it enough to live with us."

"Who the fuck put her in my shoes and skin?"

Maxine was silent for several moments. Then she said, "No one, but… isn't it true?"

"I joined this investigation to confront my fears. I" -- *fell in love* --"was starting to fall in love with you. A werewolf. Can't you just give me a little more time?"

Maxine didn't say anything.

Sonya scowled and flipped on the radio. She turned it to the loudest, dumbest rap station she could find and blasted it. And damn Maxine's sensitive ears.

* * *

Maxine surveyed the house from where she and Sonya stood a little way down the street. It wasn't much different from the mostly deserted lane in Ybor City except the houses were a little farther apart and they had ragged lawns full of trash. How could anyone live here?

She chastised herself for being judgmental and then refocused. "Stay here." She took a single step before cold hands closed on her arm.

"No fucking way. I'm coming with you."

"You're not. This whole place smells like a giant snake." She didn't add that it smelled of blood and pain as well.

"Is your alpha here?"

Trust Sonya to ask that. "Yes," Maxine admitted. "So's a dragon of some kind."

"I'm coming with you." Sonya put on her special sunglasses and handed Maxine hers, the ones she'd left in the back seat. "Come on."

Maxine caught Sonya's hand. "Like you said, no fucking way."

"Oh fine."

But Maxine could smell the lie as well as pick up on the deception from Sonya's mind. "You are staying here. Call for backup. Especially if one or both of them is hurt, we're going to need help." She added, "The basilisk isn't here in any case. Unless she's just being really quiet. The place smells like her but she's not here."

Sonya opened her mouth.

"The longer we stand here, the greater the chance that she'll come back before I can get Fehrna Susan and the dragon out."

"Oh fine." This time she meant it. "I'll call Public Relations. They'll have trackers out here as soon as possible. I wonder why they didn't find that address? I mean, it was buried under some other stuff but it was definitely findable."

Maxine shrugged. "I'll be back."

"You don't think the basilisk left it for us to find, do you? That she wanted you here for some reason? Maybe as a way to leverage your alpha?"

Maxine hadn't thought of that. But it didn't matter. "Call for backup. Tell them I went in."

"In human form. So you can wear your sunglasses."

Maxine had planned to do that already, so she nodded. "In human form." She started to jog toward the house. Behind her, she heard Sonya scrounging in the car for her cell phone.

Maxine skirted the house and came upon it through the neighboring house's backyard. She found the back door, which seemed to lead to a grungy looking kitchen, locked. She broke the lock as quietly as possible and entered the house.

She was halfway across the kitchen when her nose told her where she could find her alpha.

Downstairs from here, in the basement. She prayed that Sonya would stay far away, and hoped even more fervently that the female basilisk wouldn't come back.

She was partway down the basement steps when she heard a gunshot. She froze but then she heard something much closer: the rattle of chains. Cursing silently, she proceeded toward the basement floor.

* * *

After Sonya called Public Relations -- they didn't ask much besides the address, which didn't mean she was off the hook -- and Mark Tavery *and* Agent Wellington, leaving messages with both of the latter, she got out of her car and considered the gun she'd picked up at the basilisk's apartment. Surely the basilisk had left it there because trackers wouldn't leave such a weapon lying around. Sonya didn't understand what the purpose of leaving the gun could possibly be, but she was convinced the basilisk was hoping to lure Maxine. She'd called Maxine a dyke, which argued that she thought Maxine was female through and through. And if she'd decided female dragons wouldn't work, and since she'd now grabbed a female werewolf...

Sonya's jaw dropped when she realized what her unfocused eyed had been pointed at. The basilisk was walking briskly down the broken up sidewalk. She didn't seem to see Sonya. All her focus appeared to be on the house.

Sonya didn't know how to open the gun and didn't have time for that anyway. She pointed the potentially empty gun at the basilisk, thinking that even if it was loaded, basilisks surely had tougher skin than most magical creatures, and shouted, "Freeze!"

Instead of obeying, the female basilisk broke into a run toward the house.

Sonya tracked her with the gun, praying she would hit her mark, and pulled the trigger. The gun went off and she cried out.

But the bullet connected because blood spewed from the other's shoulder.

Sonya cried out again, this time in revulsion. She ran toward the other female. "Stop! Stop!"

The basilisk shot a look over her shoulder -- her eyes were uncovered. Probably registering the sunglasses, she hissed at Sonya and turned around. She pelted toward the house.

Sonya gave chase. She thundered up the stairs to the front door and hit it about five seconds after it had closed. She rebounded, tried the knob, found it locked, and prayed she was doing the right thing. She kicked the door down rather than risk shooting off the lock and hitting someone on the other side.

Once she was in the house, she heard sounds coming from downstairs. She saw a door partially open and headed for it. There was a flight of stairs headed down into dimness. She took these, pointing the gun straight up.

She reached the bottom of the stairs. The darkness was almost complete. With her sunglasses on she could barely see anything. She could hear chains rattling and the sound of heavy breathing.

Then she was blindsided and slammed against a wall. She collapsed, crying out in pain. Then Maxine snarled, "Get out of here, you coward," and the basilisk, for surely it had to be her, moved away from Sonya.

She'd lost the gun when she fell but she saw it nearby and scooped it up. She didn't fire, waiting for her eyes to adjust to the lighting. She also decided to squint and take off her glasses. If she was lucky, the decision wouldn't kill her.

The first thing she saw was a huge dragon coiled against one wall. There was a chain wound round and around his body. A werewolf in furry form was likewise bound.

Maxine, still in human guise and with her sunglasses very much in place, was circling with the basilisk. Before she could catch a glimpse of the basilisk's face, Sonya fired the gun five times into the female's back.

The female staggered forward -- and Maxine grabbed her by the throat, darted her head forward, and ripped her jugular.

"Sonya," Maxine ordered, her voice growly and harsh, also loud because of the gun's reports, "close your eyes."

Sonya obeyed.

What seemed like an eternity later, a gentle hand touched her arm. Sonya looked up and gasped. Maxine's face was covered with blood, but most of the mess was around her mouth. "What did you do?"

"Tore her head off so she can't come back." It was said gently.

Sonya shivered. "You're naked again."

"I had to change to wolf form to do it effectively. I couldn't let you see that, me ripping into flesh. You'd never let me touch you again."

Sonya caught Maxine's mostly clean hand, shivering a little. "I think I love you too much to judge you by what you did in order to survive."

* * *

About twenty minutes later, a strange party stood outside under the moonlight. There weren't any neighbors to see the dragon and werewolf or Maxine, who was naked, having torn her clothes in her haste to change to wolf guise. The group of them stood in the backyard, which was overgrown and running to seed. There were seven in the yard, eight including the headless corpse. The dragon and Fehrna Susan were still in their "monstrous" forms, the dragon sporting a very large erection.

And Sonya, insanely, was trying to talk to the dragon.

Maxine stood between them, ready to defend this brave and incredibly reckless woman. Even though both of the trackers and the Public Relations agent had weapons drawn, she felt justified in being there.

"It's not my fault," the dragon was saying. He sounded both petulant and shaken. "She forced me to take this little blue pill and it gave me, well..." He gestured at his penis.

"She, the basilisk, expected you to rape Fehrna Susan?" Sonya asked.

"Yes. She even took the time to explain that insemination wasn't working, that her race is dying and she has no other choice."

"Was she expecting another werewolf to show up?"

"Yes. She said another member of the wolf's pack would 'be along shortly.'"

"So. She was planning for Maxine to come charging in." Sonya shot Maxine a look. Then she returned her attention to the dragon. "Do you know how much curare she gave you?"

"No. Not enough to knock me out, obviously, but --" He shuddered strongly and shrank, changing to a human's guise. He covered his erection with his hands. "This is even more embarrassing."

Fehrna Susan shivered and regained her human form. One of the trackers gave her his long shirt. As if realizing this was a good idea, the other tracker gave his shirt to Maxine.

"She was," Fehrna Susan said, "almost the most sympathetic person I've ever met. She told us about the deaths of the basilisk young and their eventual inability to conceive at all."

Maxine took Sonya's hand and pulled her close. Greatly daring, she met her alpha's gaze for a moment. She said nothing but refused to pretend Sonya wasn't important to her.

Fehrna Susan raised both eyebrows. Then she nodded. "I assume you haven't done anything... permanent?"

"We will be," Sonya said, surprising the hell out of Maxine. "As soon as I see all of your pack and have a chance to get used to them."

Maxine felt her heart grow wings.

* * *

September 24 brought the first full moon of autumn to Florida. On the beach at Fort DeSoto, werewolves thundered across the sand and played in the shallow waves. The whole world was bathed in moonlight, making it possible for Sonya to distinguish most of the wolves she saw. She didn't know all of them by name when they were in their four-footed guises but she picked out Fehrna Susan, the alpha's mate, Michaela, and a couple of the others with whom she'd become friends since July. Maxine was easy to pick out despite her dark brown and gray coloring that easily could have been mistaken for two or three other wolves in the Fehrna pack. She wore a reflective collar around her neck, a concession to Sonya's nerves. Now there was no way she could be mistaken for anyone else, nor anyone for her.

Sonya sat in her car with the doors locked. This

was only her second full moon run and she was still a little nervous. But that was easing. She'd actually dozed off on this late evening. It was about twenty minutes past midnight and the wolves were chasing and leaping like puppies. Really large, sometimes dangerous puppies.

Still, Sonya had taken a little catnap and now she was filled with a courageous urge. She unlocked her doors and stepped out onto the sand. She hesitated a moment and then walked away from the safety of her car. She knew Maxine, when she got close enough, would be able to smell her arousal. She'd dreamed during that brief nap and was filled with a reckless need to let Maxine know.

The reflective collar winked through the night as Maxine galloped toward her, slowing to a walk about two dozen paces from her. She moved sedately forward.

One of the other wolves headed over.

Maxine snapped her jaws at the intruder.

Wagging a bushy tail, the other wolf headed back into the midst of the other pack members.

Sonya approached Maxine and dropped to one knee, putting them face-to-face. She stroked the teeth-ringed muzzle and then scratched between Maxine's ears right where her lover liked it.

Lover. They hadn't actually had full-on penetrative sex yet. That was going to change tonight. Well, this morning.

"I'm ready. I want you."

She saw Maxine's brown eyes widen and Sonya grinned. "Please?" Then she added quickly, "You don't have to stop running right now. Play until dawn. Just… after work…"

Maxine shifted right there, regaining her full five

foot seven inch height. She was bare-assed and beautiful. She was almost half hard. "Are you kidding? Run instead of joining you in our bed?"

Fehrna Susan, beautifully white and gray, approached. She didn't shift but nudged first Maxine's hip and then Sonya's.

"What does that mean?"

Maxine flashed her teeth in a happy grin. "It means she wants us to get it on." She stepped forward, kissed Sonya on the mouth, and then climbed into the back of the car and began putting on her clothes.

It wasn't exactly a short drive to Tampa from Fort DeSoto. Forty minutes, give or take five, and Maxine didn't make it easy. She'd gotten dressed but she kept doing things like blowing in Sonya's ear or singing sultry Eartha Kitt songs. Once she reached over the driver's seat and ran a thumb over Sonya's right nipple. By the time they'd reached the apartment, Sonya was damp between her legs.

Maxine locked the door, using both locks, something she rarely did. It was one a.m. but Sonya could never remember feeling less tired. And even though she knew she'd be a zombie when she dragged her butt to work at eight thirty, there was satisfaction in the idea that she wouldn't be the only one and that she'd be mated.

Maxine was wearing nothing more than sweats and she stripped out of them with alacrity.

Sonya took off her clothes more slowly, watching Maxine's eyes dilate as she removed first her shirt and then her shoes and jeans shorts. When she stood in nothing but her panties and bra, she rubbed her clit through the silky pink fabric. Ooh, but she was damp down there. She stopped rubbing abruptly when she realized just how close she was to an orgasm.

Maxine was grinning and her erection stood out straight. "One thing I'll never get to enjoy is the multiple orgasms most women delight in."

"If you have a cock ring…" Sonya suggested.

"No such luck. But I'll control myself. First things first. Getting you completely naked."

Sonya helped her there, shucking her bra and panties in two fluid movements. Then she prowled toward Maxine. "Do you want to do this on the couch or the bed?"

"Bed. Definitely. I want both of us to be as comfortable as possible."

Sonya ran a finger down the center of Maxine's chest and then swayed her hips as she sauntered out of the living room. Once she was standing beside the bed, she turned to face Maxine, licked the tips of her index fingers, and played with her nipples until they became firm points.

Maxine was hesitating at the door. "You're not in love with sucking me," she said.

"We're not going to have oral sex tonight," Sonya pointed out.

"I know, but I can't help worry that you won't like me inside you either."

"You're small," Sonya said without worries that she'd hurt Maxine's feelings. "And I'm pretty sure you can keep up a near-constant rub on my clit." She paused. "We don't have to have penetration-type sex all the time, from now on, do we?"

"Nope. Never again if you don't want to. Just to set the bond."

Sonya nodded and flopped back onto the bed. "Then take me."

Maxine shook her head. "Not that way. You're going to be riding me tonight. It will feel better."

Sonya raised her eyebrows. "You sound awfully confident."

"I am. Try it?"

"Okay." She waited until Maxine had lain down on her back and with her legs together. Then she straddled the werewolf's narrow hips.

"Let's see if I can bring out at least one orgasm first." Maxine slipped a finger between Sonya's folds and began to rub. "Ride it."

Sonya undulated her hips until she was riding the single digit. She moaned and arched as her first orgasm shook her. When she could breathe, she asked, "How do you want me to get you ready?"

Maxine had a tube of lubricant in her hand. Sonya had no idea where it had come from. "Oil-based. I know how much you hate water-based lubes." She dripped some on her fingers and held out her hand. "Smell."

Sonya inhaled and cooed with pleasure. "Chocolate. When I told you that was my favorite scent and then you bought that perfume I thought that was it, wonderful as the gesture was."

"I want you to be in heaven tonight." She grasped her short and narrow cock. "Lift up and sit on it. I'll guide it in."

Sonya did this nervously, but then she cried out in bliss when Maxine used a thumb to brush her sensitive clit. She sat on Maxine's cock and not only didn't it hurt but it felt *pleasant*. Not as good as what Maxine was doing with her thumb but good. *I think I could do this at least once a week.*

Maxine's cock twitched inside her and Sonya cried out in startled pleasure. "Shit, that feels…"

"Yes?" Maxine continued to toy with Sonya's clit.

Sonya couldn't answer. All she wanted was

more. She lifted herself up a little and then lowered herself gingerly. When Maxine's cock twitched again, she was filled with intense need. She began to ride the cock inside her.

Her eyes were squeezed shut as craving flew through her but as it crested, not quite breaking, she opened her eyes and saw Maxine was watching her with concern. "Oh, shit, that feels so fucking intense. I've never... No one's ever..." She tightened her muscles and felt Maxine twitch again, deep inside her. "I had no idea sex could be like this."

Maxine stopped looking nervous and began to grin. "Are you saying this might be more than a one-off?"

"God, yes." Sonya squeezed her muscles again and rode faster. "You're so perfect in there." Her orgasm was coming, coming...

She screamed her lover's, her mate's, name. And when she felt Maxine release inside of her, it felt like an aftershock of her own pleasure.

Twenty minutes later, after they'd shared a shower, Sonya found herself thinking of the basilisk. She confessed this to Maxine as they snuggled in bed. "I feel sorry for her."

"So do I. She was, when you come down to it, just trying to save her people."

Sonya rested a hand on her stomach. "Do you think I'll give birth to a half werewolf half human?"

Maxine cursed softly. "Oh shit, I never thought... I should have worn a condom."

"No way. If we're mated, let's really be mated."

"The ability to have a baby doesn't make us more or less mated."

"No, but I like to think that your sperm inside me does."

Maxine rolled over onto her side. She was half hard again. "Would you like a repeat?"

Sonya glanced at the clock. "It's past two." She laughed. "But ask me if I give a shit." She shoved Maxine onto her back and straddled her again. "Let the daylight hours take care of themselves."

And, after Maxine was buried to the balls inside her, Sonya asked, "How do I say I love you? What are the proper words for a mated pair?"

Maxine's eyes crossed with pleasure. "Just 'I love you.'"

"Then I love you, Maxine Brown, and I never want to be parted from you." Sonya began to move.

Practical Difficulties (Lady Troubles 2)
Emily Carrington

Maxine, a trans male-to-female werewolf, is struggling to get beyond her grief over the losses she suffered in her past. Now her mate, Sonya, is pregnant. When Maxine's ghosts rise to break the new lovers apart, they have more help than they need from her pack.

Sonya's starting to wonder whether Maxine's loyalties lie with the wolf pack she's been with for decades, or with her new mate. It's beginning to look like sabotage from all quarters. How can a new couple stay together, especially with pups on the way?

Chapter One

Sonya Johnson stared at her clean pad, scowling at its whiteness against the cocoa dark of her thigh and the pale mauve of her panties. Her period should have started four days ago. Granted, she'd stopped taking her birth control after she'd forgotten to take it for three days back in late September. But was it too much to ask that her slip wouldn't bring on pregnancy? She was a damned doctoral student *and* working a full-time job.

"Please, God," she whispered. "Let it just be late. I do not have time for this right now."

She shivered as a blast of air conditioning rushed across the back of her neck. Maybe it was time to grow her hair out and screw the cuteness of her current kinky-haired bob.

I'm a medical technician. I know enough about the human body to get this message: either stress is delaying my menstrual cycle, or I'm pregnant.

She cursed her mate before she could stop herself.

Sonya sighed, flushed the toilet, and pulled up her panties and shorts. It wasn't Maxine's fault, even if she was a trans werewolf and still had a dick. They'd both thought Sonya's pill would take care of things. They'd briefly discussed using condoms too, but Sonya privately thought at the time that that was overkill. Maxine liked teasing herself with a condom now and then, but as a form of birth control, they were weren't all that reliable.

They only succeed sixty percent of the time... but maybe I should have banked on that extra sixty percent.

She made an exasperated noise, very quietly.

The only thing that is Maxine's fault, partially at

least, is how infrequently I see her.

She'd long ago stopped tripping over the idea of calling Maxine, a male-to-female transgender werewolf, "she." Not even thinking of her mate's cock, as she did often while masturbating, could cause her confusion. Maxine was so utterly female, mind and spirit, that male genitals couldn't change her essential nature.

Sonya walked into the bedroom she and her mate shared and went to her side of the wall-length closet. She took off the striped shirt she'd been wearing and put on a sweater with a cowl neck. It was a soft orange that complemented her medium brown skin tone and had the added bonus of clinging to her curves in all the right places.

Too bad Maxine isn't here to appreciate it. She sighed noisily and then covered her mouth and glanced around, almost expecting half a dozen werewolves to pop out of the woodwork and ask her what was wrong. She kept her SearchLight-won shields in place most of the time, and her lips shut almost as much, but she still felt as if the whole darn pack could read her like a book.

Those shields were something she'd picked up at the academy in DC, learning them from the parapsychology teacher. She didn't use them much at work, at least not when she was relaxed and in her own domain -- the medtech department. But with all the psychic powers boasted by the members of her new eros pack, she felt on edge if her mind wasn't guarded.

Shaking her head, grimacing as she thought of how paranoid she'd gotten over the past two weeks, Sonya headed into the living room to sit at the desk Maxine had bought her as a mating ceremony present back in late September. It was now the first week of

October and she did *not* need to be worrying about pregnancy when her first dissertation defense was happening in less than seven days and she hadn't seen her mate for more than a few minutes at a time since they consummated their relationship.

And while that was the worst of it, not being with her mate, her third problem was almost as pressing: three of the werewolves in her new pack were openly hostile toward her. Oh, not where Maxine, who outranked all of them, could see, but whenever they caught Sonya alone…

Oh, stop thinking about it all in such negative terms. They're just pests. And as for Maxine, she sleeps here every night she's in town, doesn't she? You've made love four times so far. That's good for two weeks' worth of living together, isn't it?

Well, actually, no. Sonya had gotten the impression from listening to her friend, Luke, talk about his early relationship with his husband that sex every day wasn't uncommon. In fact, the only time her genie and dragon friends hadn't managed sex at least three or four times a week was when Mark, the dragon half of the pairing, was in crisis.

Was Maxine in crisis?

That was a good question. As Sonya sat down at her new desk to start poring over her doctoral dissertation for the millionth time, she admitted she'd been so buried in her own work that she hadn't reached out to Maxine to see if her mate was troubled by anything.

* * *

Maxine stared incredulously at the three *more* wolves who had problems this evening. "I'm trying to get to my mate," she implored. "Can't these wait until morning?"

The trio -- Tessa, John, and Christopher -- exchanged looks. Then Tessa, who was closest to Maxine in rank, said, "All right. But first thing."

There was something she wasn't saying, something the gamma wolf was holding back, but Maxine was too glad to have a chance to be with her mate to care. She breathed a silent sigh of relief. She knew she shouldn't be leaving John and Christopher, who wanted to fight out their difference, unattended for the night, but…

But nothing. If they end up fighting… She pulled out her cell phone and dialed Michaela. As the alpha's mate, Michaela was one of only two wolves who outranked Maxine's beta position. Maybe she could hold down the fort while Maxine went to see her stressed-out mate.

Sonya had sounded unsettled when they'd talked on the phone. And the two of them hadn't seen each other in three days. Sonya had been in Washington, DC, at SearchLight Academy. That was over nine hundred miles away. This meant Maxine's telepathy, which didn't always work at the best of times, had been completely foiled.

Still, she had to see to her packmates. That was a beta's job. So, only after she'd secured Michaela's help did she head for the apartment she shared with Sonya. It was after dinnertime, and Sonya had probably fended for herself for the meal.

She entered the luxuriously appointed five-room space. Sonya sat on the couch reading out of a notebook. "Still working on your dissertation, dear?"

Her darling looked up and smiled tiredly. "Half of what they said actually makes sense now that I'm not feeling cornered and ripped to shreds." But she put down the notebook and crossed to Maxine. Putting her arms around Maxine's neck, she asked, "Do I have you to myself for the evening?" Her honey brown eyes shone with need, although something lingered under the happiness. Tiredness? Stress?

"Thanks to Michaela, yes." Maxine wrapped her arms around Sonya's waist, loving the way her mate's curves fit against her own angular body. Sonya was all softness. She had a curvy butt and ample breasts. Beautiful skin, three shades lighter than Maxine's own. She always smelled of shea butter and citrus. The blend of scents reminded Maxine of her favorite candy: orange chocolate.

She had the pleasure of feeling Sonya relax against her. "Long day, dear?"

"Anytime you fly from DC to Tampa it's long."

"I'm sorry I couldn't be there to pick you up." It was Saturday; she should have been free. But..."John and Christopher are preparing to have a dominance fight and they needed counseling."

"They sure chose a bad day for it." But Sonya didn't sound really angry. "I drove myself to the airport in any case, so it made more sense for me to drive home."

Maxine liked hearing Sonya call this place home. It had been a weeks-long project to first bring Sonya's stuff here and then to find places for everything. In truth, there were still two or three boxes that needed going through. But there was plenty of room. Maxine was a minimalist by nature, the apartment was large, and Sonya had purged a great deal.

"I'm so glad you're here," Maxine murmured before lowering her lips to Sonya's. She reveled in the silken feel of her mate's mouth, kissing deeply. Their tongues danced and Maxine moaned. Very quietly, because the pack had long ears. She was instantly hard below the waist, and she rubbed her wakening cock against Sonya's thigh.

When they came up for air, Sonya's eyes were shining. "I missed you too." She laughed a little. "I really needed that kiss. It's been a sucky seventy-two hours."

"Do you want to tell me about it?" She took Sonya's hands in hers and massaged them gently.

Sonya bit her lip. "Yeah, I guess I need that before sex." She kissed Maxine's cheek and then nibbled her ear for just a moment.

"Tease," Maxine complained playfully.

Sonya grinned. "I just want both of us to forget what we're really going to be about this evening." Then she seemed to remember her rough day because she made a frustrated noise. "It was only forty-five minutes long or so, standing by myself and defending my doctoral thesis, but everyone else was there. All the other doctoral candidates and the basilisks who bent the rules so I could pursue this line of study. And they did nothing but shred my work. Hell, they shredded me." Her voice trembled just a bit. Then she scowled and her voice was firmer when she said, "I know they were being as gentle as they could, considering that I'd be tearing into their dissertations next, but... It felt like they were judging me, you know?"

"Maybe they were," Maxine murmured, stroking her mate's neck with a finger. "I mean, the two basilisks who are allowing you to get a degree that's only been held by basilisks up until now were surely applying a lot of pressure."

Sonya nodded and leaned into the slight nudge of Maxine's finger.

Maxine hugged her. "I've never had to give a dissertation, but I think it must be something like standing up before my alpha and giving a report after a terrible incident. Like an unsupervised dominance fight."

"It was awful. And I have to go back in mid December and do it all over again. After I've made most of their suggested corrections, of course." She was studying Maxine's face. "Why is reporting to our alpha difficult? I thought you liked Fehrna Susan."

"I do. Don't you like the professors who judged your work?"

Sonya seemed to consider this. Then she nodded. "Fair enough."

All traces of ire left Sonya's face. Her laughter bubbled out again and she palmed the bulge in Maxine's khaki shorts.

"I really am glad to see you. And I think someone's glad to see me too." And she squeezed, lightly and gently but with obvious promise.

Maxine groaned softly, aware of the wolves all around and above them who had very sharp ears. "Let's turn on some music."

Sonya smirked. "You don't want them to hear you scream?"

It was only a tease; Maxine knew Sonya was the one who was shy. She hadn't worried about making noise their first time here, but that had been before she remembered how easily wolves heard things. And although she was decidedly not shy when it came to asking for what she wanted in bed, she was a private person.

They retreated to the bedroom and closed the door. Sonya went to the stereo, an old model from the late 1990s, and kept mostly because Maxine knew how to use it and because she didn't like modern technology. She would probably have a record player or even a gramophone if her pack hadn't harassed her into something a touch more with the times.

Maxine was distracted from the stereo when Sonya's shirt hit the floor followed by her purple bra. Her undies would be purple too; Sonya had a thing about her lingerie matching. Maxine didn't, although she did like everything that touched her ass or chest to be lacy.

She smiled wickedly. "Stop hovering over there. I want you."

Maxine went to her mate, taking her hand and kissing it. "You're lovely." It was true, but Sonya also looked tired. "Are you sure you have energy for this?"

Sonya stuck out her tongue. Then she unzipped her jeans.

They were naked and in each others' arms within two minutes. The heady smell of Sonya's arousal and Maxine's answering need had filled the room.

Maxine was almost fully erect. She gasped when Sonya rubbed a finger over her glans. A shudder ran up her spine and she knew she wouldn't last long if she didn't put her mind somewhere else for a minute. She got off the bed and began breathing deeply.

Sonya laughed quietly. "You don't want to come right away? You really missed me."

"I really, really did. Not being able to touch you was bad enough, when I couldn't even feel your emotions…" She hesitated. In truth, she'd been unable to sense more than Sonya's surface impressions since just after the mating ceremony. Now, why would that be? Probably because Sonya was using a mild form of shielding. This was most likely more for her desire for privacy. This was a foreign concept to Maxine, but she respected Sonya's need to feel safe.

But Sonya was looking concerned now and

Maxine refused to let anything color this evening. She'd be solving pack problems tomorrow; she could worry about lack of mental connection later.

At least the distraction had calmed her raging hormones. She approached the bed again, smiling down at her naked mate. Sonya's body was so beautiful, rounded in all the right places and muscular in others. She had strong arms, short but shapely legs, and the daintiest feet.

Maxine went to these latter and kissed the top of each, smirking when Sonya squirmed. "Ticklish?"

"If you tickle me, you'll be limping out of here."

Maxine blew on Sonya's right foot... and jumped back with a werewolf's quick reflexes when Sonya kicked out.

"Can you wear a condom this time?" Sonya asked.

Maxine raised an eyebrow. "Why?"

Her mate hesitated. "Kind of for my own reasons, but mostly because I don't want to have to change the sheets. I'm exhausted."

And because Sonya didn't like the way Maxine made the bed, that task would fall to her. "Okay."

"Can I help you put it on?" Sonya asked shyly.

Maxine laughed. "Are you saying you want to touch me?"

Sonya grinned. "Maybe..." She rolled the condom on with a little difficulty that was charming because it showed how rarely she'd performed this particular task. Maxine was aware that she wasn't Sonya's first, although she was her mate's first transgender person and first werewolf.

It doesn't matter who she's had before. She's mine now.

They'd discovered that "doggy style" was the

most comfortable for Sonya, who had admitted to not liking penetration before Maxine. Now, kneeling behind her mate, Maxine slipped one finger between Sonya's labia and stroked the warm, wet bud that was Sonya's clit.

Sonya trembled all over. She'd also broken out in goose bumps.

"Are you cold, dear?" Maxine circled the little nubbin slowly.

"A little." She rocked on Maxine's finger. "But I don't care about that right now. I just want you. I've missed you so much."

Maxine stopped caressing her mate's clit long enough to slip inside her heat. Then she resumed the stroking.

Sonya moaned. "Please, keep it up. I need your touch."

They began to move as one. The glorious feel of Sonya's silken vagina around Maxine's covered member was an exquisite pleasure. The condom would slow her down and she was glad Sonya had suggested it. Her cock throbbed and her balls seemed to pulse with the pounding of her heart. She was sweating lightly.

At a murmured word, Maxine quit touching Sonya's clit. Her mate was close and wanted to make it last.

Moments later, Sonya bowed her head and cried out, barely audibly. Her vagina constricted, encouraging Maxine to pause, savoring the feel of extra pressure.

Maxine smiled in satisfaction. She waited for Sonya to say she was ready again.

"Go, damn you."

Maxine laughed. "Impatient today, aren't you?"

"I told you. I've missed you."

Maxine knew that feeling all too well. Her throat tightened briefly as she thought of all the nights she'd had to leave Sonya asleep in their bed. Then she cast the memories away and began to move again.

This time, the fire began to grow in her lower belly and tension bloomed in her thighs. She groaned and increased her pace, needing to feel the explosion. Not just because of the pleasure it brought but because when she was coming, she felt vulnerable. And feeling that way around Sonya was the most blissful experience.

They came one right after the other, Sonya first, and then Maxine. And as Maxine balanced there, not wanting to crush her beloved, she slipped her hand around Sonya's side and touched her clit one more time. "More?" she asked softly.

"Just rest your hand right there." And Sonya moved against Maxine's finger. The slickness of her clitoris was delicious.

She orgasmed a third time. Then she collapsed, obviously spent. "I --"

Someone knocked on their door. Not the door to the general hallway either, but their bedroom door.

Maxine swore. Silently. Hadn't she told everyone, every damn one of them, to stay away tonight?

Sonya muttered, "Go." She sounded disgruntled.

I don't blame her. Maxine kissed the back of her mate's neck. "I love you."

The knock came again.

Maxine snarled, "Just a damn minute."

Sonya laughed a little. "You tell 'em." She turned her head and smiled a little. "Go on. I'll be all right. Just... let's try for this again tomorrow, okay?"

"Absolutely." Maxine got out of bed and began to dress. She glanced at Sonya, saw that she was already bundling herself up in the blankets, and smirked. Sonya had a shy streak that was different than what Maxine had grown up with. It was endearing.

Fully dressed, although she hadn't bothered to put on her bra or fake boobs, Maxine said, "I love you. I'll be back as soon as I can."

Sonya yawned. "Love you too."

Maxine went out to deal with the fresh crisis.

Chapter Two

It was the third week of October. Which made it four days and change since she and Maxine had made love. They shared the bed, but usually Sonya woke in the morning to find Maxine deeply asleep. They never approached slumber's shore together; often Sonya went to bed alone.

Especially since she'd been feeling dragged out. She'd started collapsing into bed at six, only to wake up early, when Maxine was still asleep, to work on her dissertation.

And I'm only thinking about how rarely I see her because I'm PMS-ing.

Oh, but if only that was true. It had been five weeks since she'd seen her monthly flow.

Sonya tried to take pleasure in the warmth of her office. She was sweating lightly, but at least she wasn't huddled in something with long sleeves. Failing miserably, her frustration building, she did not want anyone to walk in on her right now. She needed to do some deep breathing and probably visualize the one time she'd touched a dolphin.

Of course, meditating would most likely put her to sleep. She was thoroughly done in, and the warmth of the office, welcome though it was, made her long for a nap.

Someone knocked on the door.

Okay, fine, *God*, she thought as she stood, ready to welcome whoever felt they just had to disturb her. *What's one more thing piled on my head, right?* "Come in."

Let it be Maxine, half naked and bearing a cup of coffee in one hand and a can of whipped cream in the other.

Thanks to this two-second daydream, she was able to conjure a genuine smile for the person invading her space.

Agent Mark Tavery, head of the Department of Dragons here in Tampa smiled at her. It was a sympathetic expression. "I hear the profs at SearchLight Academy were ruthless. How are you holding up?" He closed the door.

Sonya swallowed her instant need to tell Mark everything. She was *not* the sort of person who spilled her guts to all and sundry, but Mark and his husband Luke were her best friends.

Still, she longed to spew out *everything*, including how icy it was in her apartment and how lost she felt not seeing her mate for more than a few minutes at a time not even a month after their bonding ceremony. According to Maxine, the term "mate" was sacred to werewolves; it meant more than "wife" or "lover," something grander and deeper than either term. But so far as Sonya had seen, "mated" only meant living in a new apartment in a neighborhood she didn't know anything about.

With werewolves who disdained her company.

Oh shit. Had any of that crossed her face? Keeping her shields up at work was a new thing, brought on, probably, by all the time she spent with her mental guards up at home. She shared an apartment building with close to twenty werewolves, and they always seemed to be home and underfoot. It was unfair to assume they were crawling around in her mind, but many of them were telepaths. Or at least empaths. And since three of them, Tessa, Christopher, and John, were active in their dislike, didn't it follow that others might feel the same and just be better at hiding it?

Sonya yanked herself out of the rabbit hole down which her thoughts had gone and forced her lips to smile.

Mark was frowning at her. "Were they too rough on you?"

She had to smile, for real this time, even as she saw his blue eyes shift to yellow-green, signaling how much he wanted to protect her. Mark was, in many ways, the big brother she'd never had. "They were no harder on me than they were on the rest of the doctoral candidates." To forestall any other questions, she waved him to one of the seats on the other side of her desk before rounding the delicate piece of furniture herself and sitting beside him.

He raised an eyebrow but didn't pursue the subject. "Have you heard about the negotiations between the basilisk High Council and SearchLight?"

She shook her head. "Is it about the basilisks' inability to carry viable offspring to term?"

"Yes." He smiled a little. "It seems your encounter with one of their rogues last month has finally lit a fire under their collective asses."

Sonya's chest tightened as it always did when she thought of the female basilisk who had risked, and lost, everything in the name of keeping her species alive. Of course, she had also been a cold-blooded murderer who'd killed six other magical creatures, but she hadn't been without morals and her single-minded determination to save her people was something Sonya could sympathize with. "Have we learned the name of the one who caused all the trouble?"

"No. The head of the High Council, Queen Siwajen, has made it quite clear that she considers that matter closed." He added more quietly, "There are rumors that the basilisk you and Maxine killed was one of the queen's own attendants."

Sonya winced.

Mark squeezed her hand briefly. "She bears you no ill will."

"I wish there had been another way to stop her, whoever she was."

Mark nodded and Sonya wondered if he felt that way every time he had to "dispose" of one of his fellow dragons for the safety of the world.

She firmly turned the conversation back to why he'd come down to see her.

He brightened. "I came to say that I talked to your boss, Agent Corelli, and we both agree you're the best person for the job."

She waited, hoping only that he wasn't going to heap more work on her head.

"Once the negotiations are underway, after all involved have decided to actually get past the posturing and begin serious talks, there's going to be a research team created to help diagnose what's wrong with the basilisks' ability to have children.

"Based on the dead young one left in your office back in July, a dragon and a werewolf do indeed produce a basilisk. So, various groups are being asked if they will contribute DNA to SearchLight to figure out how this is possible, and to also determine if two basilisks can still make another of their kind when science helps them along."

She still waited. This was all very interesting, especially when viewed in the context of her current doctoral thesis, "Reptilian Magical Creatures: Treatment and Dissection," but she sensed there was more to come.

"The bulk of the posturing revolves around dragons and werewolves not wanting to mix their DNA or share any information about themselves with a third party other than SearchLight. And the dragons are iffy even on that part.

"So, all of this is to say that we won't be needing your help for at least a month. Probably longer."

Okay, she was through with waiting. "What do you need my help with?"

He looked at her as if she had missed something crucial. "Heading the team that will research basilisk, dragon, and werewolf DNA."

Sonya gaped at him. "Mark," she whispered, forgetting in her astonishment to call him Agent Tavery since they were at work, "I'm only a senior medtech!" Then, blushing, she added, "All right, so I was promoted to Agent Corelli's assistant, the head of the GP department, but…"

Mark nodded. "Your position is new, but you will have your first doctorate in less than six months. You have the experience we need in leading a team. Plus your studies in dragons, werewolves, and basilisks, who don't exactly let most humans study their physiology. I've always meant to ask. How did you swing that, anyway?"

Sonya flushed. "I know royalty."

Mark's eyebrows rose. "How?"

"The daughter of the current queen was my roommate. And when she found out I wanted to make dragons and basilisks my focus but didn't know how to go about getting permission, she put a word in for me."

Mark grinned. Then he returned to the topic at hand. "Also doing research and documenting that research. Not to mention soothing hurt feelings."

"How do you figure that last?"

"Thanks to your work back when you first started, when I was busy killing murderers and you had to tell their families that they'd died, you've met and negotiated with more than half the medtechs in the US. And since the dragon third of this dragon, basilisk, and werewolf game of Twister won't negotiate with anyone but me, working with someone here in Tampa makes much more sense. We're already importing a werewolf for that side of the debate plus a master negotiator to oversee the whole thing."

Sonya wanted to throw up her hands. She wanted to storm out. She wanted to tell Mark to shove his logic. Instead, she said, calmly as she could, "I'm flattered but…" *I'm probably pregnant. And I'm working full-time. And I'm finishing my doctorate this semester.*

The look on his face, a mixture of understanding and confidence, stopped her tongue. "You've already told Agent Corelli I'd do this."

"No. But he already told me you would."

"He didn't talk to me."

Mark nodded. "I know. And there are other medtechs, but not ones with your level of experience with both dragons and werewolves. We need a team leader who can check the others' work."

"But I'm not a DNA sequencer!" she half wailed.

Oh, fuck. Get it under control, Johnson. You're overreacting. Wasn't that supposed to happen in the first trimester?

She closed her eyes for a moment, picturing the dolphin she'd been allowed to pet. The creature had been tame and yet still possessed a freedom and wildness in its gaze. When she felt like she had herself in check, she looked at Mark. "I'm in the middle of my dissertation."

"You should be done by the end of December, right?"

"If they like the changes I've made." She still saw his confidence in her abilities. It was all over his face.

"Please tell me there are compensations, not just prestige."

"No prestige," he admitted. "But you'll be making time and a half on any overtime you have to pull."

That was something at least. She was a salaried employee, which meant overtime wasn't rewarded financially. "Will you be getting overtime?" she asked, thinking of the baby Mark and his lover were expecting.

Mark smiled without humor. "No. But don't worry about us. We're managing. But back to you. If you really don't want this extra task, I can finagle things with Agent Corelli."

I'd be gone even more than Maxine. Which means we won't see each other at all. Maybe Maxine would be making more time for her, especially once Sonya had proof she was pregnant.

She'd be getting that proof today.

She tried to weigh her mounting exhaustion, her apparently newly sharp tongue, and her unresolved issues against a growing excitement. She *wanted* to do this job. She loved leading teams, and the challenges of working with high-ranking members of different species made her blood sing.

"I'll do it."

Mark's relief was obvious. But then his expression changed. "You're worried about something else besides this job. You were worried when I came in."

Damn his telepathy anyway. Even though Maxine was a telepath, her powers weren't very strong or reliable. Mark's were legendary. Sonya made her shields stronger and admitted the smallest part of what was pissing her off. "It's an icebox in my apartment.

The werewolves like it that way."

"You could change the thermostat."

"If it was that easy, I wouldn't be shivering in a sweater all the time. It's broken."

"Who do you go to for repairs?"

"I have no idea."

"Ask your mate."

Sonya laughed bitterly. "Sure. When I see her for more than five minutes at a time." And that was too much information. "I need to get back to work. Thank you for giving me this opportunity."

Mark got to his feet. "Sonya, if Maxine is --"

"Not your problem," she said firmly. "I'll talk to her. Promise."

Once he was gone, not just out the door but out of the hallway as well, Sonya went to collect her purse. She needed to get to the human doctor who was going to tell her what she already knew: that three days without birth control, even if it had been an accident, had consequences.

She walked down the hall and up the stairs, her feet dragging. Maybe she'd start taking the elevator and screw keeping her girlish figure.

Her thoughts turned to her mate as she got into her car and turned the key. Having a pup would be a challenge for her, especially considering everything she was going through right now, but would it be a blow to Maxine?

They didn't talk much about Maxine's one and only son, James, who had died in infancy when his body tried, instinctively, to shift from human to werewolf in response to the call of the full moon. That not talking much made Sonya think Maxine was more upset about his death than she let on.

Over and above James's death had been

Maxine's first mate's suicide. She'd been suffering from postpartum depression, or that was Maxine's assumption decades later.

Sonya was less worried about their pup surviving infancy; he or she would be half werewolf, half human. And, at least according to all the research SearchLight had done, which was admittedly not much when weighed against all they knew of humans, half wolves couldn't change guises. But the postpartum depression threat worried her because she knew women it had happened to. And because, as a medtech, even one who specialized in magical creatures rather than humans, she knew the life-changing disease was caused by hormonal changes, the adjustment to becoming a mother, and fatigue.

Was she even ready to have a little one to look after?

"Oh, fuck it. Let's at least see if I'm pregnant before I freak out."

But it was too late. She knew she was pregnant, and she knew, without a doubt, that "freaking out" was exactly what lay in front of her.

* * *

That evening, with the knowledge that she was indeed pregnant swirling around in her guts, Sonya paced around the apartment. She both saw and didn't see the art on the walls and the tasteful furniture. She didn't want to appreciate Maxine's perfect taste when it came to decorating, but seemed unable to keep herself from admiring the little touches that made this five-room space a home. The cut flowers in their delicate vases, the multi-colored afghan on the back of the couch, and the one pane in the large window that had been replaced by stained glass all combined to mark this as a place where Sonya should feel safe and content.

She did feel safe. No one would dare harass her here, not when her mate was the pack's beta. But as for content... *How could anyone be happy being a kept bird in a gilded cage*? That was unfair and Sonya immediately felt guilty for the thought. Maxine was busy; that wasn't a crime.

And it wasn't as if Sonya didn't have other friends.

She considered calling Luke Tavery. Mark's husband, a genie who had sex changed himself into a female half human, half dragon so he could have Mark's baby, was definitely Sonya's closest friend. Even though she'd known Mark longer, it was Luke she'd truly bonded with.

But if I call him, the whole pack will know I'm miserable. And I will not *air Maxine's and my dirty laundry.*

She threw up her hands in utter frustration. It was too damn hot to go for a walk, she didn't really feel like pounding out her fury on a track somewhere, and sitting down to work on her dissertation was simply out of the question.

However, the heat from outside could have other uses. Sonya opened two of the windows in the living room and sat on the windowsill, loving it as a hot breeze from outside warmed her.

Someone knocked on her door. She crossed the room and opened the door. Where she might have snapped at the other person a few moments ago, driven as she was by her hormones and being uncomfortable, now she felt more like herself. She even managed a smile. "Hi, Michaela."

Michaela's delicate eyebrows were raised. The beautiful, German-born werewolf was Fehrna Susan's mate. She outranked Maxine and unlike the rest of the pack, she went out of her way to talk to Sonya. "Are you all right?"

I must smell like all of my frustration. Taking a deep breath, Sonya stepped back and invited her in with a wave of her hand. When the door was closed, she asked, "Is everything all right?"

"Besides you pacing like a zoo animal? Everything's fine."

Sonya groaned. Then she went over to the radio she kept on the windowsill and turned it on. "Who sensed it?" *So I can tell them to stay the hell out of my head.*

"I heard the clack, clack of your high heels."

Sonya looked guiltily down at her shoes. "Oh, damn. I'm sorry."

"You shouldn't be," Michaela told her. "It's just that I was worried about you. Why are you stalking around?"

"I'm cold." Sonya blushed. "Forget I said that. Please?"

"All right. For now. But only if you give me a more pressing reason for your pacing."

"The pack's driving me nuts," Sonya said after a moment. She would not be telling about her pregnancy. Maxine deserved to hear about it first.

"They are?"

Sonya nodded, running with partial truth in the hopes that Michaela wouldn't sense there was more. "I get 'yes, ma'am, no, ma'am' and all other forms of polite speech but no one really talks to me."

Michaela frowned. "Well, that's something I didn't know. Who, specifically, is giving you trouble?"

Sonya shook her head. "I am not tattling on fellow pack members like a first grader."

"It's not tattling," Michaela said patiently. "It's making sure everyone coexists happily. Unless there's something else really wrong?" She smiled slightly. "Like why you're wearing a sweater when it's ninety degrees?"

"The whole building is kept like an icebox."

"You can raise your thermostat."

Sonya sighed. "It *is* something else, but it's for Maxine and I to discuss."

"Maybe instead of pacing, you should take a rest. You look tired."

Sonya shook her head, opened her mouth to lie about how worn out she felt, and pressed her lips together. Werewolves could sense lies, even if they weren't psychic wolves. People smelled and sounded different when they lied. "That's none of your concern."

"Is it related to why you haven't been down for the pack potlucks since you joined us?"

"Please, Michaela, I know the potlucks are pack builders, but…" How could she explain that there seemed to be many more than twenty wolves in the basement dining room when they were all gathered together? She knew it probably wasn't true, but it seemed they moved like one pair of hands, doing exactly the same thing at the same damn time. Not to mention the way Tessa and the two just beneath her in the pecking order made her feel unwanted. That really would be tattling.

"I see," Michaela said, probably in response to her silence. She turned back to the door. "If you don't want anyone knowing how agitated you are, keep the music on and pace in your bare feet." Then she was gone.

Sonya did one better. After she'd given Michaela

fifteen seconds to walk away from her door, she went to her desk, took out her diary, and began to write in it. She started out making a list of pros and cons about keeping the little one growing inside her. But soon her musings dissolved into scribbles and jottings about how much she missed Maxine.

Chapter Three

The basement of the apartment building where the Fehrna pack lived had terrible cell phone reception. So, before she came down here, Maxine had texted Sonya to let her know she wouldn't be available even by phone. Sonya had responded with, *Whenever you're done, I have news.*

Maxine had foreknowledge of the "news." Someone in the Department of Dragons had let it slip to someone in Werewolf Watch that Sonya was going to head a kind of testing of basilisk DNA. Certainly this was a coup; Sonya hadn't exactly studied DNA in her schooling. More: Sonya wasn't even through with her first doctorate that specialized in physiology, not genetics, except on the most basic level.

So, Maxine had sent her mate a smiley face and then headed down to deal with John and Christopher's dominance fight with a mostly light heart.

Dominance fights shouldn't be entered into lightly but these two had gone through the counseling, administered by Maxine personally, and they were as prepared for the consequences as two people could be. So, Maxine had named tonight, a Tuesday when most of the pack was busy elsewhere, so there would be less of an audience to drive the tensions higher.

Her charges stood at opposite ends of a mat, ready to do battle. Maxine lifted her hand. When she lowered it, the fight would begin.

The basement door opened and Michaela stepped in. "Hold up a minute, everyone." She walked to the center of the mat and made sure both male wolves saw her. "John, Christopher, you're going to have to wait a few minutes. There's another matter that requires Maxine's attention."

It must be serious to forestall a dominance challenge. Maxine followed Michaela quickly out of the room. To her surprise, she was led into the kitchen and Michaela went to the farthest corner. Once there, she spoke in a low, intense voice.

"Are you aware that your mate is having problems with the pack?"

Maxine opened her mouth, searched for something to say, and shut it again when nothing came.

"You're not. Sonya has been keeping it to herself." Michaela sighed. "Maybe that's normal among human pairings, but it's not what will work here. We are all one community. Werewolf packs are a family. We may not all like each other, but we all respect each other. We all work together. For the common good of all."

Then she got to the point. "If Sonya can't function within those boundaries naturally, maybe it's time she had a lesson."

Maxine remembered the "lessons" her former mate, Carrie, had been taught. Carrie, a werewolf, hadn't needed instruction in how rank worked. But she'd been uncomfortable with sharing who she was with the rest of the pack. And that wasn't how the community functioned best. "Let me do it," she said as protectiveness rose in her chest. Dominant wolves could be a little forceful when imparting information to those they figured should "get" it without their help. And though Michaela was usually a good mentor, Maxine harbored the fear that it was Michaela's teaching that had pushed Carrie even deeper into her loneliness. "I'll help her accept the pack."

"Have you already introduced her to the idea that sharing her feelings is expected? That it will help the pack run more smoothly?"

Maxine frowned. "I guess not. She shares with me. I thought that was enough considering how independent and unused to cooperative living she is."

"On another note, Sonya may simply be having trouble remembering, or understanding, how well we hear everything. I stopped her pacing not ten minutes ago. The clack of her high heels was driving me crazy."

Maxine considered telling the more dominant wolf about Sonya's new work responsibilities. But Michaela had never worked outside the pack, let alone for SearchLight. She probably wouldn't understand. And besides, Sonya was Maxine's mate, Maxine's concern. "I'll talk to her."

"Don't scare her," Michaela admonished. "She's a loving soul and she seems to have a lot on her shoulders. Moving to the middle of a wolves' den would intimidate anyone, and less than six months ago she was terrified of us."

Maxine nodded. "Do you want me to talk to her now?"

"Go on. No time like the present. And don't worry about the fighters. I'll supervise."

"Thank you," Maxine said genuinely. Then she left the kitchen, heading for the stairs. She lived on the third floor with her mate. She'd had the same apartment since she and the pack moved from Montana in 1979. Carrie hadn't ever lived in this apartment. She'd been dead three years before the Slaughter of '78 when dragons had descended on the northwestern part of the United States.

With memories of Carrie fresh in her mind, Maxine admitted she was afraid to talk to Sonya. All the times she'd tried to talk to Carrie about being open… *Well, let's just say she wasn't exactly receptive.*

Steeling herself, Maxine entered their apartment. Sonya was asleep on the couch, a notebook marked "Doctoral Thesis: Basilisks" closed on the floor next to her. She had two more stashed somewhere; Maxine had seen them. One was marked "Dragons" and the other "Werewolves."

Maxine hesitated, not wanting to disturb her. She looked thoroughly done in, as if she was still adjusting to the trip back from DC. But that made no sense; SearchLight Academy wasn't even in a different time zone.

She approached the couch and a floorboard creaked under her foot.

Sonya blinked, yawned, stretched... and then smiled when she saw Maxine. "You're home early. I thought you'd be gone all night. Don't dominance fights, and their aftermath, take a while?" She rose slowly, stretching again. When she pressed herself against Maxine, her body was ample and warm and she smelled of shea butter.

Maxine drank in everything her senses gave her, reaching out with her telepathy to see if she could get more that way. What she received was a mixture of relief and joy and caution. It was dim, as if Sonya had shields up. Humans could use mental blocks; they were just not as strong as, say, a natural telepath's. Maxine wondered why her mate felt like she needed protection, but probably it was part of her desire to keep things hidden. "Are you all right, dear?"

Sonya smiled at the pet name, as she always did. She even wrinkled her nose a little, trying to imitate how a deer would sniff around. Then she laughed, but uneasily. "I need to talk to you." She retreated to the couch, pulling Maxine gently after her. "I'll share the less important stuff first, although it seems wrong to call anything I'm doing at work 'less important.' I'm going to head the --" She stopped and frowned. "You already know about this. It's all over your face. How do you know?"

"The office grapevine," Maxine admitted. "Is this going to interfere with your dissertation?"

"According to Mark," Sonya said slowly, "it shouldn't." She smiled. "Trust you to know what's going to bother me most. At least in this." She sighed. "Okay, so I was hoping to bandy that around for at least five minutes and get up the courage to tell you what's really going on, but I guess I'll just have to plunge in."

"What if I tell you I think I know?"

Sonya shook her head. "Unless your telepathy is a lot stronger or I've been talking in my sleep, I've kept this stuff to myself."

She sat forward, dropping Maxine's hands and staring across the room. "I'm tired of being cold all the time. Not just physically, although that sucks. Being cold-shouldered by the pack. Everything is 'yes, ma'am' and that's about it."

Maxine started to explain about Michaela's words to her, but Sonya went on.

"Let's talk about the thermostat first. It's broken."

Maxine's gut tightened, not because of what Sonya was saying but because of how she was avoiding what was really bothering her. Standing, needing to give herself a little distance, she crossed to the wall readout. "Yeah," she said after a moment of fiddling with the dial. "It's stuck on fifty-eight." She didn't turn back toward Sonya, hoping the space between them would encourage her mate to talk.

"I'm getting 'yes, ma'amed by most of the damn

pack," Sonya said, her anger obvious in her voice as well as her choice of words. Sonya swore rarely.

"By whom?"

"Everyone. Well, at least the ones who will actually talk to me in the first place. This doesn't apply to you, Michaela, or Fehrna Susan, but no one else will engage with me. Being plopped down in the middle of a neighborhood I don't know is bad enough. I'm not really the go out and explore on my own type. But doing it when everyone's distantly polite? It's infuriating."

"I can't do anything about 'distantly polite,'" Maxine said. "Maybe it's because they don't know you yet."

"Werewolves tend to be less nervous about meeting new people than humans are," Sonya said. "They're usually open and welcoming."

Maxine didn't know how to respond to that. She turned back toward her mate. Sonya still sat, staring across the room. "Is that all that's bothering you?"

"No, but..." Sonya looked at her, meeting her gaze. "Come sit with me? I don't see you enough and it hurts when you're so far away."

Maxine hesitated. She wanted to stay where she was. Memories of Carrie complaining about "distant" pack members and not seeing Maxine enough swirled in her head. But she could see the real need in Sonya's eyes and she crossed to her, sat down, and took her hands. She even tried to smile reassuringly, although her heart wasn't in it.

Sonya looked away and then back. "I didn't mean to, but I'm pregnant."

Maxine's world tilted on its axis. "You're... what?" Surely she hadn't heard that correctly.

Sonya nodded. "I'm pregnant. I went to a doctor

this afternoon and confirmed it."

"How? What about the birth control?" She felt instantly guilty. She should have been wearing a condom all those times… "Did I do this to you?"

Sonya smiled a little. "In a very real sense, yes, but I don't blame you. I forgot my pills for three days in a row, and then…"

She went on, her eyes glistening with unshed tears. "I know you don't want to risk any more children coming into this world and dying, but…"

True, as well as a fear of Sonya dying, but Maxine's mouth seemed stuck shut.

"I'm sorry," Sonya said miserably.

That sorrow got through Maxine's silence. "You didn't do it on purpose. I guess… I guess we'll be having a pup."

"Well, I don't have to go through with the pregnancy," Sonya said softly.

Maxine shot to her feet and stalked away from the couch. When she thought she could speak without shouting, she turned to glare at her mate. "You'd get rid of a… a… new wolf?" She'd wanted to say "miracle" or "blessing" but neither word was strong enough.

Sonya's eyes flashed. She was angry too, it seemed. "It's my body. You are not going to dictate what I do with my own womb."

"No, but…" Maxine tried for something that didn't sound male-dominant. Usually this wasn't a problem. She didn't think much like her biological sex. But now… "Can't we at least talk about it before you decide to kill our pup?"

Sonya shot to her feet. "Damn it, I haven't decided anything." She strode past Maxine and to the door. "I'm going out."

"Alone?" It wasn't that Sonya couldn't defend herself; she had a brown belt in karate and had used it in Maxine's presence. Her skills were impressive. But in her delicate condition...

"Well, I'll drive to Luke's, but we'll go out together."

A kernel of resentment inspired Maxine to say, "Luke's an outsider. You're having trouble with the pack, but you won't stay to work it out. You're seeking people outside the pack." Then she wished she could take it back, because that sounded possessive and untrusting. "Sonya, I'm --"

"I'll be careful," Sonya said in her best professional voice. The voice she barely used, even at the office, because it meant she was absolutely furious. "I'll be home later tonight."

Maxine wanted to tell her all sorts of things. Don't drink was chief among them. But she knew she'd exhausted their line of communication, at least for now. "Call if you need me."

Sonya nodded and she was gone.

Maxine walked quietly to the couch and sank onto it. But the piece of furniture seemed to hold the memory of Sonya's anger, and she stood back up. Prowling around the main room, she looked at the walls, seeking an escape. She paused beside the large back window that looked out onto the garden behind the apartment building. From here, she could see the trellis heavy with sky blue, a large-blossomed flower with a yellowish center and light, almost hazy, blue petals. Sonya often cut one or two of the blooms and put them in a vase on their dining room table.

Her gaze shifted to the single pane she'd replaced with stained glass. It was an abstract image of an egret, a bird, white and leggy, that populated this west coast of Florida.

The pack had done all it could to reestablish itself in this new place. They'd been here, in this building, since 1980. The year between moving to Florida from Montana and finding this abandoned apartment building, had been fraught with difficulties. No wonder they'd worked so hard to make this place home. And Sonya was fitting right into that, from the flowers she picked to the way she'd made that little corner of the main room her office.

She could have used the spare bedroom. True, but maybe Sonya had been thinking about pups all along, wanting to save the space for a little one of their own.

"No," Maxine whispered. "No, she wouldn't be talking about abortion if that had been her plan."

It occurred to her that the whole pack would know soon that Sonya was planning to murder their unborn pup. Neither she or Sonya had thought to turn on some music and so mask their words.

"Murder is too harsh a word. It's just a collection of cells right now." But her gut twisted at the idea of losing a pup of hers.

She turned from the window and found herself staring at the painting, bright and colorful, that she'd hung on the wall across from the couch. It was Carrie's work, done in happier days before they found their son, half shifted and dead, in his cradle.

The memory of finding him that way, with fur covering half his body and his bones only partially reformed into a wolf's likeness, made Maxine's stomach clench. But she'd seen a therapist for over two decades to work out her stabbing grief. Now, even though she'd never be able to recall James's twisted form without that tightening in her gut, she wouldn't throw up or run, screaming, through the apartment building as she had more than once when they first moved here.

Shame threatened to bury her, but she talked that down too. She'd been a different person when she was in hell. Like the country song said, when you were going through hell, you just kept going.

But that brought her back to Sonya, because it was Sonya who loved country music like that song, and it was Sonya who'd quoted that song once after her mother had written her a letter that basically said to never darken her doorstep again. Sonya had been crying, but she'd also smiled through her tears and said hell was other people.

Hell certainly was other people. Maxine rested a hand next to the canvas and stared at the wild bursts of color that could look like any variety of images if stared at long enough. Today, a blotch of reddish brown resembled a person standing on a clifftop, their silhouette dark against the hazy blue of the high Montana sky.

Maxine's gut seized like a tightened fist and she clutched at herself, doubling over. She needed to get to a bathroom. Right now.

But the urge to vomit was so strong, she didn't quite make it to the toilet. Especially not when Carrie's scream, a scream that had sounded both despairing and triumphant, split her head, a lightning bolt of remembered sound.

She fell to her knees and gave up everything on the tiles.

Her mind raced even as she puked. Whoever had said throwing up meant you couldn't think of anything else had been different than Maxine. She remembered how Carrie had huddled into herself when she jumped, hugging her empty, still swollen belly. She could recall with hellish detail the jeans and yellow, flowered shirt Carrie had worn. Her favorite shirt, the one she would never wear after James was born because she didn't want him to spit up on it and potentially ruin the delicate fabric.

Rage flashed through her and she howled her fury, the puking having passed for now. She'd thought this depth of rage was beyond her now, but as she remembered Carrie's final words, she discovered it was Carrie's final act on this side of reality to hurt her.

"If you hadn't spent so much time with the pack and so little time with me, maybe I would have had a prayer of a good future."

The words had seemed stilted and rehearsed, but they'd stung anyway, cutting through all of Maxine's defenses and trying to slit the throat of her commitment to the pack.

She was done throwing up. Sighing as much from sadness as relief, she got to her feet and started for the mop and bucket in their closet next to the kitchen. "She's dead. Isn't that, can't that be, the end of it?"

Apparently not, because she remembered Carrie sobbing, *"You don't love me. You only love your responsibility."*

But Maxine didn't love her duty; she loved the pack. They were hers to take care of. Even though she wasn't the alpha, it was to her that many of the others came with their troubles. What was she supposed to do? Give up being who she was for a partner?

"I'm upset about two things," she said. "The idea of losing, voluntarily, a pup I've helped make, and I'm afraid that Sonya doesn't understand my responsibility to the pack."

She started cleaning up the mess, and now she

kept her words inside her head because they were too terrible for accidental ears.

Carrie... Her stomach clenched again but she fought it down as the image and sound of Carrie's final moments on Earth rushed past her. *Carrie was depressed. Justifiably so. If I hadn't had Fehrna Susan and Michaela helping me, I might have wanted to die too. But Carrie never had them. She never liked either my alpha or my alpha's mate.*

She moved the mop firmly, putting her frustration and touch of panic into the cleanup. *Sonya isn't like that. She just said she doesn't see me enough, and I've been awfully busy over the last, well, month or so.*

She rested in this knowledge, the idea that she'd have more time soon, and was soothed by the idea. Now, what to do about her mate saying she was going to let their pup die?

"No. That's completely unfair," Maxine said to herself. "Sonya did *not* say that. She said she's thinking about it. And she is exhausted already. I mean, maybe I can take over some of her duties, anything to help..." She sighed. "There's nothing I can do. Sonya is busy because of school and work and I can't help with either of those things."

But she could make sure she was here to assist with dinner prep. And she could pack Sonya's lunches.

Well, maybe. She was busy too. The pack seemed restless lately, and the dominance fight between Christopher and John was just the most recent proof.

Her cleaning done, she took the mop to the bathtub and rinsed it. Then she put mop and bucket back in the closet. Returning to the living room, she stared at the spot on the colorful painting that had caused all the trouble. It still looked like Carrie.

Without pausing to think about what she was

doing, Maxine took the painting down and turned it to face the wall. She didn't want to throw it away, but she wanted it out of her sight for a while.

Something had resolved in her mind while she did this simple chore. She wanted Sonya to keep the pup, their pup, but she was more worried about losing Sonya.

As soon as she gets home, I'll find a way to make her comfortable, to let her know that she's not going anywhere, that she's mine. That sounded possessive, but she didn't care. She loved Sonya and wouldn't lose her the way she'd lost Carrie.

So determined, Maxine set about straightening up the apartment and baking one of Sonya's favorite treats: brownies with caramel in the middle.

* * *

"I gotta see your sweet, sweet smile every day…" Maxine stopped singing because she heard someone approaching the apartment. She'd only been singing in an attempt to keep her spirits up.

Sonya entered, smelling of many people and alcohol.

Maxine opened her mouth to demand if Sonya drank while pregnant, but kept the accusation behind her teeth. "Hi, dear," she said meekly.

Sonya came to her and hugged her.

The smell of alcohol was on her skin, not her breath. She'd been around people who were drinking, not imbibing herself. Maxine relaxed.

Wouldn't it be easier, some corner of her mind whispered, *if the baby died in utero?*

Maxine shivered and pulled Sonya still closer. "I'm sorry."

"I'm not mad at you anymore," Sonya answered. "We all make mistakes." She drew back a little. "But I need you to know something. This is my body, and the baby is more a part of me than of itself right now."

Maxine nodded hesitantly. She didn't like where this was going.

"I haven't decided what to do. But I know you don't want to lose our pup. I promise, I'm hearing you and listening."

"I don't know what I want," Maxine confessed. Losing the pup in utero would be bad enough, but often when pups were carried by humans, making them half werewolves, they were born prematurely. So early that their little lungs couldn't support their breath. She shuddered. "But destroying a life seems wrong."

"To me too."

"Then why would you even consider..."

Sonya turned away, crossing her arms tightly over her stomach. "Neither God nor Fate asked me if I wanted to upend my life." She shivered.

Maxine used this as a reason to cross to her and hug her from behind. "You're cold. I'll get the thermostat fixed."

"I don't want just one more reason for you to be out of our home," Sonya snapped.

Maxine considered that. Carrie's old accusations, that Maxine loved the pack more than she loved her mate... those were coming back to haunt Maxine now. "All right," she said carefully. "Our electrician is Heidi. She's in 2C." Heidi was a gentle soul. She'd treat Sonya with respect. Some of the others, like Tessa, who was just under Maxine in rank, might use the opportunity to be a bully.

"Thank you." Sonya turned in the circle of Maxine's arms and rested her cheek against Maxine's shoulder. "I love you. Even when I'm mad, I love you."

"I love you too."

They went into the bedroom and Sonya got under the covers quickly.

Maxine hesitated. She did not want Sonya to be chilled but she couldn't imagine being under all those blankets. "I'll sleep on top."

Sonya snuggled against her and for a while, as her mate dropped off to sleep, Maxine was comforted. Then, she couldn't help thinking of the covers as a symbol of the wall between them. They hadn't really talked about the baby. She didn't even know how Sonya actually felt about a life growing inside her.

She lay awake most of the night.

Chapter Four

Sonya woke the next morning with Maxine still snuggled against her. Her mate had remained on top of the covers, and Sonya longed for the touch of Maxine's naked skin against her own. She'd gotten into a nightgown last night, although she barely remembered doing so, she'd been so wiped, but the lovely werewolf who shared her bed slept nude.

There was an ache in her belly that she knew had nothing to do with hunger. She'd dreamed of sex all night long and consequently woken wet and wanting.

She rolled carefully over until she faced Maxine. Then she kissed her mate's brow. "Good morning," she murmured. She longed for sex, but what she really needed was touch. When Maxine didn't wake immediately, Sonya rested her lips against the werewolf's silken forehead. She inhaled the scent of the oil Maxine put in her hair. It was a heady and aromatic blend of spices she couldn't name, but which made her mouth water.

She pressed her legs together as her clit throbbed.

Maxine stirred. She blinked sleepily at Sonya. Even though she'd been the early riser when they first met, she'd had a lot of late nights recently.

"Good morning," Sonya repeated, her voice soft.

Maxine yawned, covering her mouth. "Morning. What are you doing up so early?"

Sonya glanced at the clock behind her and chuckled quietly. "It's almost seven. As for why I'm waking you up, I was hoping we could make love."

Maxine grinned, her eyes shining despite their blurriness a moment ago. "Absolutely."

Sonya wriggled out from under the blankets and stripped out of her nightgown. She felt like she was dripping but knew that was an illusion. Still, the room filled with the smell of her need.

She glanced at Maxine, saw her mate's nostrils flare, and grinned herself, unashamed.

Maxine was up and rounding the bed. "Let's try -_"

Her cell phone, connected to the charger on her side of the bed, rang.

Sonya cursed. "Now?" she half whined.

"I'll make it quick." Maxine went to her phone and answered it.

Sonya wished she had a werewolf's sharp hearing. She wanted, more than anything in that moment, to know who was disturbing them.

Maxine said, "I'll be there in two minutes." She hung up and met Sonya's gaze. "I'm sorry, but Michaela needs help. She's having trouble calming Travis."

One of the wolves Sonya didn't know well yet, except to know he was a precog bisexual wolf mated to Tessa.

"I'll be back in... well, I was going to say a few minutes, but I don't know how long it's going to take."

Sonya plopped back onto the bed. "Okay." After all, she reasoned, she'd known she'd married a beta. With all the responsibilities inherent in that position. Still, with her clit throbbing in time with her heartbeat, she longed to tell Maxine to just play hooky.

Maxine kissed her briefly. Then she started getting dressed. In less than a minute, she was gone.

Sonya flopped backward and lay with her legs spread. She wanted touch so badly that her breasts ached. She caressed them, lingering around the nipples until they were hard points.

With that part of her body temporarily satisfied,

she trailed her fingers down over her belly. Goose bumps followed the path of her hands and she shivered pleasantly.

Closing her eyes, she envisioned Maxine touching her, her darker skin a beautiful contrast to Sonya's own. The difference in their skin color was a gorgeous thing, liquid milk chocolate and richer brown like spring earth.

She touched her pubic hair lightly and loved the spark of lust that rushed through her entire body. In her mind's eye, it was Maxine who was playing with her. She imagined she could smell her mate's spicy oils and the faint deodorant she wore.

Spreading her legs wider, she caressed the insides of her thighs and teased her way between her labia. Arching, she met her fingers halfway, moaning softly, almost inaudibly, mindful of the pack.

She *was* wet, her bud slick with moisture. Using one finger, she rubbed her clit clockwise and counterclockwise, stopping to press it when a spike of need shot down her back. She lifted her hips again and slipped a single digit into her vagina. She didn't usually masturbate that way, preferring to stay on her clit, but she was picturing Maxine pleasuring her and Maxine's fingers were always so tender.

A shiver ran up her back, blossoming in her head. She swore she could see stars and she moaned her mate's name, still quietly.

Her orgasm broke over her then and she trembled through it, pressing her clit and rocking against her finger.

But after her climax passed, a wave of sorrow overwhelmed her. She sobbed, once, before finding it within herself to control the noise she made. She couldn't stop the tears that trickled down her cheeks.

Yes, she'd gotten her pleasure, her release. But what she wanted was Maxine.

Maxine in her bed. Maxine between her legs.

Maxine back in her life for more than a few moments at a time.

She lay in bed, hating herself for crying but unable to stop. Even being a medtech, knowing pregnancy would make her emotional, she still despised the tears.

After a while, she quieted. Then she rose, went to the shower, and washed off the evidence of her orgasm. Then she got dressed for work.

* * *

Sonya knocked on Heidi's door after work the next day. She was nervous, but mostly because she'd been getting the cold shoulder from the entire pack and this would be the first genuine interaction. Surely she'd be able to strike up a conversation with someone who was fixing her thermostat? She had a great deal of respect for people who worked with their hands and made their living by fixing others' problems.

The werewolf who opened the door was slight and short, but her arms were well-muscled and her legs, clad in tight jeans, were just as impressive.

Sonya smiled. "Hi."

"Ma'am."

The smile froze on Sonya's lips. *Please, God, please don't let it be another case of polite speech.* "My thermostat is broken and Maxine suggested I seek you out." She tried widening her smile. "I won't bite. I promise."

Heidi flinched.

Sonya retreated a step. "Um, maybe if later would be better…"

"No, ma'am. I can help you." She came out into the hall and closed the door. But she seemed to be stuck in one spot just outside her apartment.

Sonya frowned. "I'll show you where I live?"

Heidi nodded and relaxed just a trifle, or at least she seemed to if her posture was any indication.

Sonya went up the stairs and opened her door. She stepped back, but Heidi wouldn't precede her.

Confused, and feeling awkward, Sonya said again, "I won't bite." And tried the smile once more.

Heidi flinched.

Helpless to do anything else, Sonya demanded, "What is it? What am I doing wrong?"

Heidi shook her head but said nothing.

Sonya went in, hoping Heidi would follow.

She did.

Okay, at least I managed that much. She felt ridiculous pointing out the thermostat, so she stepped aside and waited to see what would happen.

Heidi darted a look at her, seemed to come to a decision, and crossed the room to the troublesome piece of electronics. Her shoulders were tense and whatever stress she'd felt earlier had returned.

Feeling profoundly frustrated, Sonya sat down on the couch. "So… How long have you been with the pack?"

Heidi didn't answer.

Sonya tried three more conversational gambits with the same result. Finally, as her annoyance boiled over, she snapped, "What's wrong? Why won't you talk to me?"

Heidi had turned her back to the wall and was staring at Sonya's shoes. "You smell like prey. And you're terrified of us."

Then, trembling slightly, she began to work with the thermostat again.

I smell like what? A wave of fear rolled through

her and she hugged herself briefly. Then she noticed Heidi looked even more on edge and tried to calm down. She knew enough about werewolves to understand they read emotions through smell like most humans recognized the same via body language.

I'm not scared of werewolves. Anymore. She hesitated. *Well, maybe a little, but only because they do everything together when they're home and don't give me any space to be myself.*

Sonya didn't move or say anything else until after Heidi was done and gone. Then, mindful of making her movements known, she turned on music, took off her shoes, and began to pace.

But after circling the main room like a vulture for several minutes, she knew her anxiety was worse rather than better. She put her shoes back on and went in search of Maxine.

She knew exactly where her mate was; they'd discussed Maxine's heading a "controlled play session" where the werewolves could work out some of their stress from a day of being among other magical creatures and humans.

Maybe, her mind whispered, *being present for a controlled play session wouldn't be wise if you're giving off fear pheromones.*

Sonya stalked past the voice and marched down to the basement. She shoved the door open when she'd reached the wrestling room.

The wolves were deep into their exercises. Maxine was barking out orders and her class was moving with deliberate precision. They were graceful and beautiful.

And absolutely terrifying. Sonya pressed herself against the wall and tried to breathe normally.

Maxine glanced at Sonya after a minute or so and

told everyone to take five. Then she crossed to Sonya. "Is everything all right?"

Absolutely not, Sonya thought as hard as she could.

Maxine's expression didn't change, so maybe the message hadn't gotten through.

Aware that everyone was watching them now, and being naturally averse to airing her dirty laundry in public, Sonya said as calmly as she could, "Please wake me when you come in. No matter how late." Her voice shook despite her best efforts.

Steeling herself, she glanced around the room, forcing herself to look at the dangerous people who had been moving with deadly precision only moments ago. Then when she could bear to look at them no more, she caught one of Maxine's hands in hers and kissed it. "I love you." She hoped all the werewolves in the room could hear her sincerity. Probably they could hear the frustration too but fuck it. And fuck them.

She smiled at Maxine, turned, and fled.

* * *

Maxine shuffled her feet, shifting her weight. If she stood out here long enough, someone would come by, see her, and ask what was wrong. She absolutely did not want that to happen. But still, she couldn't make herself go into the apartment she shared with her mate.

Her mate.

Those words were supposed to mean a pairing, a joining of two souls in the yoke of union. To run in harness meant depending on each other for direction and guidance. To rely on your partner's strengths and compensate for their weaknesses.

Hadn't she and Sonya both understood this when they agreed to be mated? Surely they'd discussed it. They'd even put off having sex for months after their sexual attraction had bloomed because they wanted to make sure this was what they wanted. It hadn't mattered that the alpha above all alphas had decreed that sex no longer had to equal mating. Because Maxine's pack still believed in that tradition, because Maxine believed in it, they had waited and Sonya hadn't protested. Didn't that mean she understood what it meant to be mated?

Maybe not, because she was determined to see herself as her own property instead of as part of the pack. She didn't understand the history of werewolf pup deaths or she wouldn't talk so casually about abortion. And she didn't grasp the truth that she was one of many now, responsible for her fellows as they were responsible for her.

But what if this one dies too? Not like James, but dies nonetheless? Or what if he lives, and Sonya suffers from postpartum depression? That was what had killed Carrie, Maxine firmly believed. Not her own divided loyalties as she struggled to take care of the pack and her first mate. James's death had only made a bad situation worse.

Oh, moon goddess, but those were Maxine's greatest fears. That she'd get to see her beautiful pup… only to watch the fruit of her mate's womb turn blue and die. And then, to make things much worse, to bring Maxine to the very end of her own desire for life, Sonya would kill herself.

It was unfair to think Sonya was like Carrie, but postpartum depression wasn't even fully understood now. Back in the 70s, it hadn't been much more than a rumor.

Maxine squared her shoulders and tried to think positively.

There was a way to tell if the pup had a greater chance of survival. If he or she was born with a ridge of fur down his or her spine, then they were more likely to live. Did SearchLight even know why? Maybe, but the werewolves didn't.

Was it the same for half werewolves? She didn't know. Despite having biologically fathered a pup before, there was much she was unsure of. Because the werewolves didn't know. *But I'm a member of SearchLight this time. I can help by doing research.*

Her sharp ears picked up the sounds of someone climbing the stairs. Desperate not to be caught out in the hall with her face full of anxiety and knowing she couldn't compose herself in time, Maxine rammed her key into the lock and swiftly stepped into the apartment.

She closed the door quietly, not wanting to wake Sonya if she was asleep. She saw this hadn't been necessary. Her lover waited on the couch, looking tired but determined. Maxine could see the set of her jaw.

She moved toward the stereo, but Sonya said, "I'll get it." She raised the remote, which Maxine never used, and soft music filled the living room.

"If we keep our voices down, we'll be fine."

Maxine hesitated. She was afraid to sit too close to her lover. *And I'm thinking of her as my lover rather than my mate. Just like I did with Carrie in the weeks before she committed suicide.* Maxine resolutely sat on the couch and took Sonya's hands. Something had resolved itself in her mind; there was that much to be grateful for. "I couldn't stand it if you killed our pup. If he or she dies of natural causes, that's fine, but... What?" For Sonya was shaking her head.

"That's not what I want to talk about."

Maxine forced her voice not to rise. It shook

instead. "Maybe we should. I know it's your body, but to talk so casually about killing --"

"There wouldn't be anything casual about it. But it doesn't matter now. I've decided to keep it."

Maxine let out her breath in a rush. "Thank the moon goddess. What changed your mind?"

"Nothing. I was never planning on an abortion. I just hadn't decided what to do." Sonya pulled her hands away and knotted her fingers together in her lap. "Maxine, we need to talk. About the pack. And your role in it."

Maxine winced. "Carrie --" She stopped as it registered that her dead mate's name had just left her lips. In front of her living mate. "Sonya, I'm --"

"I thought something was wrong, but I didn't realize you were comparing me to *her*. I would never commit suicide. I would never give up on our baby. And I would never..." She sighed. "Maxine, let's just pretend that didn't happen, okay?"

That was all right with Maxine. "About the pack..." But she didn't know what to say about that. Or her duty to them. It was part of who she was as well as a function of her position.

"I either really pissed off or worried or scared Heidi today. I think I scared her because she kept flinching. I damaged our relationship." She snorted. "What relationship? All she says is 'yes, ma'am.'" She paused. "Except when she told me it's my fault for acting scared. Like prey I think is how she put it."

Sonya got up and began to pace. She didn't have her shoes on and her tread was as light as a cat's. "I love you, but sometimes, when misunderstandings and lack of communication are between us, I wonder if I did the right thing by becoming your mate."

Maxine jumped up and seized Sonya by the

shoulders. "Don't you dare talk about breaking our bond."

Sonya blinked at her, and the pain in her eyes was so deep and so obvious that Maxine wanted to cry.

"Please," Maxine whispered. "Please, let's not think about that at all. Let's try to patch what's broken."

Sonya nodded. "Okay, but I don't have the slightest idea how to start."

Maxine brought her back to the couch and they sat down. "Tell me what helped you decide to keep our pup."

"Partially the high mortality rates for werewolf pups. More because I want to bring a part of you into the world. I love that I'm carrying a piece of you inside me that will grow and change, have its own ideas and challenge our authority."

Maxine hugged her, kissing her deeply. She parted Sonya's lips with her tongue and plundered her mouth, claiming her. "I love you too," she whispered after drawing back slightly. Then, because it was bugging her, she added, "Can you call the pup he or she? It sounds weird and disrespectful to hear you call him or her 'it.'"

"But what if our child, sorry, pup, is nonbinary? Then saying he or she would be wrong too."

"How about 'them'?"

"Or *sai*," Sonya suggested.

"That only covers trans," Maxine pointed out, relieved to have something as innocent as gender to discuss.

Sonya chuckled. "True. Okay, them it is, although that sounds like I'm going to have twins." She laughed. "Your eyes are huge. Are you going to start praying to your goddess for that miracle?"

"Maybe…"

Sonya kissed her. "I'm exhausted. There's no way I could make love to you tonight. But with the thermostat fixed, at least we can both sleep on top of the covers. Me in a nightgown and you deliciously naked."

"Maybe we can shoot for tomorrow morning…"

"I'll hope for that, then."

Chapter Five

It was the pack's potluck night again, the last Saturday in October. Now that Sonya was aware of her visceral reaction to many wolves being together in one place, she'd been avoiding them like the plague. She did *not* want to expose them to her fear, especially since the "prey" comment had really gotten to her. She knew how predators thought of prey and she didn't want to inspire the wolves to do something that might lead to...

Oh, stop right there. If you're about to say you're avoiding them for their sake, you're full of shit. You're staying away because the nightmares have returned, because dealing with a mass of wolves all doing the same thing at the same time is terrifying, and because the only time you feel safe is either at work or when the door is locked between you and them. Maybe you wouldn't be so afraid all the time if Maxine was with you, but she's not. Face it. You've basically married someone who doesn't have time for you.

I refuse to believe that. Even if I do, I don't. That made little sense, but Sonya believed firmly in the "fake it till you make it" mentality. It had gotten her through many a tight spot before this.

Okay, and yes, that was her heart telling her that this was about her *mate*, her true love, and that she couldn't avoid thinking about it forever. But just for now? Was that so bad?

Sonya scrubbed harder at a pan that had lately held lasagna and now resisted her attempts to make it spotless so it could be put away. She was in the kitchen down in the basement.

When Maxine had told her it was part of the beta's mate's duty to attend the potlucks, Sonya had agreed to come. But she didn't have to like it. Maxine said she'd been "letting Sonya get away with not coming" because she wanted her to settle in. But now, she needed to attend.

Her duties included showing up a little early to help with preparation, smiling, keeping her thoughts to herself, and trying in general to pretend that she was a part of the werewolf group.

No matter that they seemed not to want her.

She acknowledged that if Maxine had been around more, or more *something* that Sonya couldn't identify, the cold shoulders from the rest of the pack, not to mention her own fears, wouldn't have bothered her so much.

Well, maybe not, she thought. *Or maybe I'd be even more on edge due to the contrast.*

At least Michaela was kind to her. Sonya thought if even the alpha's mate was cold to her she might break down and cry.

Two other members of the pack were preparing long racks of ribs. Sonya knew Tessa fairly well, at least from what Maxine had told her. Tessa was just beneath Maxine in the pack. Technically, she was just under Sonya, but she never seemed to notice Sonya. She chafed against Maxine's orders and was a constant source of annoyance for the beta.

The other wolf, who worked as a butcher in a grocery nearby, was John, the winner of the latest dominance fight. Sonya had learned that from Michaela. According to the alpha's mate, this would make John a little difficult to deal with for the next couple of weeks because he'd be feeling his oats. "Not precisely King Shit of Turd Mountain," were Michaela's words, "but arrogant. Steer clear of him until he settles down unless you want to get into a verbal."

Michaela called arguments "verbals." And emphasized, at least to Sonya and probably to other members of the pack, that these were to be avoided. If the matter was truly serious, a wolf should bring it to the attention of a higher-ranking member and leave it in their hands. "It's not that I don't trust you to stand up for yourself," Michaela had reassured Sonya when they'd had the talk about higher authority. About a week after the mating ceremony, this had been. "But it's my job, as your mate's immediate superior, to smooth things over when Maxine can't. Usually she can. She's very competent. Try not to argue with wolves far down in the ranking. It will make them uncomfortable and paint you as a bully. Which we both know you're not."

Tessa was right below Sonya, and John just below her. Sonya considered trying to ignore whatever they were saying. Maybe they didn't think she could hear them. But then she caught her name and all but felt her ears sharpen.

"… not worthy of our beta," John said.

"Absolutely not," Tessa responded. "Sonya is disrespectful of our ways and refuses to try and learn them."

"Besides," John said, "any baby she births will be half werewolf at most. Probably not long-lived."

Sonya's stomach knotted. She had *not* thought of that. She knew that for most werewolves, shifting at the full moon, or whenever they wanted, was central to how they thought of themselves. How would any half wolf, half human from her and Maxine's union be accepted by the pack?

"That bitch doesn't deserve our Maxine," John said.

Sonya spun, her mouth open to yell at them for

calling her a bitch.

Before she could say anything, the kitchen door opened and Michaela swept in. "Sonya? Do you have a minute?"

Sonya hesitated, but only for an instant. She did not want to make waves and, she reminded herself, "bitch" meant something different to werewolves than to humans. Didn't it?

Besides, if I argue with them, have a "verbal" in Michaela-speak, I probably will get scared instead of being able to hold onto my fury. I will not be anyone's prey. She followed Michaela into a small storage room and Michaela shut the door.

She looked stern, the first time Sonya had seen her that way. It made the hair on the back of Sonya's neck stand up.

"I know you're not doing anything on purpose," Michaela said, "I know that. Your aura reads as too pure for maliciousness. But the fact is, you made Heidi profoundly uncomfortable the other day. It took her this long to bring it up with me and only after I'd noticed something was wrong."

Sonya opened her mouth. Closed it again.

"I can see you have no idea what you did wrong."

"No," Sonya said, "I know I hurt her somehow. She was afraid of me. Or angry with me."

"In a way, it was both, although it wasn't you she was afraid of, but her own reaction."

"I don't mean to be scared," Sonya said, feeling defensive and small.

"Obviously. And you're not scared of all of us. Just the ones you don't know. And that's most of the pack. But your fear put Heidi in a very bad position. She's not a dominant wolf, used to defying her instincts without someone there to help her. And her instincts labeled you as food."

Michaela was actually angry, maybe furious, Sonya saw, and she was intimidated. She retreated a step. "I didn't mean to hurt her."

"I explained that to her. But you've been here over a month. It's time you either seek help or get over yourself."

That pissed Sonya off. "If you damn wolves wouldn't do everything together like a damned cult, maybe…" She stopped, horrified at how species-ist she sounded. "I'm sorry," she whispered. "I don't really mean that."

"No," Michaela murmured, "I can read in your face that you don't. Pack is for protection, not subverting your own desires. Pack is for supporting each other, for coping with the stresses of the world."

"They stress me out," Sonya confessed.

"Let Maxine help you."

Sonya wondered if telling Michaela that Maxine wasn't ever home enough to help her with anything would make things worse. She decided it would, and kept her mouth shut. "I'll try," she said very quietly.

Michaela nodded and some of the ire went out of her expression. "You have a loving heart, Sonya. We are not your enemy." She brushed past Sonya and left the storage room.

Sonya let a few exasperated tears fall, then allowed a few more out in the name of feeling humiliated. Then, when she had control of her emotions and her face, she went back to the kitchen.

Tessa and John were gone. That was a relief. At least she didn't have to deal with them. She started toward the space that was currently being used for a dining room. Then she realized all the looks and snide comments she might have to endure. She did not have the strength for that just now. Biting her lip and feeling terribly small, Sonya retreated to the sink and went to work on the lasagna pan again.

* * *

Why in the name of the moon goddess's big blue tits was Sonya hiding in the kitchen? She'd come down here, true enough, and she'd been applying herself, at least according to the wolves Maxine had asked. Just checking in to make sure there weren't any further misunderstandings. She knew about the trouble between Heidi and Sonya. It had surely been a mistake because Sonya would never purposely make anyone uncomfortable. That simply wasn't in her nature.

Of course, it could have to do with Sonya's nervousness around the other wolves, but for as long as Maxine had known her, Sonya had been a bull-by-the-horns type of lady. Her hiding made little sense.

She's making me uncomfortable right now by not being here.

Yes, but that was different. Maybe Sonya was simply… Maxine fumbled for an excuse. *Maybe the smells of the food are making her queasy in her delicate condition.*

She seized upon this idea… until it unraveled in her hands. Sonya might be nauseated by the smells of the food, but then surely she wouldn't be in the kitchen, where the smells were undoubtedly stronger.

So, why else might Sonya be avoiding this dinner?

Whatever the reason, it's probably the same one that's been leading her to skip these potlucks every week except for the one after our mating ceremony. If I can find that out, maybe I can figure out how to help both of us.

Maxine stood up, cutting Tessa off with a gentle

wave of her hand. "I'll be back in a minute."

Tessa shook her head and caught Maxine's wrist. "Let her be. She's obviously in need of some alone time."

Maxine pulled away, kindly, and smiled a little, an expression she didn't feel. "She's been alone too much lately. I'll be right back." She started away.

Only to be distracted when she heard someone say, "Tilthos Charles will do what?"

Tilthos Charles was the head of the entirety of werewolf kind. All right, so only the werewolves in North America actually had to obey him, but his influence was growing, as Firos William's had before him. Maybe soon his name would be spoken with awe by wolves all over the world.

Maxine turned toward John, the one who had spoken, and listened.

Christopher, sitting only two seats from John, spoke with a gleam in his eye. "He's going to head the whole damn negotiation circus when the basilisks and werewolves and dragons all sit down to talk. Now I think that's stupid, but who am I to challenge the alpha above all alphas?"

"Why not?" John taunted. "You already proved you're an idiot."

Maxine stepped in smoothly, restraining Christopher with a hand on his shoulder. "Tell me why you're questioning Tilthos Charles," she said softly.

And by the time everything was hashed out if not resolved, it was well past midnight.

Chapter Six

For Sonya, it had been a miserable two weeks since the last potluck she'd attended. It was now the second Saturday in November. She'd taken Luke and Luke's husband, Mark, out shopping. Luke needed more maternity clothes because he'd outgrown what Sonya had provided earlier in the pregnancy. And although Mark made more money at SearchLight than she did, everything the dragon made was going to pay a leprechaun who was keeping Luke's pregnancy not quite a secret, but kept neighbors and most non-SearchLight people in the dark about Luke's condition.

And when Sonya put it to herself like that, it seemed Mark and Luke were having a much more miserable month than she. Still, she felt pretty damn awful.

So, in the midafternoon of that second Saturday in November, she sent Mark away to find her something to "settle" her stomach. She needed a minute alone with Luke.

He was, even sex changed and halfway through his pregnancy, the more sensible of the two male Taverys. Perceptive too, because he at once took her hand as soon as Mark was out of earshot and asked, "What's wrong?"

Tears at once pressed behind her eyes and Sonya blinked hard. Two escaped in spite of her attempt to keep them at bay and she scrubbed at her right cheek, grimacing. Would her hormones ever be normal again? "I hate living with those damn werewolves. They're so superior, they're always right and they barely leave me alone to lead my life. Except they sometimes leave me alone too much. And I *know* I can't have it both ways." She held up a hand when he opened his mouth. "Give me a second."

He waited obediently.

"If I complain to Maxine, she's, one, got to be home for more than a couple of hours so I can complain. Two, she's going to assume this is all hormones brought on by the baby and not give me proper consideration. And three, every damn werewolf in that whole damn place will have heard me, know we're having marital problems, and jump all over that. Because they already think I'm not right for Maxine." She'd kept her voice very low, not wanting anyone to hear. Now, she shook her head, grimaced again, and said, "Luke, I don't exactly want to leave, but something has to change. And despite what Michaela thinks, it's not all my fault. Yeah, I'm on edge when there are a lot of them in one place, especially when they're all doing the same movements like a trained robot army of the damned, but…"

She sighed and rubbed at her eyes again.

Luke, God bless him, didn't immediately start giving suggestions. That was one of the things she loved about him, and why she'd chosen to wait until Mark was gone before allowing herself to burst. Instead, he took her in his arms, his rounded belly preventing them from truly embracing. He kissed her cheek and whispered, "It sounds like it absolutely sucks."

Sonya knew she was crying again. She didn't bother to stop it. She simply nodded against Luke's shoulder.

When she felt a little calmer, she stepped back and met his dark blue gaze. "What can I do? She won't listen to me."

"First, you have to decide what the most important problem is."

That wasn't what she'd expected. "Huh?"

He nodded. "I know, that's like trying to decide what's more dangerous, a rabid dog or a zombie."

She smirked, amused in spite of herself. "Okay. What will that do?"

"It will help you figure out what Maxine needs to hear first. Because if she's really there as seldom as you say, communicating is at a premium."

Sonya said, "But her not being there is the problem. The worst one." She stopped. Considered those words. "Okay, so I need to talk to her about her being gone so much. And what do I say if she tells me it's her duty to take care of the pack and our love has to be second to that? I mean, I understand it's her responsibility to care for the pack, and I'm not jealous or anything, but I did not sign on for being married to the werewolf equivalent of a long-distance truck driver who's never home."

"Then," he said slowly, "you need to decide."

"On?"

"What's more important to you. Being mated to her or having the potential for a lover you can truly rely on." He squeezed her hand. "Can you stand a story as an example?"

She nodded. If she had something to think about besides her own misery, she might be able to hold it together. Again: damn fucking hormones.

"Until I figured out the ending of this story, that Mark only works excessive hours when he's under strain, I was pulling my hair out. You see, there have been three times he's worked too damn hard. Number one was when he still hadn't managed to shed for the first time. The second was after Reese... Well, you know. And the third was just this past winter, when he was grieving over the idea that he'd never have children of his own. Once I realized what caused him to be away from home, I was able to solve it. But until then? I thought he didn't love me anymore. That's a terribly vulnerable position to be in. It can make people angry. Scared. Bitter."

"You really think Maxine has some kind of reason, beyond taking care of the pack, for spending so much time away from home?"

"I don't know her well. But if there's still the caring person you fell in love with somewhere in there, she'll probably have a deeper reason."

Sonya hugged him again. "I love you, Luke."

He laughed and she caught a slight throat clearing behind her.

Without turning, she said, "If you didn't have Mark, do you think I could have you?" Then she laughed outright as Mark wrapped a protective arm around Luke's waist.

"Mine," the dragon said. And even though he was smiling, she knew he meant it. It was, she realized, how she still felt about Maxine. In spite of everything. And it made her feel good to know that was the truth.

* * *

Maxine was prepared to be annoyed at Sonya. She'd skipped pack potluck. Again. To go shopping with Mark and Luke Tavery.

And why hadn't Maxine talked to her before this? She'd tried, but two things had happened. First, Sonya had tearfully apologized for hurting Heidi's feelings and had baked the werewolf a batch of three dozen chocolate chip cookies because she found out they were Heidi's favorite. Maxine had supervised their visit at Michaela's urging, and Heidi and Sonya were becoming friends.

Second, Sonya had prepared not one, but three

meat-heavy stews for the first potluck of November. She'd said she didn't feel well, though, and stayed in the kitchen. Again the truth of her words had been in her mind, although now Maxine wondered if it was "not feeling well" in terms of physically or emotionally. Maxine wondered how the smell of food could possibly be less in there and why, exactly, Sonya was feeling queasy in the evenings.

So, she was ready to be furious at her lover and never mind that she should be calling Sonya her mate. But when she opened the door, beneath the sound of soft rock playing, she could hear Sonya throwing up.

Maxine dropped both her bag, stuffed with different things for the pack, and her frustration. Then she rushed into the bathroom.

Sonya had her shirt off; it lay against one wall, looking strangely forlorn. She knelt before the toilet and heaved.

Maxine found a washcloth, soaked it in cold water, and wrung it out, then squatted beside Sonya. She put the cool cloth against Sonya's forehead and cheeks, trying to help the only way she knew how.

Sonya took the cloth after a particularly violent episode. She flushed the toilet and wiped her sweaty face. "If this is what awaits me each time I'm pregnant, this will be the last time."

Then she glanced at Maxine and a repentant look flitted over her features. "I didn't mean that. I love carrying our pup. This is just exasperating."

"Is something wrong with our pup?" Maxine asked. "Have you seen a doctor about these…" She gestured vaguely at the toilet.

"It's just morning sickness. Evening sickness. Whatever."

"Is it? I thought morning sickness happened,

well, in the morning."

"It can also occur in the evening. It depends, I guess, on a number of factors. In any case, I went to see my doctor today and she said it was completely normal."

"A doctor who only specializes in humans?" Maxine asked, unable to keep the worry from her voice.

"And I talked to Fehrna Susan. She said everything seems fine."

That eased Maxine's mind. She made a move to help Sonya to her feet but Sonya held up a hand.

Then she was puking again.

Maxine felt helpless as she watched and listened to her lover. "Is there anything I can do?"

"Stay home more?" Sonya smiled, maybe trying to turn it into a joke.

"I'm home as much as I can be," Maxine told her seriously. "The duty of a beta…"

"What about your duty to your mate?" Sonya ejected again, groaning and holding her stomach.

Maxine's own stomach knotted. She'd had similar discussions with Carrie once upon a sadder time. Except Carrie's comments hadn't been so direct, but had been shrouded in passive-aggressive bullshit. Maxine preferred Sonya's way of doing things. At least she came right out and said what was bothering her. "I was thinking about that. Maybe if you had more friends in the pack, my absence wouldn't bother you as much."

With Carrie, it hadn't been a case of more friends being needed. Carrie had simply thought herself above the rest of the pack. Sonya wasn't like that. She was loving and appreciative of others' strengths. "Michaela pointed out that I haven't taken the time to introduce you to anyone so they're all strangers to you, which may be leading you to be nervous around them."

"It would help to have friends," Sonya said quietly.

She wasn't looking directly at Maxine. But that was all right, Maxine told herself. "I'm sorry it took me so long to figure out that was why you were having issues with the pack. Michaela called me a dunce and I guess I am. But I just... It's been really busy around here." She laughed a little. "I swear, I haven't been so overworked since I was trying to get through the academy." That made her think of Sonya's work with SearchLight's doctorate program. "How's your dissertation going?"

"Better." Sonya sighed and got to her feet. "I really don't want to clean that right now, but I guess I'd better."

"No, what you're going to do is sit down and relax. I'll clean up."

"Do you have time?"

"I do. The one good thing about potlucks is everyone's too stuffed with food to get up to much." She considered saying something about Sonya missing the dinner to go hang out with friends outside the pack. Then she decided not to. Mark and Luke Tavery were basically Sonya's only social life beyond the pack. Maxine decided she could accept two people who weren't part of the pack. Especially if they made Sonya feel better. She helped Sonya into the living room and settled her on the couch. "How was your day?"

Sonya smiled, and it was an uncomplicated expression. "Mark's a mother hen and Luke's handling his overbearing tendencies with good grace. He's due in February or thereabouts, by the way. Maybe as late as April, but probably sooner. They just don't know how long a dragon-human hybrid carrying a mostly dragon baby will react to pregnancy."

So much happiness was bubbling out of her that Maxine felt a brief stab of jealousy. Then she repressed it when she realized Sonya was probably actually thinking about their baby. "You're really happy you're pregnant, aren't you?" She sat on the couch, deciding the bathroom could wait a while.

Sonya nodded. Then she bit her lip and looked down at her hands. "Does that bother you?"

"Why would it?"

"Because you're so worried about our pup living. And here I am, planning what color to paint the nursery and what to name our little blessing."

Maxine smiled. "There are human children named 'Blessing.' I'll be here as much as I can. It's just been hard because while the whole pack usually needs me, they don't all need me at the same time. If I didn't know better, I'd think they were planning when to ask for my help."

She stopped, realizing this was the first time she'd thought of her responsibilities in a negative light. She didn't like that.

Sonya was looking at her with an unreadable expression on her face.

Maxine said, "I'll make sure you make friends." She realized she couldn't make such a promise without sounding overbearing and amended it. "I think you'll settle in here. Given time. I want you to be part of us in every way." This, she discovered, she still meant despite the unexpected burden it placed on her shoulders. She'd assumed Sonya, who studied werewolves, as a sideline to her reptilian emphasis, would know most of the ins and outs of pack life. *I still love her. No matter my frustration. Thank the moon goddess.* She leaned forward and kissed Sonya.

Or tried to.

Sonya pulled away. "My breath," she said. "Let me go clean up the bathroom and my mouth, and then maybe…" The hunger in her eyes was undeniable.

Maxine's groin tightened. "I'll clean the bathroom. Then you brush your teeth and get into something more comfortable."

Sonya grinned at her. "Sounds like a plan."

When Maxine came into the bedroom twenty minutes later, she found Sonya reclining, naked, on their bed and playing with herself. The air was already aromatic with the promise of sex.

Her breasts were fuller and there might have been the slightest increase in the swell of her belly. Maxine stripped as fast as she could.

Her cell phone began to ring.

Sonya cursed and rolled off the bed. She glared at the phone and then at Maxine. "Well? Aren't you going to answer it?"

Maxine snapped, "That's unfair. What if something's really wrong?"

Sonya looked away and there was no way to read the emotion in her voice when she said, "You're right. Go ahead. It's your duty." She began dressing again, slipping into a nightgown.

It wasn't one of her revealing ones and Maxine hesitated, not wanting to answer the phone.

It had stopped ringing, but it started up again at once.

Maybe, if she could take care of this quickly… She answered her cell.

Chapter Seven

Sonya knew she was sick with loneliness. She hadn't seen Maxine *at all* since last Sunday when Maxine had made introductions around the pack. Now it was the Thursday of the following week. Thanksgiving, according to the human calendar.

She couldn't shake the feeling that newlyweds weren't supposed to be separated as much as she and Maxine were. *But... how am I supposed to know? Maybe this is normal. Maybe, especially maybe, for werewolves with high ranks.* Were Michaela and Fehrna Susan apart this much? Sonya knew Michaela didn't work, but that the alpha was a doctor.

Almost like Sonya.

But I'm not the one who isn't making time. I mean, soon I'll be busy, yeah, but I've managed to be here, waiting for her. Was that unfair? She was juggling a dissertation and a full work schedule, but the dissertation part was done mostly at home. Maxine couldn't exactly solve everyone's problems from the comfort of the couch.

Tears pushed at Sonya's eyes and she let a couple fall. Then a few more. Because, she realized, it didn't matter if she was being fair or not. The truth was that she was surrounded by virtual strangers and she was facing the prospect of being tied to someone she never saw. Of raising a baby in that environment.

Anger broke through her loneliness and pain and she whispered, "Fuck it. I will *not* allow any child of mine to be raised where they're not wanted. Or at least where their mother isn't appreciated and cherished. They'd grow up with my bitterness to teach them. That's not going to happen."

But, a part of her mind argued, *Maxine loves you. She's just busy.*

"Fuck her busy. This is not some depressing lesbian novel where the heroine pines away for lack of love." Her mind made up, she rose and started for the bedroom, meaning to start packing at once.

But then she froze. This wasn't a case of separation and divorce. From what she knew, werewolves did not let their mates go. Ever.

Sonya felt cold. She hugged herself around the middle, recognized it as a protective gesture, and knew she needed help.

Mark and Luke couldn't help. Mark would simply storm in here, pack up her stuff for her, and keep her sequestered at his and Luke's condo. That wouldn't do, both because they didn't have the room right now and because Maxine would bring down the whole weight of the werewolf community on their heads. That would be a lovely way to start the negotiations between dragons, werewolves, and basilisks.

Likewise, she couldn't appeal to SearchLight. As powerful as the organization was, they tended to stay out of most magical disputes unless they involved innocent and sheltered humans. Sonya would be seen as having walked right into this. She was part of the Fehrna pack now.

Could she go to Fehrna Susan? No. From what she'd seen so far, pack rules seemed rigid and in favor of the higher ranking person. She had, it appeared, fewer rights than Maxine because she was lower in rank.

Sonya scowled. "All right," she muttered. *So, my alpha can't, or won't, help me. SearchLight absolutely can't. And I won't let Mark and Luke get into that position. Who's left to help me figure out the tangles of marriage to a werewolf?*

She'd been marching around the apartment in her socks. Now, she stopped in front of the fridge and scanned the emergency numbers Maxine had posted there the night after they'd first made love. Because, the werewolf had said, there were just some times she wasn't going to be right there to help.

"Isn't that the fucking truth?" Sonya scanned the list, her gaze flicking past Fehrna Susan's cell number, Michaela's, and the number for the head of the local Werewolf Watch office, Agent Wellington. Down at the bottom of the list another number. "Tilthos Charles, only to be called when all else fails," and an upstate New York phone number.

Sonya hesitated, but only for a moment. She was furious. She wanted to kill someone. And surely that state of mind wasn't good for the baby. She strode into the living room, grabbed her cell off the desk, turned on the stereo nice and loud, and went back into the kitchen.

I won't get him. He'll be busy.

And she was right. The person who answered the phone had a slight Spanish accent and introduced himself as Luis.

"I need Tilthos Charles," she said before she could lose her nerve. "I'm one of his wolves." She swallowed. "Okay, so I'm a human but I'm mated to one of his wolves."

"You're pack," Luis said. "Give me just a minute."

What am I doing? If he can help, it will mean the end of Maxine and me. Do I really want to take that step? She almost pushed the little red icon to disconnect the call.

Our baby will grow up in a miserable household. That is not acceptable.

"Hello? This is Tilthos Charles. To whom am I

speaking?"

"S-Sonya Johnson." She swallowed again, but this time it hurt. "I'm mated to Maxine Brown, beta of the Fehrna pack in Tampa, Florida."

She could all but hear a gentle smile in his voice. "We're lucky to have you, Sonya. How may I help you?"

Tears threatened and she forced them back. Except this made her voice rough. She coughed and a few teardrops trickled down her cheeks. "Oh God, Tilthos Charles, I hope you can."

He asked, "Are you safe?"

That startled her. "Yes?"

"You sound unsure. Let me put it another way. Are you in physical danger?"

"No."

"All right. That's good. Are you where others can hear you?"

"I have the music up pretty loud."

"You should be okay, then. As long as you keep your voice low. Are you sitting down?"

"No. Pacing helps me think."

"I understand. Please, Sonya, tell me what's going on."

"The pack hates me," Sonya burst out. "They're calling me an outsider. And saying my baby won't be full werewolf. That'll give them a reason to hate the baby too. But that's not the worst. Maxine is avoiding me. She hates me." She heard how that sounded and retracted it. "I mean, probably she doesn't hate me but she's always gone. I'm always alone." That wasn't true either. "All right, so Michaela, the alpha's mate, and Heidi, the electrician, talk to me now. But the rest? They hate my guts."

She took a deep breath. "I refuse to raise our

baby in the midst of this hostility. And if I have to raise her alone, I'd rather be alone all the time. Not trapped in a loveless marriage. But I know werewolves don't get divorced. What can I do, Tilthos Charles?" She sobbed. "What can I do?"

He spoke without pity but with fierce rage that seemed to be barely in check. "What are Maxine's reasons for leaving you alone so often?"

"Duty to the pack."

"Idiot wolf," Tilthos Charles muttered. "*You* are pack."

Sonya felt a flash of protectiveness. "She's trying to do the job of two. Because I won't help."

"Won't? Or haven't been allowed to help?"

Sonya hesitated. "I'm not going to the potluck dinners."

"Why?"

"Because," she said softly, feeling small and lost, "they're like a cult, doing everything together and not letting me breathe." That sounded as though she was judging the wolves. She winced but didn't know how to gentle it.

"Werewolves operate best as a pack," Tilthos Charles said quietly. "Did you grow up mostly alone?"

"Except for my father." He hadn't really been her dad, but he'd been there for her. Until he died when she was just a kid. "Yeah, I guess I did."

"Then learning to lean on others for strength is a foreign concept to you."

She blinked, startled. He understood.

"Please, tell me what else is bothering you. We'll come back to the pack's synchronized swimmer routine in a minute."

That made her smile briefly.

"She's blinded by her duty and by the fact that

she's been with these wolves for decades," Tilthos Charles said. "She's relied on them through many struggles and has trouble seeing them as flawed. Or at least that's what it sounds like."

Sonya realized she was nodding and said, "Maybe."

"Probably. I assume you've tried talking to her."

"Yes, sir."

"If I stepped in, it most likely wouldn't solve anything. Maxine needs to realize what she's doing wrong on her own."

"What is she doing wrong? She's beta. She needs to take care of the pack."

"As I said, you're pack too. And every person has to find a balance between working life and home life. It can be done."

Sonya sank down into a crouch against the breakfast bar. "What can I do? Divorce isn't possible."

"Severing a mating bond is completely possible. But counseling is recommended first. Because once you're separated, there's no going back. Some humans get remarried after a divorce. That is not our way. Once the relationship is sundered, it cannot be reformed." He paused, and when he spoke again, it was very gently. "As for the rest of the pack, they're not truly your concern. No one can have universal approval. But you may have friends in the making."

She decided to bring up the "prey" comment. After she'd explained it, the alpha above all alphas murmured, "I know about your case. You were mauled when you were twelve."

She shivered. "Yes, sir."

"You're brave, falling in love with a wolf. But bravery doesn't mean you'll be over all your fears at once. The pack functions best when it's working as one, but each member has a solo part to play as well. If you can find a way to fit yourself into that, and Maxine should be there to help you, then you'll see their synchronized swimmer routine as less of a threat."

He paused and then asked, "Do you have a support network outside the pack?"

"Yes, but I will not involve them in this." She realized how angry and defensive she sounded and explained, "Mark is a dragon. He's... protective. He would make matters worse."

To her surprise, Tilthos Charles chuckled. "I know Mark Tavery very well. He certainly wouldn't stand for you being neglected."

She tried to be amazed by the idea that Tilthos Charles knew a dragon from Florida. Then she reminded herself that he had, not so long ago, been a professor at SearchLight Academy and had probably taught Mark. Just as he'd taught her during her first year.

"Do you want me to talk to Fehrna Susan?" he asked.

Sonya said quietly, "No. I think she'd come down on Maxine's side."

"You're seeing this as taking sides? Forgive me, but I think that's a little skewed."

He said it gently, but she was furious instantly. "How should I take it? She's against me."

"Fehrna Susan or Maxine?"

"Maxine."

"I doubt that, but I've been wrong before. What it sounds like is that she's *for* the pack and she doesn't realize how she's hurt you. Can you stand a little advice?"

"That's why I called," she answered, feeling abruptly exhausted.

"Do something that will get her attention. I don't know where your strengths lie, and you know her better than I do. Don't issue ultimatums."

Sonya sighed. "I don't know what else to try."

"In that case, take yourself out of the situation for twenty-four hours. Gain a different point of view. Then come back. See what has changed." He paused. "Do not leave without giving your mate a heads-up as to where you're going."

Sonya said, "Mark and Luke are having their baby shower. I'm due there in an hour. But I can't ask to stay the night."

"Why not?"

She didn't have any answer for that.

Tilthos Charles said, "I'm sure they wouldn't mind. And feel free to keep your reasons to yourself if you're worried about... involvement." He sounded mildly amused.

"Okay," she murmured. Then: "Okay," more firmly, as she made up her mind. "They'll definitely let me stay for a single night. Thank you, Tilthos Charles."

"I will be calling you soon to see how things are going. If you're ever in a position where you can't talk, just say so."

"How do you have time to tend to a single wolf?"

"Usually, my mate handles some of these calls, or my beta's mate, but... well, let's just say my beta's mate had a feeling about this call. I've actually been waiting to hear from, and I quote, 'someone from Tampa, a pack member who isn't a wolf' for some days."

She marveled. "Is that supposed to be my role? Informing my mate or my alpha about --"

"No," he said at once. "Ethan is a precognitive.

His talents are unique to him. Your job is to figure out what your talents are and use them to the best of your ability for your own betterment and the betterment of the pack."

I feel less alone now. This realization made her smile. "Thank you, Tilthos Charles. I'll call you when this is resolved."

"I'll give you three days. That's more than enough time to continue living in a version of hell."

She opened her mouth to say living with Maxine wasn't hell, but she thought of the baby, of their welfare, and said instead, "Thank you."

* * *

Maxine stood out in the hall, listening to the loud rock music thrumming through the door. This almost surely meant Sonya didn't want to be disturbed.

That doesn't apply to me, does it?

She reached out mentally, seeking her lover's emotions.

The first wave that hit her was so strong she staggered a step. Sonya's shields were all the way down. Any moderately strong empath or telepath would be able to feel what she felt.

Paradoxically, the wave was indefinable. Sonya felt something very strongly but figuring out what was like trying to determine the predominant color in a kaleidoscope. Slowly, her emotions settled into two distinct feelings: anxiety and anger.

Maxine laid her hand on the door as a way to ground herself in reality. Then she reached out for any thoughts that might accompany the intense, but wordless, sendings.

"What can I do? Divorce isn't an option."

Maxine yanked her telepathy back into her own head. Divorce? *Divorce?* Yes, it was possible, although rare. Was that what Sonya really wanted?

She couldn't stand it. She had to talk to her lover. *My mate, damn it. My mate, no matter how upset I am and no matter how we're drifting apart. She's still my mate. I still love her.* She moved to unlock the door.

And another burst of emotion flooded her mind: panic.

Not from Sonya, she realized only an instant later, but from below her, maybe on the first floor or even in the basement.

Cursing, Maxine left the door. She *would* talk to Sonya when she was done with the current crisis. And then she was going to ask Michaela if there was any way, under the reign of the moon goddess, that she could have a little time with her beloved.

* * *

The microfiber couch was covered by a quilt. Sonya snuggled her face against the soft arm and tried to stifle her sobs.

She'd spent the last three hours trying to sleep. The condo had gone silent around her as Mark and Luke took themselves off to bed and Mark's huge family had left for their hotel. She did not want to wake either half of the exhausted couple who'd just hosted a baby shower for their coming bundle of joy.

Will there be anyone around to help me celebrate my baby? Sure, on a practical level she knew she had Mark and Luke, and that they would do their best for her. But they'd have a daughter of their own soon. Sonya had no family that cared about her, especially since she'd joined SearchLight. She had work friends, but with the possible exception of Jenny, a fellow medtech, and Jenny's wife, there wasn't anyone else.

I wonder if one of the reasons I fell in love with Maxine was because I was hoping for a community, a built-

in family with her pack. Of course, she had been fearful of the wolves when first she joined them, but until it had been pointed out to her, she'd thought that anxiety was dead and buried. Thinking back on everything that had happened, she realized she'd been viewing Michaela as an older sister and hoping for others of the pack to fill family-like roles. She hadn't thought she was that desperate for friends, but looking back on the past three months or so, it was terribly easy to see her loneliness as a factor.

It's almost funny. I never knew I was lonely until I fell in love with Maxine. She gave me a sense of home, a feeling of belonging I hadn't realized I was missing. Could it be all these issues I'm having with the pack are because I'm seeking more than my due? Maybe I'm meant to be a loner among them with only Maxine as a touchstone. Maybe I've just been greedy, wanting more.

But that didn't make sense. Packs were all about togetherness. That was what both infuriated her and was the thing she'd longed for. Although not to the extent she'd encountered it. She'd been seeking a group of people that came together occasionally and did things as a family. The wolves were just... too dependent on each other.

Which was, she saw now, judgmental. So if she was being excluded, it was intentional.

Even if Maxine, somehow, came to her senses, could Sonya be happy in an environment where she'd always be treated as an outsider?

Maybe that's not the question. Maybe the real thing I should be asking is, do I want to be an outsider in the pack or an outsider in the wider world? Because I'll most likely be excluded either way. I can't exactly have human friends who don't know anything about magical creatures. Even if my pup doesn't change with the moon, what if they demonstrate other wolf-like qualities? Like a longing to hunt, or desiring, above all else, to be with their pack?

She'd never understood mothers who would deprive themselves of freedom without having someone to share the load. Now she knew that some of them had been promised help before having it taken away.

"Sonya?"

She sat up quickly, briefly dizzy with the hasty movement. "Mark? Did I wake you?"

He sat beside her and pulled her into a hug without saying anything.

She stiffened, but not because she didn't appreciate his empathy. She just wasn't used to him touching her so intimately. He was demonstrative with only one person: Luke.

He started to let go, but she buried her nose against his collarbone.

His arms were tight around her back again and she relaxed.

When her tears had come and gone, she asked quietly, "When did you learn to just stay silent and wait for the other person to talk?"

"Luke's rubbing off on me." He chuckled; it vibrated in his chest under her ear. "I'm not half as good as he is, but he's asleep and I want him to stay that way for a bit. Trust me; if I discover I'm upsetting you rather than giving comfort, I'll ask him to join us and fix my fuckups."

Sonya smirked. But it trembled on her lips and fell away. "What woke you?"

"Your thoughts," he admitted.

She winced. "I thought I was keeping them to myself."

He sounded embarrassed when he said, "I guess

I have something in common with Tilthos Charles. I can sometimes read thoughts even through shields."

Strange that he should bring up the alpha above all alphas… "I talked to Tilthos Charles today. He said you'd help me if you could, and if I let you." That hadn't been exactly what the alpha wolf had said, of course, but the general feeling was the same.

"I knew Tilthos Charles when he was Charlie to me." Mark snorted. "Back when he should have been Professor McLaughlin but I was so lost and so in need of a friend that he stepped in to help with some of my bigger problems. I didn't know him well enough for the friendship to go both ways at the time." He sighed. "But here I am, talking about me and not listening to you."

"I like hearing about you too. It helps me forget my troubles for a while."

They were silent together for a bit, and Sonya gradually became aware that Mark was shirtless. She blushed and sat up fully. She peeked to make sure he was wearing something, anything, and saw he was in sweatpants. She relaxed.

"Do you want to talk about it?"

"What thoughts did you pick up?"

"Mostly emotions, probably because your thoughts were racing and barely touched your conscious mind. You're furious and also heartsore."

She nodded. "Yeah, that's true."

"Tell me about it?" he invited.

So, she rehashed everything she'd told Tilthos Charles. When she was done, she saw not sympathy in his eyes but rage.

He blinked and it was gone, but it had absolutely been there.

"Don't do anything rash," she said. "I'm a big

girl. I can take care of myself."

"All right, I'll keep my dragon in check. I just want to say one thing: I've never seen you happier than you were with Maxine in the beginning of your relationship, but if that was only the honeymoon period, you can get out of it."

Sonya's chest tightened and she said, "I don't want to leave her." There it was, out and bald. Hearing herself say it aloud gave her strength and she went on. "I'm going to try one more time before I give up. I'm going to ask Michaela to keep the rest of the pack away and I'm going to lay it all out for her. Tilthos Charles said to do something that will get her attention. I think I'm going to show her what I want the nursery to look like and make her a meal she won't forget. Show her how much I love her, and hopefully she'll show me the same."

Sonya got to her feet. Then she glanced at her watch and laughed. "But not at one o'clock in the morning." She sat back down and yawned. Now that her mind was made up, all the stress she'd been under was catching up with her.

Mark rose, squeezed her hand lightly, and said, "Get some sleep. You're welcome here as long as you want to stay." He hesitated and she saw that he wanted to say something.

"Go ahead."

He smiled a little. "If it's true love, she'll do for you what Luke did for me: bring out the best parts of your nature and celebrate them. But that doesn't mean it will be easy. Like the song says, love is not a victory march."

After he'd returned to his room, Sonya settled her head on the couch and tucked her legs up so she was in a half fetal position, the way she slept best.

Visions of the future nursery filled her head. She marveled that she'd been repressing these ideas for so many weeks and also that it hadn't occurred to her to get Michaela involved in keeping the pack at bay and give Maxine a break. If she *was* a member of the Fehrna pack, she deserved the perks that went along with that truth.

Chapter Eight

Sonya didn't sleep much past seven. She was tired still, but her heart wouldn't be quiet. She rushed through breakfast with Mark and Luke. She wouldn't have even stayed for that, but Luke insisted, and he was the most marvelous cook.

The dragon and genie lived on the outskirts of Tampa. Sonya headed into the center of town, grateful that she'd taken today off of work. Mostly she'd done it because she'd been planning to spend a few hours helping Luke choose toys for the baby dragon. Now she had the time to woo Maxine properly. Her mate wouldn't leave for work until eight forty-five since the apartment building was close to SearchLight's Tampa campus. That wasn't enough time to set everything in motion, but definitely enough to at least convince Maxine they had to talk.

Maybe even enough time to seduce her.

She pulled into the parking garage and saw a moving van of the type people drove themselves. She smirked briefly, thinking of jokes about U-Haul lesbians and wondered if another new person was moving into the pack.

After parking, she headed for the outside door that led into the stairwell. But then she saw her desk, *her desk*, waiting by the van.

Her knees turned to water and she staggered, catching herself with a hand on the wall.

What was her desk doing out here?

"*It's for you*," she remembered Maxine saying when the beautiful work of wood and wicker was delivered. "*You need a safe place to work where I won't accidentally put something down on your papers.*"

"*It's amazing*," Sonya had breathed, feeling weak

with awe at the glorious nature of the gesture and the furniture.

"*So are you.*"

Sonya spotted two wolves working around the van. One was inside, probably shifting things, and the other was examining the desk.

There was no sign of Maxine.

So. This is the way she tells me I'm not wanted, is it? This is the way I find out that the pack is more important to her than I am?

She marched over to the two wolves, recognizing them as John and Tessa, the two who had talked about her behind her back just loudly enough that she heard them. *All right. So. This is how Maxine stabs me in the back.*

She felt a moment of indecision. What if Tessa and John were acting of their own volition? It was certainly possible, wasn't it?

No. Pack hierarchy would prevent them from doing this. Besides, they don't have a key to our apartment. She paused. Amended that. *Maxine's apartment.*

"Where's Maxine?" She demanded.

The two wolves looked at each other and then back at her.

"I don't know," Tessa said.

Her eyes didn't shift away from Sonya's face and she didn't even hesitate.

That meant what she was saying was most likely a lie. People who thought about their answers usually flicked their eyes right or left. That was something Sonya had learned at SearchLight Academy. *Humans can't tell instinctively when someone lies*, she remembered a professor saying. *You have to use your senses.*

"Tell me the truth," she demanded, standing straighter and glaring directly into Tessa's eyes.

The wolf looked uncomfortable for a moment. "She's helping someone."

"Where is she?"

"Maybe talking with Michaela and Fehrna Susan."

Which meant she wouldn't want to be disturbed. Well, fuck that. Sonya turned on her heel and dug her cell phone out of her purse as she headed for the building again.

"Please," John called. "Don't make this harder on Maxine."

That froze Sonya's feet and her blood. She stood, irresolute, and then decided she didn't exactly want to confront Maxine face-to-face when she might deck the wolf. She went to her car, got in, and locked the doors behind her. She dialed Maxine's cell phone.

"This is Maxine. Leave a message."

"You fucking coward," Sonya snarled. "Packing up my stuff and then not even deigning to answer your fucking phone?"

Her guts twisted and she clamped her mouth shut for a moment. She would not be sick right now. She would not.

Her stomach settled after a moment and she continued in a different vein. "I love you, but if you can't see that or you won't see it, if the pack is more important than I am, I know where I stand. You're not going to be a part of our child's life, though. I won't have them confused about how relationships work. They will learn positive things about partners." She ended the call.

Then, burying her head in her arms and leaning on the steering wheel, she burst into tears.

* * *

Maxine emerged from the basement. The

moment the door to the rest of the building opened, her cell phone chimed. She looked down and saw she'd missed a call from Sonya. She also saw, by the light flooding in through a window, that it was morning.

Moon goddess, but she was tired. She would have almost thought Christopher wanted her to be exhausted and away from Sonya if his distress hadn't been so genuine. He'd been upset, although he couldn't put it into words, and she'd spent a fruitless night trying to figure out why he was so distressed.

The only reason she was leaving now was because he'd shifted to his wolf form and refused to talk to her anymore.

She'd have to bring up his anxiety and obvious pain with Fehrna Susan. Her alpha would be able to ferret it out. So thinking, Maxine pressed the little phone icon and accessed her voicemail.

Sonya's rage poured through her, through her ears and into her heart.

Then there was a pause before Maxine heard her say, "I love you, but if you can't see that or you won't see it, if the pack is more important than I am, I know where I stand. You're not going to be a part of our child's life though. I won't have them confused about how relationships work. They will learn positive things about partners."

Maxine stared at her phone for several moments while her brain fought to understand what had happened.

Finally, her heart cried, *She's leaving. You've driven her away.*

Unable to move for a few more moments, Maxine tried to deny this voice. *No. She's doing exactly what Carrie did. Demanding a 'me or nothing' way of life that excludes the pack. I can't give up on the pack.*

To which the other voice replied, *Is she? It seems to me that all she did was accuse you of packing up her stuff.*

Which made no sense.

"I need answers," Maxine whispered. And she would be damned if she was going to seek them over the phone when the technology wouldn't give her any of Sonya's emotions.

She took the steps up to the third floor two at a time. But the apartment they shared was empty. And devoid of all of Sonya's things.

She packed up? But then why would she accuse me of doing it?

She thundered down the steps and out into the garage, meaning to stop any moving van, assuming there was one. Because there had to be, didn't there? Sonya couldn't fit that huge desk in her car.

She spotted the van at once. It was deserted, all the doors locked.

Sonya wasn't there.

Maxine pulled out her phone, meaning to call Sonya after all because they *needed* to talk. And that was when she spotted Sonya's car.

She ran to it, looked inside, and saw Sonya asleep with her head on the steering wheel. Her eyes were red and swollen, probably from crying.

Maxine tried to open the door. It was locked.

She cursed, considered ripping the thing off its hinges, and controlled herself enough to knock on the window instead.

Sonya rubbed her face and blinked. Then she saw Maxine and before rage filled her face, Maxine saw relief.

She opened the door and got out. "What?" she demanded. "Come to make sure I get out before --"

Maxine took her hands. "Why did you pack your things?"

Sonya gaped at her. "You packed them. Well, had Tessa and John do it anyway. I guess the pack even takes precedence over kicking me out of our home personally."

Fire bloomed in Maxine's belly. But then she saw the tears standing in her mate's eyes. "I didn't pack everything up."

Sonya stared and the tears spilled over, running down her cheeks. "I didn't either. But the van's packed."

"Who…"

"Tessa and John, like I said. But they weren't acting on your orders?"

Maxine saw the hope in her mate's gaze. "No. They weren't. I'd never kick you out of your home."

Sonya began to cry in earnest and when Maxine hugged her this time, she didn't pull away.

They stood that way for several moments while Maxine's thoughts raced and sweat broke out on her forehead. "I… I don't understand. How could they… Why would they?"

"They hate me." Sonya hiccupped. "The whole pack hates me."

A sliver of hot rage stabbed Maxine's heart and she snapped, "Don't blame everything on them."

Sonya laughed without any humor. "But if you didn't pack up the van and I didn't, who else is to blame? I see, Maxine, you'll defend them until your dying day no matter what evidence is brought against them."

Maxine opened her mouth to argue the point. Then understanding flared in her mind like a lighted candle. "No matter who did it, you're not trying to leave me. That's what matters."

"I will leave," Sonya said, although her face was still against Maxine's shoulder. "I will, if you don't make room for me. I can't let our pup be raised with someone who's never around."

"If you left," Maxine said logically, "our pup wouldn't have me anyway."

"Fine," Sonya muttered. "But I'd be in agony, watching you ignore me every day and the baby would grow up learning *that*."

"Learning what?" She felt Sonya tense in her arms and said as gently as she could, "I just want to get all our cards on the table. What's wrong with our little one learning the value of hard work?"

"Nothing, but you're working hard at the expense of our family." Sonya drew back. "Unless Michaela and every other mated wolf ignores their mate in this way…" She didn't finish. "Mark and Luke find time to see each other."

"They don't have a pack." But, for the first time, these words sounded hollow and Maxine admitted, "Michaela and Fehrna Susan find time to see each other. But I don't know how they manage it."

"Probably by having you do everything else." She hugged Maxine hard. "Don't misunderstand me. I'm not blaming them. It's probably as unconscious as you being a workaholic. But it can't last. Not if you want to keep me."

"I do." Maxine kissed Sonya's cheek. "Desperately. But I don't know where to go from here."

"Then let's talk to the alpha. That's what she's there for." She paused and then added, "I already talked to Tilthos Charles."

Maxine felt her stomach drop and her balls draw

up unpleasantly. "What did he say?"

"To do something you'd notice. I was planning to make you a huge and fancy meal and then talk about my ideas for the nursery. It's about damn time I really showed you how important this pup is to me."

Maxine relaxed, but only a little. "We need to talk to Fehrna Susan." She pushed Sonya back just a little, keeping her arms around her mate. "Please look at me."

Sonya did. Her honey brown eyes were full of hope and anxiety.

"I love you. I know you can't feel that like I feel your love for me, but please believe me. I love you. I just... I guess I don't know how to do it right. Can you give me time to figure it out?"

She didn't answer directly. "Tilthos Charles suggested we go to counseling."

Maxine felt the pressure of taking on yet another commitment. Then she thought, *But if I don't, I'll lose her.*

The very idea made her feel like crying. "I'll probably suck at that too, but I'll go. And I'll learn. I promise I will."

Sonya kissed her and as her tongue nudged Maxine's lips apart, the simple fact that they hadn't kissed in over a week hit Maxine.

She closed her eyes and drank her mate in.

* * *

An hour later, Maxine sat near the head of the tables that had been organized into one long line. Pack order was clearly delineated. Fehrna Susan was at the top of the rectangle, Michaela to her left, Maxine to Michaela's left, and so on. Sonya sat with her hand firmly on Maxine's knee as if to restrain her.

Or maybe she was grounding herself. Judging by

the fury in her gaze, she needed some stability.

Maxine hated it that her meager telepathy was overwhelmed by the sheer number of people in the room so that she couldn't read her mate's emotions.

"All right," Fehrna Susan said and everyone quieted, even though they hadn't been doing more than murmuring. "Who, precisely, loaded that moving van?"

Maxine watched Tessa shift uncomfortably in her seat before speaking. "It was my idea, Alpha. John helped, but it was my idea."

Sonya snapped, "Why?"

Fehrna Susan nodded. "Answer her, Tessa."

The gamma wolf hesitated but only for a moment or two. "Because you don't know anything about our ways. You're not helping the pack. You're holding Maxine back from her duties --"

Sonya actually laughed at that one. "She's been gone almost the entire time since we were mated."

Tessa grimaced. "All right, fine, I'll give you that."

"How was Christopher involved?" Fehrna Susan asked.

Tessa gaped. "How did you know…" She pulled herself together. "He agreed, after losing to John, that he'd help us. He didn't want to, but we pulled rank on him."

"The fight wasn't about dominance then, or at least not just about dominance." The alpha sighed. "You wanted help and John instigated the confrontation. Christopher's crisis last night was just a little too convenient. The fact that he wouldn't change back to human guise without my influence and answer questions is even more telling."

Tessa shrank in her chair. "I want her out of our

pack," she said, but she told the tabletop rather than meeting anyone's gaze.

"Is it because I'm human?" Sonya demanded.

"You're not allowing me to lead this interrogation, Sonya," Fehrna Susan said, probably more gently than she would have to one of the wolves.

Sonya looked like she was going to answer. Then she said, "I'm sorry, Alpha."

"You're learning," Fehrna Susan said. "Christopher? What do you have to say for yourself?"

"I have no defense, Alpha."

"Forgive me," Sonya said, "but I don't understand something."

Maxine squeezed her hand. "Wait until --"

"No," the alpha said. "She's trying to learn. Go ahead, beta's mate."

"Wasn't Christopher under orders? Wasn't John?"

"This isn't the military and even in the military you can always appeal up the chain of command. It was their responsibility, if they saw something wrong, to report it. Blindly following orders is not encouraged here."

Sonya bit her lip. "But..." She stopped. "I'm sorry I don't understand, but I have another question."

"Go on."

Sonya gripped Maxine's hand. "Why is my fear such a trigger?" She blushed. "I mean, I know you're werewolves, but I wasn't even conscious of how I felt until Heidi pointed it out."

"Often, our feelings have scents even when we're not aware of them," Fehrna Susan answered.

"We understand why you're scared now," Heidi put in. "Not just that you are afraid, but why we've scared you. And you've agreed to actively work on it."

She said this from her seat on Fehrna Susan's right. Then she blushed. "Sorry, Fehrna Susan. It's just…"

"You like Sonya." The alpha smiled. "I understand. Any other questions, Sonya?"

Maxine watched the woman she loved press her lips together. "Probably you'll get to all the others I have."

"I know you don't trust me yet," Fehrna Susan told her. "But give it time. Trust is earned." She turned back to Tessa. "What is the core of your problems with our beta's mate?"

"She doesn't understand anything about being part of a pack."

"No one's bothered to teach me," Sonya snapped. Then she looked down, seeming to shrink in her chair. "That was uncalled for. I'm sorry." She glanced at Maxine. "And I'm sorry I said that at all. I don't want everyone to know the difficulties we're having."

"That's part of being in a pack," Fehrna Susan said. "We all look out for each other."

Maxine lifted Sonya's hand to her lips. Her own fingers were trembling. "I'm sorry I wasn't listening."

"I don't want you to lose face in front of them," Sonya said, gesturing with her head to indicate the rest of the table. "If they don't respect you, they'll challenge you. And I don't want you to get hurt."

"You really think that's how dominance fights are begun?" Michaela asked, obviously flabbergasted. "I really haven't taught you anything about werewolves, have I?"

"It's obvious some education is in order," Fehrna Susan said. "Education for Sonya to learn how the pack works, education for Maxine to learn how to balance her duty to the pack with time for her mate. And maybe," she added, smiling sardonically, "some education for me since I missed much of this brewing." Then her expression hardened. "And definitely some education for the three wolves who decided to take it upon themselves to dissolve a mating bond."

Tessa, John, and Christopher looked supremely uncomfortable.

Tessa said, "Please, Alpha, I need to say something."

"Go on."

"I was just hoping to protect the pack."

Fehrna Susan nodded. "I understand that, but you overreached your boundaries by focusing on a pack member who's higher than you are. Yes," she added, and Maxine saw a look of frustration cross Tessa's face, "Sonya is higher than you are. It doesn't matter that she's human. She's mated to my beta."

"I don't care that she's human," Tessa said. "She doesn't know anything of our ways."

"We've already established that her ignorance wasn't willful." Fehrna Susan stood. "All right, Michaela and I will be setting up lesson schedules for the five of you. Unless anyone else has any other business, this meeting is adjourned."

The room began to clear, but Maxine only had eyes for Sonya. "Are you satisfied?"

Sonya nodded. "Our alpha obviously has everyone's best interests at heart." She put her arms around Maxine's neck and leaned into her. "You do too. That's one of the reasons I love you."

They went upstairs together, Maxine all but floating. She knew the next few days and weeks were going to be a bitch, but she'd managed, through little merit on her part, to keep her mate. And she wouldn't run the risk of losing her again.

Though there was still the fear of losing both pup and mate to death, she tried to keep that out of her face. There was nothing Sonya could do about it, and it would be best to shoulder the burden alone.

Chapter Nine

Sonya cursed as the banner fell down again.

Maxine snickered. "Are you sure you don't want me to do that?"

"And have you stop setting up the cradles? Fat chance." Cradles, she thought. Not one, but two. She *was* pregnant with twins. Now using the inclusive term "they" seemed even more appropriate.

Maxine didn't banter back, and Sonya glanced over her shoulder to see that her mate was looking miserable.

She crossed to Maxine, leaving the banner on the floor. It was Frost Thaw morning, February 13th, which meant two things. It was actually decent weather outside. And, miracle of miracles, she was done with the first trimester and her stomach had settled down.

She had noticed that look of pain on Maxine's face before, but each time her mate said it was nothing for Sonya to worry about. The touch of condescension in her voice had pushed Sonya away. But now, armed with some knowledge about Maxine's past that she'd lacked, Sonya was ready to take her on.

Let's start with the missing painting. Sonya took Maxine's hands and kissed the knuckles tenderly, lavishing attention on each one until her mate smiled a little. Then Sonya met her gaze and asked, "Did you take Carrie's painting down because it was bothering you?"

Maxine blinked, a startled expression. "I didn't think you had noticed. Not because it wasn't huge, but because you didn't comment on it."

"I like that artwork. So full of color."

"It never bothered you that I kept my dead

mate's creation?"

"The ones who die never really leave us, and I just assumed you were doing like me, keeping what best reminded you of them."

"You don't have anything from your family."

Sonya chuckled. "No? Where did that cedar box with the carvings of dolphins on it come from?"

"Who gave it to you?"

"The man who helped raise me, Papa Harvey." She kissed the back of Maxine's right hand. "Why did you take it down? And where did you store it?"

"Michaela's holding onto it for me. I didn't want to see it. It was reminding me of her death." Maxine's eyes were overly bright.

"You know, postpartum depression isn't the death sentence it probably was in the 1970s. I'm not going to say we've perfected how we deal with mental health, but we're certainly further along that path," Sonya promised, her voice soft and fervent. "I will seek you first before I seek oblivion. I will seek all my friends, both those in the pack and those outside it, and I will find a therapist if it comes to that."

Maxine nodded and her face was pinched with worry again.

Sonya hugged her close, pressing herself against the place that was usually hard nowadays whenever they were alone for more than five minutes. "Please tell me what's really scaring you."

"It's not something you should worry about."

Sonya resisted the urge to snap. Instead, she answered, "I love you. You're often my strength and my shelter. Let me be the same for you."

Maxine broke. Sonya saw it in her face before she said a word. "What if our pups die?"

Sonya shook her head, pulling Maxine against

her when her mate tried to get away. "Our pups are half werewolf. The mortality rates are much less."

"No, they've just changed. Humans carry their young for a shorter time than werewolves. That means a premature delivery. And often, at least thirty percent of the time according to the research, the pups don't survive. Because their lungs don't work. Or even worse things happen."

Sonya took Maxine out of the nursery and to their bedroom. She sat her mate down on the bed and kissed her cheek. "Listen to me. That's what NICUs are for."

"Nick-yous?"

Maxine's pronunciation made it obvious she'd never heard the word before. So, Sonya spelled it. "Intensive care for infants," she clarified. "SearchLight has them as well as humans-only hospitals."

"Our pups would stay in the NICU until they could breathe on their own?"

"And until they could do everything else independently. Poop, eat, whatever."

Maxine gaped. Then she sagged with obvious relief.

Sonya asked, "You're not worried about them not being able to change with the full moon? I thought that was central to werewolf society, the hunting as a pack."

"It is. And they'll probably grieve when they're old enough to understand. But at least they'll live to be that age." She hugged Sonya close.

Sonya melted into her mate's arms and closed her eyes. She couldn't get quite as close as she'd managed in months past, but she didn't care. Being held so possessively did wonders for her sense of wellbeing.

"So," Maxine said, "we really can start arguing about names for the baby. Right, Dr. Johnson?"

"That's something else I wanted to talk about," Sonya said. "I was thinking about changing my last name. What do you think of Dr. Sonya Brown?"

Maxine, being a werewolf, was much stronger than a human. She picked Sonya up and spun her around.

Sonya squealed with delight.

When Maxine set her down and she could breathe again, she asked, "Does that mean you like it?"

* * *

They'd retired from the Frost Thaw festivities early. Maxine had been manning the main drum, but she happily passed it off to Tessa, who was at least competent with the instrument even if she didn't have Maxine's flare or creativity.

Sonya had been dancing all evening, leading the circle dances with different partners who were unmated. She'd stepped, if not flawlessly then at least gladly, into the role of beta's mate.

They'd been having sex at least four times a week for the past two and a half months and Maxine was in a constant state of "do me now."

Like right at this moment. As they left the party and headed upstairs, she walked behind Sonya so she could watch her round ass that did not jiggle but was beautifully full and curvy. Maxine's cock, which she'd carefully tucked, was trying for freedom.

She smacked Sonya's ass when they were on the landing between the second and third floors.

Sonya gasped, jumped a little, and then shot a look full of heat over her shoulder. "Are you saying you want what I've got?" She made her hips sway a little more as she started up the final flight.

"Abso-fucking-lutely."

"You know, once the pups get here, you're going to have to curb that profanity."

"Yes, ma'am." Maxine pinched her where the pinching was good and Sonya squeaked.

Once they were in their apartment with the music playing and their clothes off, Maxine took a moment to study Sonya's full breasts and rounded belly. "You're positively glowing, dear."

Sonya smirked. "And you're positively stiff. Dear."

Maxine glanced down at herself, specifically at her cock, and laughed. "I guess he can't stand being ignored all day. He needs you."

Sonya touched the bed. "I want to ride you tonight."

It was her second favorite position, maybe because when she was on top, she controlled the action or maybe just because she liked fighting gravity as she slowly lowered herself onto Maxine's wood.

Whichever it was, Maxine knew if she didn't stop such thoughts, she'd come right here and now.

She settled herself on the bed, rolling a condom into place because they both had decided they liked avoiding the mess. Especially, Sonya had pointed out, with pups coming, they wouldn't have as much time to change the sheets. Whatever bullshit some men touted about not being able to come with a rubber on, Maxine loved the way she was teased. She would come, but this slowed her down a little.

Sonya was above her then, her legs spread on either side of Maxine's thighs. She was lovely, and she smelled heavenly.

Maxine trailed the fingers of both hands up the insides of her mate's legs, coming together at her beautiful clit. She stroked Sonya's bud, reveling in the way Sonya allowed her eyes to drift shut and her breath to quicken.

Soon, Maxine's fingers were wet with fluids and she moaned in anticipation of her mate's orgasm.

Sonya tossed her head like a horse, her kinky hair bouncing. She shuddered all over and moaned.

Maxine stroked faster, more firmly, until Sonya was trembling all over. The sight of her, so taken up with pleasure, made Maxine's cock throb in anticipation.

Sonya came, shuddering and whispering, "Maxine, Maxine…"

Her brow was dewy with sweat; this seemed to make her glow more.

After Sonya had recovered, Maxine carefully guided her cock into the waiting warmth.

Warmth? Heat. Inferno. *Perfection*. She closed her eyes in an attempt to keep it together. When she could breathe just a little easier, she let her eyelids flutter open. "Please, dear. Move."

Sonya did, tightening and relaxing her muscles around Maxine's cock. Lust sometimes made Maxine want to push, but she held herself back, aware that Sonya loved the relative shortness and narrowness of her shaft.

But maybe some of what she craved was on her face because Sonya said, "Thrust."

"Are you sure?"

Sonya pulled up a little so that Maxine was barely inside her. "Thrust. Now."

Maxine did and Sonya met her partway. They moved together like dancers who'd been partnered for years. Talking and asking for what they both wanted had certainly helped in that area.

The build of tension began in Maxine's belly. She clenched her ass cheeks in an attempt to hold it at bay. But moments later she was coming, crying out softly and trembling all over.

She reached out and touched Sonya's clit again. Sometimes, her mate didn't want this, but Sonya gasped, "Please, please..." and Maxine stroked her to another orgasm.

When they were lying side by side a few minutes later, Sonya having washed because she was fastidious and Maxine having soaped her hands because she knew Sonya's sensitivity to smells, Sonya asked, "How long before you're ready again?"

Maxine laughed. "Give me twenty minutes."

Sonya propped herself up on one elbow. She was smiling into Maxine's eyes. "I love you, but I want you sooner than that."

Maxine kissed her. "My fingers are always ready."

Tactical Difficulties (Lady Troubles 3)
Emily Carrington

Work and pregnancy are driving Sonya crazy. Her mate's concern about her well-being isn't helping because that concern takes the form of overprotectiveness. But when Sonya is kidnapped, she finds strength in herself and her mating bond that she never knew existed.

Chapter One

Agent Corelli looked nervous. He was sweating lightly as if he'd run the distance between his office and hers in Florida's August heat. Even though they were both sitting, he fidgeted. "This is an important coup," he said for the second time. "Sonya, if we lose their trust, we'll never regain it."

"I've led teams before," she said, trying to soothe him. Her boss was not normally an anxious man. Rather, an anxious fae. SearchLight did not, by and large, promote anxious people to the heads of departments.

Maybe he was feeling nervous because his little corner of the world was often overlooked and now had been thrust into the spotlight. He had been the one to draw the spotlight, but perhaps its brightness was too much for him. It was obvious to Sonya the dragons, basilisks, and werewolves would eventually reach a compromise. Was it possible Agent Corelli was surprised that even the little research as Sonya had done would become important?

He responded to her comment, but he was obviously distracted. "And we wouldn't have chosen you if you weren't qualified. But your doctorate is so new it squeaks."

"It's not as if I'll be doing the DNA sequencing," she tried again. "I'll just be the facilitator because I've worked with dragons and werewolves before."

"There's no 'just' anything in this situation."

Sonya decided to keep her encouragements to herself. Excitement bubbled through her with the effervescence of a briskly shaken bottle of soda. She, Shaquilladay Johnson's daughter, was doing something of which her mama had never dreamed: she was leading a scientific team.

For a moment, she was filled with a bitterness so strong she had to swallow. There were many things her mama wouldn't get to see or enjoy, everything from her daughter's financial and social success to her new grandchildren, due in five months' time. Sonya had mostly left her broken home behind her. Between her work, her friends at SearchLight, her mate Maxine, and her mate's werewolf pack, who were now accepting Sonya with open arms, she had regretted the loss of her old life only a little.

"Sonya?"

She pulled herself out of her funk and smiled at Agent Corelli.

"You're not worried about this at all, are you?" he asked.

"Nope."

Agent Corelli sighed. "All right. You've picked your team?"

"Jenny will head the collection of dragon and werewolf DNA and Tom will manage the same for the basilisks. They each have two DNA sequencers under them."

He nodded and stood. "And you're comfortable with public speaking?"

A lance of fear penetrated her heart, but she fought to keep any reaction off her face as she nodded. Maybe he could sense her fear -- some fae were supposed to be able to do that -- but she would act as if he couldn't until proven differently. She had defended her dissertation before nine other people, two of which were experts in comparative biology. But she had never spoken to more than one high ranking official at a time, and that was what made her nervous.

He finally smiled. "You're one hell of a brave

lady."

After he was gone, Sonya closed her eyes. Who, exactly, would she be speaking in front of? Well, that was easy. The delegates from the three communities participating in this research project: a basilisk or two, a couple of dragons, and as many werewolves. She found herself wondering who would be representing the different species and considered the possibility that it would be Mark for the dragons and some SearchLight werewolf for the wolves. Then she laughed ruefully. SearchLight prided itself on staying neutral. There was no way Mark or any other SearchLight agent would be a delegate.

At least that means I won't be dealing with issues of internal rank. Just… lords and ladies and the basilisks' High Council. Dragons had ladies and queens; it was a matriarchal society that scorned males for the most part. Werewolves were more egalitarian when it came to gender roles, especially since first Firos William and then Tilthos Charles had taken over the North American packs and made it quite clear that all wolves, straight or not, were equals in the sight of the alpha above all alphas. But Tilthos Charles, while he was the alpha above all alphas, also worked for SearchLight. Who would be speaking on behalf of the wolves in that case? Surely, the basilisk queen, who was technically the head of the High Council, wouldn't attend. Would she?

Deciding she could put this aside for the moment, Sonya called her beloved to share the news.

* * *

Maxine stared at her mate. Sonya was lovely, of course, with her cocoa dark skin and cap of short, kinky, beautifully natural hair. Her skin was two or three shades lighter than Maxine's and her eyes were a breathtaking honey brown. She was even more attractive today because her gaze shone out with triumph.

But how could she feel that way? The LGBTQ psychic werewolves were being discriminated against. Just like always. And this time, it was their own leader who was doing it. And Sonya might be human, not a werewolf like Maxine, but didn't she understand the plight of her pack family? Her eros, meaning LGBTQ, pack family?

"Tilthos Charles is giving the basilisks permission to overlook us," she said slowly and rather more loudly than she meant to. "Sonya, don't you understand that? He's saying, 'sure, ignore and belittle a subsection of my people. That's just fine.' And you're sitting there… smiling!"

Sonya's grin became a smirk. "It sounds like you're gainsaying the alpha above all alphas."

Maxine started to speak. "Okay," she said carefully, "that is what it sounded like. But he's not here to listen in and…" She shook her head, her braids thumping gently against her shoulders. "What I really don't get is why you're happy about it."

"Because, quite frankly, my dear, it won't last. The basilisks want to shoot themselves in the foot by not including the most willing participants in their little genetic experiment? When all the packs in North America were polled, it was the eros packs who responded most positively to giving their DNA. All werewolves should respond favorably because learning about basilisk reproduction could conceivably help werewolves carry pups more easily. But if the straight wolves are reluctant because of tradition or secrets or secret traditions? And if the basilisks only want straight DNA?" She laughed. "Let them fuck themselves over."

Now Maxine saw the joke and she chuckled. Then she asked her beloved, "Will you make love to me?"

Sonya's eyes widened playfully and her humor was replaced with a devilish look. "How fast can you get undressed?"

It actually took a few minutes because as Maxine removed each article of clothing, shoes and socks, jeans shorts, bikini panties, and skintight T-shirt, Sonya wanted to stroke the newly exposed skin.

Maxine paused dramatically before taking off her bra and fake boobs. Maxine was a transgender wolf, a male to female that would have been called a transwoman if she'd been human. She thought of herself as female, even at the times when her cock ruled her head, because she was not a guy no matter how she'd been born. She'd figured out her transgender self when her name was Maximillian and that little kid had been seven. This had been a good century before the word "transgender" was even in use.

They were at a pause, with Maxine's fake boobs on the nightstand. Maxine tried to push past the memories, but Sonya had already seen something was up. She'd stopped her striptease and was patting the bed next to her, inviting Maxine to sit.

Feeling foolish, she sat. "I'm sorry. I just… drifted."

"Tell me?" Sonya offered softly. And she took Maxine's hands.

Maxine looked down at the beauty of their two skin tones. It was sort of like looking at a wood carving. Somehow majestic even as it was soothing. Also, this time with Sonya was undeniably *theirs*, something no one could take away.

"I don't want to waste --" she began.

"Hush. Time with you is never wasted."

Maxine eased beneath that gentle murmur. "I don't usually give a shit about my penis and balls," she said. "And I don't really now, except that they made you pregnant."

Sonya waited.

That was one of the things Maxine loved about her. Leaning forward, she kissed her mate, slipping her tongue into Sonya's warm and welcoming mouth. When she had the strength to go on, she sat back. "I don't regret our coming pups. Never think it. But I'm feeling sort of guilty for the sperm that took over your body."

Sonya grinned but she sounded absolutely serious when she said, "I love you for saying so, Maxine. You're such a woman when you say things like that." She did laugh then. "And here I thought I wasn't a lesbian." She rested a hand on Maxine's thigh and then ran one finger up the half erect shaft between Maxine's legs.

Maxine shuddered with pleasure.

"I'm so lucky to have a trans wolf with a female's heart, a male's parts, and a warrior's spirit in my bed. Don't regret what I'm glad happened." She colored a little, and then she stood. "Now, will you let me finish stripping for my mate? She's made me wet and I want to lose my underwear."

The unseen burden rolled off Maxine's shoulders and she sat up a little straighter. "Please. Get naked."

Sonya had already removed shoes, socks, skirt, and blouse. Now, she slipped her panties over her round and gorgeous ass and down her legs. Her bra had a front clasp. It was lacy, that bra, and Maxine couldn't sit still longer. She rose and ran the tips of her fingers over the material. She stroked her thumbs over her mate's nipples.

Sonya moaned quietly. "Music," she whispered.

Maxine blinked, and then blushed. She had given away her feelings at a normal volume with the radio off. Probably no one in the pack-filled apartment building cared what she said, but never had she been so aware of revealing her secrets. It made her feel naked.

She crossed to the ancient stereo that she kept because it was easy to use and modern technology annoyed her. She turned on a jazz recording. Then she was back, undoing the clasp between Sonya's breasts.

Sonya's beautiful ladies were revealed then, size C melons of fullness that were, just possibly, a touch larger than the last time Maxine had held them. Sonya was definitely pregnant. Her rounded belly was a little bigger and her nipples were...

Maxine bent and took one of the wonderful buds between her lips.

Sonya moaned again.

Below her waist, Maxine's cock woke to complete erection. Maxine groaned far back in her throat. Then she used one of her slightly-longer-than-human canines to tease the nipple she'd kissed.

Sonya shivered and wrapped her hand around Maxine's cock. She squeezed gently before palming Maxine's balls and rubbing them with her thumb.

Stars seemed to explode behind Maxine's eyes and she stumbled backward until her legs hit the bed. She sat. "Come," she whispered.

Sonya didn't. Instead, she licked one finger and slipped it between the labia that hid her vagina like curtains. Her eyes were slits and the pleasure on her face made Maxine's mouth water.

"You come to me."

Maxine got up on shaky legs and approached.

Sonya retreated until her ass touched the wall. Then she turned around, presenting that perfect moon of her anatomy. "Take me."

Maxine first cupped her mate's ass, enjoying its firmness and the way her touch caused Sonya to tremble. Then she went back to the bed, grabbed a condom out of the nightstand, and rolled it on. It wasn't necessary, not with Sonya already pregnant, but neither of them liked the cleanup afterward.

She also took the time to coat her covered member with a slippery and faintly scented water-based lube.

Sonya glanced over her shoulder and said, "Hurry up!"

When Maxine felt like she was going to burst, she returned to her beloved and brought her to orgasm with a few strokes of her fingers.

Sonya cried out softly and then demanded, still breathless with her pleasure, "Fuck me."

Maxine entered her in one movement. It was agonizingly slow, that thrust, but she wanted nothing more in the world than her mate's pleasure.

Sonya tightened her muscles and pushed back.

They were joined. One.

Maxine began to move and Sonya matched her pulling back and pushing in. They moved together, like a dance, and Maxine hid her face against Sonya's cap of beautifully kinky hair. It was coarse and rubbed against Maxine's cheeks delightfully.

Sonya came again, murmuring, "Maxine, Maxine," four or five times.

Maxine thrust once more. Twice. Thrice. And

then she, too, was letting go. She hugged Sonya to her and rode out her orgasm.

Sonya's phone rang.

"Let it go to voicemail," she murmured. "I'll get it in a few minutes."

Maxine didn't argue.

Chapter Two

When Sonya woke early on Friday morning needing only to pee and then go back to sleep for another hour or so, her phone was buzzing. She'd turned it to silent before going to sleep. She *had* dealt with last night's crisis and soothed Tom's ruffled feathers about having to listen to a junior medtech who happened to be one of the best genetic sequencers on the East Coast. What could the problem possibly be now?

Maxine was still deeply asleep; Sonya took the phone with her into the bathroom. She took care of her business and then retreated to the kitchen so she could call whoever it was back.

It turned out to be Jenny.

"Good morning," Sonya said cautiously. "How can I help?"

"Merle Judah won't quit calling me," Jenny snapped. "He's having trouble finding places for his wolves who want to volunteer for the DNA swab to stay."

"Can't they just do it like those commercial human DNA organizations? Send it in the mail?"

"One of the basilisks' requirements was that everything be done on site."

Sonya sighed. She'd forgotten about that. "Are his wolves straight or LGBTQ?" Then she laughed. "Straight of course, since the basilisks are shooting themselves in the foot by not allowing the non-straight werewolves to participate. Did he contact the local straight pack here in Tampa? Surely they'd take --"

"They're playing host to three other packs right now. Some sort of annual mixer."

Sonya remembered about those; it was how

werewolves from straight packs avoided inbreeding. But it was a damn inconvenient time for that to be taking place. "All right, what about a hotel?" Merle Judah was the alpha who'd taken over Firos William's pack when that wolf had been killed. Wouldn't he have access to funds?

Jenny sighed. "That's a good idea. I'm not sure why I didn't think of it."

"Why the hell is he calling you with these problems in the first place? He's a fucking alpha werewolf. Let him deal with this himself."

"I was so focused on them having to stay with other wolves…" She laughed a little. "I'll call him back. And I'm sorry I had to wake you up this early."

"Tell him if he has any more problems to talk to me directly. You are the head of werewolf DNA sequencing, not werewolf lodging."

After hanging up, Sonya muttered, "This whole thing is going to be a shit show, isn't it?" She didn't actually mind other people having circuses, not when she could step in and out of their drama as she pleased. But being stuck as the ringmaster of another's circus sucked.

Not my circus, not my monkeys could not apply here.

"Do you want to talk about it?"

Sonya looked up, smiling tiredly at her mate. "I always wake you up even when I'm trying to be as quiet as possible."

"Dangers of loving a werewolf." Maxine, naked and beautiful, her penis dangling between her legs as a silent promise, crossed the kitchen and wrapped her arms tightly around Sonya's waist. "Come back to bed and I'll soothe you."

Sonya knew her nipples were hardening. She

grinned. "It will only make us sleepy again."

"Or give us something to think about all day," Maxine suggested.

They went back to their bedroom hand in hand. Sonya was already wet; she could feel it slicking up her clit. Just to tease Maxine, she dipped a finger between her legs and touched off a shock of pleasure. Maxine was a telepath. Even though she was not a strong telepath, proximity helped. The closer they were, the more she could feel Sonya's emotions. And arousal. Sonya caught the widening of her mate's eyes and knew she'd picked up on the spike of need.

Glancing down, she grinned at the response playing with herself had caused. She cupped Maxine's lightly hairy balls and smirked when her mate's cock rose from half to full mast. "No condom; I don't want to take the time." She flopped onto the bed and spread her legs. "Claim me."

Maxine mounted her moments later but didn't push in immediately. "You're sure you're wet enough?"

Usually they had a little more foreplay, but Sonya didn't need it today. She said as much. Her eyes rolled back in her head when Maxine thrust into her, possessing her body in a way that Sonya found completely intoxicating.

Rocking her hips, Sonya matched her movements to Maxine's. Then she had to bite back a scream as Maxine, balanced on one hand, used the other to stroke her clit. It was blissfully perfect, the sensation of being filled and yet set afire by a single finger.

Sonya came.

When she emerged from the shaky world of bliss to reality, she grinned up at Maxine. "Please. Move."

Maxine always waited until she was done

orgasming, and Sonya loved her for it.

They rocked together again, Maxine's rhythm speeding up as her own orgasm neared. Her lovely eyes were slit almost shut and she was trembling all over.

Pleasure began building in Sonya's legs and lower belly. She tightened her muscles as much as she could and rode out Maxine's climax. She needed a little more to come for a second time and she reached down, caressing her clit.

Meeting her mate's heated gaze, she stroked herself to completion.

Then, as if a switch had been flipped inside her, she began to sob.

Damn fucking mood swings, she thought as Maxine held her. She cursed the day she'd started having them, even though she knew they were part of being pregnant.

"I'm fine, I'm fine," she said over and over.

"I know," Maxine murmured.

But Sonya felt the tension in her mate's embrace and knew that her plunging and rearing moods, untrustworthy as an untrained horse, were a burden for her beloved.

And that made her cry more.

* * *

Sonya's up-and down, ocean-wave changes of mood were going to drive Maxine to distraction. Sitting in her office a full four hours after making love to her beautiful mate, Maxine could barely concentrate.

Luckily, there wasn't much she was doing today. Because she was mated to the head of what her boss, Agent Wellington, had nicknamed "The DNA Festivities," she wasn't allowed to help much with the werewolf part of things. It was seen as a conflict of interest. So, instead of tending to this or that minor crisis among the werewolf delegates or their escorts, she was helping to plan that June's summer solstice party.

It was a relief to not have something critical, but in a way, it was frustrating too because she couldn't find anything to distract her from the storm of Sonya's moods.

Not even Carrie, her deceased former mate, had been this anxious or prone to crying. And Carrie had been one moody wolf.

Maxine endured the stab of guilt that came whenever she thought of Carrie in the negative. Then her thoughts swung back to the current issue: Sonya making passionate love with her before falling into a bout of sobbing that had lasted almost ten minutes.

Even with Sonya saying she was fine, it was obvious she wasn't. Her tears were the proof.

Maxine's cell phone chimed quietly. She jumped a little, startled that anyone was contacting her while she was at work because no one ever did unless it was an absolute emergency.

It wouldn't be Sonya; she'd call on the office phone. Hopefully that meant everything was okay on her mate's end.

Maxine looked down, saw the text was from her alpha, Fehrna Susan, and prepared herself for a problem.

The text simply said, *Call me*.

Maxine did.

When Fehrna Susan answered, she didn't mince words or waste time. "You're worried about Sonya. Why?"

Fehrna Susan wasn't a telepath. "How do you know that?" was out of Maxine's mouth before she could call it back.

"I saw you leaving for work this morning. You were riding her heels. Hell, you were practically wearing the same pair of shoes."

Maxine felt herself blush. It never occurred to her to lie or prevaricate. Her alpha had a nose finely tuned to the smell of dragonshit. "She's so moody lately. I don't know how she's going to react moment to moment.'

"And that's all?"

Maxine's temper flared but she tried hard to keep her irritation from her voice. "Isn't it enough?"

"Absolutely. Especially since you seem to have forgotten what pregnancy does to some females." Despite the harsh-sounding response, Fehrna Susan's tone was gentle. "Maxine, my caring and thoughtful beta, do you not realize that Sonya isn't in control of her emotions right now? She's in thrall to the hormones rushing through her body."

Maxine almost snapped that she knew that. Then she replayed what her alpha had said. "You mean... you mean she's not really upset?"

"No, she is. But not because of anything she or you have done. She's feeling sad or angry or ecstatic because of the necessary mixture of hormones charging through her veins like an invading army."

"She really is upset," Maxine said slowly as she digested it, "but there's nothing I can do about it?"

"There absolutely are steps you can take to alleviate her stress. Respond to her moods with genuine concern and try to help her laugh when she's sobbing. Treat her still with the respect you will always have for her, and simply love her. All of her. Even her mood swings."

Maxine thought about that for several moments.

Then she said, "I should've known all this."

"No. I was unfair before. Your experience with Carrie was completely different than your experience with Sonya. What you need to do is not beat yourself up, and stop trying to fathom why she's crying or laughing. Simply be with her as she goes through each change. She'll be grateful for your support and you'll grow closer as a result."

Fehrna Susan paused before adding, "And for right now, your time would be better spent coming up with names for the twins she's carrying. You can bet Sonya's doing the same when her head's clear."

Maxine grinned. Thinking up baby names sounded a lot better than worrying. "I'll do that."

"Good. And take a breath. You're going to be a wonderful mother."

Maxine had come up with about two dozen names, both male and female, when Michaela, Fehrna Susan's mate, both a strong empath and a powerful precognitive, called. Then Maxine had no more peace.

Chapter Three

Sonya's stomach was as sudsy as a washing machine. She sat at a round lunch table that seemed to simultaneously put her at the head of the gathering and yet pass her over. She knew, unquestionably knew, that this was impossible. It was a circular table, for God's sweet sake, like the one supposedly used by King Arthur so that no one knight could claim superiority over another.

Oh, stop analyzing the table. All the tables in the cafeteria are round. This was true, but it still seemed deliberate to her. As did the seating arrangements. Surely Mark Tavery, who was escorting the dragon delegate and her bodyguards, and Luke Tavery, Mark's husband, who would be standing with the basilisks, wouldn't choose to sit apart. But there they were, Mark on Sonya's right, followed by Tilthos Charles, Luke, and then Jack Sowerby.

Everyone was eating. Well, everybody but Sonya. She glanced from face to face and saw no anxiety or tension. She wished fervently she could feel as they did. Or at least hide it as well as they.

"You have something on your mind," Jack Sowerby said.

Sonya wanted to wring her hands. Instead, she poked at her salad. "Agent Sowerby…" She saw him smiling and realized he wasn't an agent anymore. "Um, I'm sorry. I'm not sure what to call you." Did he hold a doctorate?

"Jack is fine," he answered, "but if that makes you uncomfortable, Mr. Sowerby is also okay."

His smile was dissembling. She found herself voicing one of her chief concerns almost without permission from her brain. "Mr. Sowerby, if you're the head negotiator, how can I possibly help?"

"You're seen as the expert," he told her gently. "The delegates will respond to you in a way they won't allow themselves to respond to me."

"But I'm not a DNA expert."

"No, you're an expert at analyzing other species' characteristics. You were the one to discover, incontrovertibly, that joining a dragon to a werewolf makes a basilisk."

She opened her mouth, thinking to confess that all had happened by accident.

Tilthos Charles saved her from the admission. "The greatest leaps forward in the world of science are sometimes made through trial and error. Many people wouldn't have trusted the legends long enough to see if they were true. That is your strength; you believe that there must be a shred of truth if a hypothesis has been carried through so many years."

She said miserably, "That sort of implies I'd believe in the world being flat if enough people passed it down through oral tradition."

Tilthos Charles shook his head. "You give yourself too little credit, Dr. Brown."

Sonya grinned. She liked being called Dr. Brown.

"You're giving the legends a chance to be true, not closing your eyes to reality."

She felt herself relax under his regard. It loosened her tongue and she said, "Thank you."

"All right," Tilthos Charles said, "now that we have established Dr. Brown's role in all this, I have a question. How did you finagle things so that both of you, Mark and Luke, were on this detail? I had thought SearchLight is against sending couples. Especially when you're supposed to be on maternity and paternity leave."

Mark and Luke's baby, born of Luke in female form because Luke was a genie and could change guises, was less than two weeks old.

Sonya saw Mark and Luke exchange a half exasperated, half proud look.

Luke waved his hand and Mark said, "Jack almost asked for Travis Wong to step in on behalf of the dragons, but he's human and the Lady Nicole had a fit at the very idea. As for Luke, he's the only person working for SearchLight who has both the knowledge of basilisks and the security clearance for this assignment. As soon as everything's resolved, we'll be getting delayed leave."

"Who's taking care of Zia?" Jack asked.

"My mother, Miriam Tavery," Mark answered.

Jack smiled. "I always liked Miriam. Raising you couldn't have been easy and she handled it with grace." He flashed a grin when Mark flushed. "Forgive me, Mark. I couldn't resist a tease."

Luke spoke up, probably to get attention away from his husband. "Who, exactly, is everyone guarding? I know my delegate is Duchess Antoinette Bouhouche, daughter of Queen Imane. And Mark's is the Lady Nicole from Ontario, Canada. But who is standing in for you, Tilthos Charles?"

The alpha above all alphas smiled. "Discreet as a freight train. But I'll bite. Merle --" he pronounced it "MER-lah" --"Judah. Even though he's only been head of his pack for three years, is competent to represent the wolves' concerns."

"How did that come about?" Jack asked.

Tilthos Charles answered, "He inherited the former Firos pack. And since I can't, by virtue of my affiliation with SearchLight, serve the wolves' interests, it was determined that Merle Judah would be the best substitute."

From there, the conversation moved on to Tilthos Charles's coming retirement from SearchLight. Sonya finally found herself able to eat, and she worked her way through her salad while the four males at the table discussed everything under the sun except the coming delegates.

As they talked, she realized that she was the only female and felt outnumbered.

She chewed this over for the rest of the lunch hour.

* * *

Maxine met Sonya for their fifteen-minute coffee break. They didn't usually meet, but Maxine had something to share and she absolutely didn't want to wait until they were walking home together. Mostly because this would probably make Sonya furious and it wasn't good to go home to the pack who could read every gesture and look with anger ascendant.

Maxine was not a big believer in "get it over with," but she felt the urge to do that in this instance.

"What's wrong?" Sonya asked.

"Are you the telepath now?" Maxine asked, amused in spite of her agitation. She liked it that Sonya could read her moods. It was further proof that they were overcoming the struggles that had dogged the beginning of their mating.

"It's all over your face." Sonya drew Maxine to a bench. "We don't have long though. Do you want to hold this until we're home?"

Maxine shook her head. "This needs to be said where you'll have a chance to react to it and the pack won't know."

Sonya sighed ruefully and smiled just a tiny bit. "I'm going to get pissed, aren't I?"

"Maybe." She sighed. "Probably."

Sonya gripped Maxine's hands. "All right. Let me have it."

"Do you know Michaela's psychic powers?"

"Powers? Plural? I thought most wolves who have any psychic talent had one."

"That's true. It's not common to have more than one, and to be strong in either, let alone both, is rarer still. Almost unheard of. But Michaela is blessed or cursed with strong precognition and intense empathy."

"She sympathizes with others, do you mean, or does she have the werewolf gift of empathy where she can read others' emotions if not their thoughts?"

"Read and sometimes influence, that one."

Sonya frowned. "I never thought about the abilities the rest of the pack must have," she admitted. "I just assumed, I suppose, if I thought about it at all, that they were all like you. Which is silly, because I know there are many more talents than just telepathy." She waved all of this away. "Why is Michaela's empathy and precognition a problem?"

"Because," Maxine said, and then she hesitated.

"Go on." Sonya smiled again; it was still a small thing. "I'll do my best not to fly off the handle."

"Michaela says it's dangerous for you to associate with the escorts and delegates. That something terrible is going to happen to you. Or the pups you're carrying. Or all three of you."

Sonya was quiet for a moment. Then she said, "Because I'm going to be speaking in front of them all?" She winked. "Because I can believe that. I'll probably have a heart attack when I have to actually stand up in front of all those powerful people."

Maxine huffed a frustrated sigh. "It's not a joke. Precogs are not to be taken lightly."

Sonya sobered. "I understand that, but think of it this way: I'll have Mark and Luke there. Luke, who is so tremendously powerful that SearchLight has to regulate his magical strength. And they can't really even do that, just ask Luke to restrain himself. He's all but a god. Considering that, do you think there's anything that can be thrown at me that Luke can't stop?"

"You're not Luke's responsibility."

"No, but he and Mark are my best friends, besides you. Wouldn't he want to protect me?"

"If he has to protect his delegate, he's going to do that first."

Sonya was quiet. "Okay," she said at last. "I see your point."

"And the danger may not come when you're all gathered together. It's circling around you like a cloud, Michaela said." Maxine frowned and recalled it precisely. "Like a 'cyclone made by strong winds,' is how she put it."

"Maybe I could get someone to protect me specifically."

Maxine breathed a sigh of relief. "I could --"

"If something happens to me, our pups will need you. Besides, even if you're trained in investigations, you're not a fighter."

"Not according to SearchLight, but I --"

"Absolutely not. I will not let both of us die and leave the pups without parents."

"But if you die, the pups won't have a chance."

"They might." Sonya closed her eyes and bore down on Maxine's hands. "We have to get back to work. But I'll find someone to protect me. Okay?" She kissed Maxine's lips, softly and chastely. Then she drew back and stood. "Go. And don't worry about this anymore. I'll make sure Michaela's concerns are taken seriously." She left then, walking briskly.

Maxine watched her go for a couple of breaths. Then she rose and headed more slowly back toward her desk. Sonya hadn't blown up, there was that much to be grateful for. She was often unreasonable when it came to matters of safety.

All right, so that wasn't fair. Maxine had nothing to base that on. She just knew Sonya was strong-minded and a little pigheaded when it came to the pack.

But hadn't that changed since Maxine wasn't spending every waking moment taking care of the pack? Yes. So, why had Maxine been so sure Sonya would explode? For that matter, why had Sonya been convinced of the same?

Because it might have interfered with work. Yes, that was it. Sonya loved her work. She was ecstatic about having these extra duties, even if she was agonizing over the public speaking part.

She's a workaholic. And was that so unusual? Maxine was the same way, although in regards to the pack, not her nine-to-five job.

So why am I annoyed, if I'm the same way? She sighed and admitted it was probably because, deep down, she was just a touch sexist. It was okay for her, born as a male, to overwork, but now that Sonya was in a delicate condition...

No. Sonya was carrying their pups, but that didn't make her weak or "delicate" or anything else that she wasn't already. She was eating for two, and suffering mood swings because of hormones, but that didn't make her anything other than what she was naturally.

And once the pups are born? Who will be staying

home with them? Oh, but if that wasn't a sexist question, she didn't know what was. SearchLight offered a six month leave for mothers and fathers, both the one who carried the child and the one who had gotten them pregnant.

It would behoove Maxine to be just as forward thinking as her employer. Then again, she thought as she entered her building and headed for the stairs, if someone else was in charge of this blooming fiasco, Sonya wouldn't be in danger.

She resolved to talk to Jack Sowerby. Maybe he could find someone who didn't have a threat-cloud hanging over their head.

Chapter Four

Sonya was in a rage. Her temples throbbed and her hands shook as she fumbled in her purse for some lip balm. She was so furious that she dropped the damn tube. She cursed.

"What's wrong?" Maxine went for the yellow stick.

"I can get it myself," Sonya snapped. "I'm not helpless." She scooped up the offending bit of plastic, unscrewed the top, and nearly dropped that as well. She finally managed to get some on her overly dry lips.

"What's wrong, dear?"

Don't 'dear' me. She was thankfully able to keep from saying this aloud. She began to walk faster. Maybe she could outrace her fury. Or at least get away from her mate.

Maxine kept up easily. Damn werewolf.

"What's wrong?" she asked again.

Sonya shoved her lip balm away. "You're interfering in my life."

Maxine, bless her, didn't pretend not to know what she'd done wrong. "I was protecting you."

"By going behind my back?"

"I was trying to save you the stress of --"

"And your way of doing that was by complaining to my boss? Not even just my boss, but the head of this whole damn affair?"

"I wasn't complaining. I was just worried about your delicate condition."

Sonya rounded on her as her anger flared. "I am not delicate. People were having pups long before this."

Maxine made a shushing motion with her hands that was patronizing and annoying as fuck. "Keep your voice down. We don't want to expose --"

"Oh, fine. *Babies*. And that's not the point. You shouldn't have --"

Maxine snapped, "They're my children too. I have a right to try and protect them." Then, quieter, "Especially with the high mortality rates."

"Which will be less because our *children* will be half human," Sonya whispered.

Maxine all but growled, "There is still a thirty percent chance they could die. I consider that too high." Maxine visibly pulled herself together and hugged Sonya. "I'll try to stop obsessing about what can't be changed. I still want to protect you. I shouldn't have said 'delicate condition.' That was sexist and I know it. I'm just so -- damn -- worried!"

"All right," Sonya said. "All right. You're worried. I respect that. But let me handle the guard situation. I was going to talk to Agent Corelli on Monday. He respects precog impressions." She poked a finger at Maxine. "But I insist you refrain from going to my boss or to Agent, hell, Mr. Sowerby again. I'm an adult. I can make my own choices. I will not do something stupid that will get me or our little ones killed."

Maxine was silent for several heartbeats. Then she sighed. "All right. I won't. Not unless you're in real danger. Like something Michaela can articulate."

Sonya, annoyed but not wanting to argue, said nothing.

Maxine took her hand after they'd walked half a block. She sounded tentative when she suggested, "Maybe we should talk about baby names."

Sonya jumped on this. She didn't want to fight with her mate. And Maxine was as good as her word. If she said she wouldn't worry at Mr. Sowerby, she wouldn't. "How about Fenris? He's a legendary wolf from --"

Maxine pulled her hand free and swatted Sonya's ass. "Name our," she whispered the next words, "werewolf 'wolf'? Are you insane, woman?"

"No. I just want him to know he is a wolf, even if he's half human."

Maxine seemingly couldn't argue with that because she suggested, "What about after a book character?

"What, like Flix from *For Love of Mother-Not*?"

"I was thinking more like a *Lord of the Rings* character."

Sonya swatted Maxine's ass this time. "If you're going to suggest Legless --"

"That's Legolas," Maxine said, most likely pretending high offense.

And so, the awkwardness was behind them. At least, Sonya thought, for now.

* * *

The weekend passed peacefully enough, and with just the right amount of sex to make Sonya relax without wearing her out. She would have never thought too much sex would be possible, but she was tired these days. Her morning sickness, which had mostly occurred in the evening, truth be told, seemed to be a thing of the past. She was entering what Luke, when he'd been pregnant with Mark's baby and sex-changed by his own genie magic, had called "the sweet months." This was the time, supposedly, when she wouldn't be big as a house but be able to sleep through the night and still enjoy a cuddle or boink with her mate. She didn't have to pee every fifteen minutes, not yet at least, and her sex drive was high.

Now it was Monday again and she was excited

about the delegations arriving from different parts of the country to sit down, have final negotiations if necessary, and celebrate the beginning of this new venture in science. The basilisks wanted children and the dragons and werewolves, whose forefathers were the basilisks, were willing to help them get there.

Sonya stood outside in the warmth of Florida's February. It wasn't beautiful like this all over the state, but here in Tampa, the winter months were the best of the year. She'd dressed in a business suit instead of her usual scrubs or business casual, the dressy tops and skirts she often wore for Maxine's benefit as well as her own natural desire to feel sexy.

The first limousine to pull up was baby blue. Sonya had seen many light colored cars in Florida, but every limo had been black. Or maybe there had been one or two white ones. But certainly not the color of an early morning sky. She had to smother a smile; surely it would be taken wrongly.

She wished she had a werewolf's nose so she'd know which representatives were disembarking. The back door on the curbside opened and she longed for Mark and Luke and Tilthos Charles to be with her. But they were arriving with their delegates.

The first person to emerge was either a delegate or a guard, not one of the escorts she knew. Very finely dressed, it was impossible to tell their status, royal or otherwise. Then she saw that the one who stood in front of Searchlight's main building was male and she thought, if he's a werewolf, he could be Merle Judah. If he's a basilisk, he's surely a bodyguard.

Then a beautiful, long-legged and decidedly dark-haired woman got out. She was Mediterranean in her looks, but when she spoke, she had a slight Southern accent.

"Good morning. Are you Dr. Johnson?"

Sonya curtseyed. "It's actually Dr. Brown, madam. Welcome to SearchLight."

Beside her, Jack Sowerby bowed. "Duchess Bouhouche, you honor us with your presence."

She smiled graciously and offered him her hand, which he kissed.

This, then, was the basilisk representative, daughter of an actual queen.

Meanwhile, two more guards had emerged and Luke was also out in the February sunshine, his golden hair gleaming.

I'm just admiring everyone's looks today. Am I horny?

The Duchess Bouhouche had turned to her. "Please, we are equals, we two. Please call me Antoinette."

This made Sonya feel a little awkward, and not only because she was aware of the rampant anti male sexism implicit in that statement. "Madam, I'm not sure if --"

The duchess tossed her head imperiously. "You'll be working on my people's genes. We must therefore trust you. 'Duchess Bouhouche' is reserved for those with whom I will not become good friends."

Sonya realized that the basilisk's accent might be Southern but the structure of her speech was very European. Had she been raised here? Meanwhile, the royal lady was awaiting an answer. Sonya struggled with herself for a moment and then smiled. "I'm honored to call you Antoinette."

"Lovely. Now, we must wait for our other guests." She gestured curtly to one of her bodyguards and he scurried over with an umbrella, which he positioned over her to provide shade.

The next delegate arrived in a Mercedes. *Make that three Mercedes.* The first car held two guards and the driver. The second car held Tilthos Charles and someone Sonya assumed to be Merle Judah. And the third car held more guards. At least, she was assuming that was how it worked. That was, at any rate, the way that made the most sense.

And when Tilthos Charles introduced his riding companion, Sonya found she had been right.

Merle Judah was possessed of dark and curling hair, a rather large nose, and arresting brown eyes. Sonya could almost feel the power pouring off of the alpha wolf. She wondered why she didn't feel Tilthos Charles's power in the same way. Didn't he outrank Merle Judah?

"Duchess Bouhouche," the alpha said and took her hand, kissing it delicately.

"Alpha," she said rather coolly. Then she glanced at Mr. Sowerby and added to Merle Judah, "It is a pleasure to see you again."

He took his place beside her after offering Sonya a quick and much less gracious hello.

The third arrivals, which had to be the dragons, arrived in an honest-to-God horse-drawn carriage with seats that looked like leather and large, yellow wheels. It was pulled by six horses. Sonya wasn't familiar enough with horse breeds to know what kind they were, but they looked like the ones used on the Budweiser commercials. Huge.

There were five people in the carriage: two females and three males. Mark was one of the latter, and Sonya knew the delegate in this group because she'd met her last year.

Approaching the carriage as the Lady Nicole was handed out by one of her bodyguards, Sonya curtseyed. "Lady Nicole."

"Agent Johnson," Lady Nicole greeted her.

"Forgive me, my lady, but it's Dr. Brown now."

The dragon matriarch nodded. "I hope you didn't change your family name for some male."

Sonya chose not to be offended. "I changed my name for my mate, Maxine."

With everyone arrived, it was a short journey to the conference room. Sonya stood outside with the delegates and escorts as the bodyguards checked the room for danger.

Two SearchLight agents, identified as such by their lanyards and badges, approached. They stopped a little distance away and spoke quietly together.

She caught only one word: TruWolves.

She didn't mistake it for true wolves or anything else but one word, blended together, that meant danger. Over the last couple of months, Maxine had been teaching her the history of North America's werewolves. She'd spoken of the TruWolves, of their members, who were all LGBTQ psychic wolves and some half wolves. They were a terrorist group, although they hadn't been heard from since Tilthos Charles, or maybe just someone closely associated with him, had killed their leader, Gary Gavin, a transgender wolf known also as GG.

As Sonya turned toward the two agents, Tilthos Charles passed her. He did not look happy.

He addressed them in a barely audible murmur. Then, leaving them looking chastened, he stopped beside Sonya. "Whatever you heard, don't pass it along. They have no business bringing up such rumors even if they are trackers."

She nodded, accepting his words both because he was the alpha above all alphas and because Mark spoke highly of him.

Finally, the room was determined to be safe and everyone stepped in. The guards stood against the walls and the escorts sat, each one, to the right of his delegate. Jack Sowerby sat at the head of the rectangular table and Sonya was directed to sit beside him.

After the meeting was started, and after the pleasantries had been exchanged, an old topic was brought up: the inclusion of the LGBTQ werewolves in the DNA samples.

Sonya sensed this had never really left the delegates' minds. Even Lady Nicole, who was a dragon, came down on one side of the argument, on the side of the werewolves, which seemed to surprise Merle Judah. It startled Sonya for sure, because dragons and werewolves were enemies of old.

As everyone's voices began to rise, and Jack Sowerby worked to keep everyone calm, Sonya resisted the urge to chew her lip nervously. She had no idea how to prevent an argument like this, especially when not even Jack Sowerby seemed to be having any luck.

Merle Judah stood, glaring at the duchess. "Lady --"

"Duchess, wolf, and don't you try to lord it over me."

Sonya's stomach knotted and she waited for everything to erupt in violence.

Chapter Five

Sonya's heart pounded and sweat broke out on her brow. She pushed her chair back a little, needing to get away from the fighting even just a tiny bit.

You're the facilitator. Do something. But who was she to stop these enraged people?

And that was when she heard a different voice in her head, one that didn't belong to her. One that was male and full of quiet authority. She knew it immediately even though she'd somehow expected the werewolf's mental voice to be different than the one he used more commonly. If pressed, she would have said that everyone's voice sounded different in their own head so shouldn't telepathy be different than regular speech?

Maybe it was for others. But Tilthos Charles sounded just like himself when he said silently, *"Sonya, we need your help. Jack's not getting anywhere because he's not an authority when it comes to medicine. You're a doctor. You can talk sense into these people. Even if you can't get them to agree, to see the truth, maybe you can bring them under the influence of your knowledge."*

She opened her mouth to speak, that was how close he seemed even though he was halfway down the table.

"Reply this way. Right now, no one else knows we're talking. I don't want this to come from me. It will seem like I'm interfering. He gave the impression of being amused in spite of the troublesome circumstances, the sensation of his humor there and gone in less than a second. *"Of course, I am, but that's beside the point. This must appear to come from you, a neutral party. Will you try?"*

"But I'm not an expert, Tilthos Charles. I'm not an

expert when it comes to DNA."

"True, but you're a doctor. That's what the basilisks asked for. And you are knowledgeable enough to understand the fallacy of their arguments. Will you try? You can't make things worse."

His confidence that she couldn't send everyone over the edge reassured her. She took a breath and rose to her feet. "Duchess Antoinette? Merle Judah? Lady Nicole?"

They, all three, turned to her as sunflowers turned toward the sun. Merle Judah seemed on the edge of saying something but subsided when Tilthos Charles put a hand on his arm.

Sonya's knees were trembling. She worked hard to keep her nervousness out of her voice and off her face as she said, "There is no fundamental difference in DNA. There are minor changes, but those dictate hair color, eye color, and skin color. Superficial discrepancies."

When in doubt, share a tale.

That was her own thought and she welcomed it. "May I share a story?"

Antoinette smiled.

Merle Judah sat back down.

"Back before the Civil Rights movement of the 1960s, and for years afterward despite advances in being able to vote and affirmative action that gave my people the chance to find gainful employment, there was a stigma against interracial marriages." She paused, remembering that race wasn't really something most magical creatures cared about. "White people and black people, those of Asian descent, and those whose ancestors were in this land centuries ago, weren't allowed to intermarry. Their children were called mongrels and other unpleasant names.

"When DNA sequencing first emerged as a feasible line of scientific study, many people looked for essential differences between the races to support their prejudice. They found none. We are one species, indivisible."

She paused for effect.

"So are werewolves."

She still had their full attention; none of them had moved. So, she pressed her point home. "The greatest number of potential contributors to this admirable, necessary project are psychic wolves."

Silence.

Then, from Antoinette, "But even human races are different on some level. And do not tell me it is only skin deep, melatonin deep, because I know your very skeletons have differences."

Damn, but she was knowledgeable. Sonya had hoped for accepting audiences. Now, she pulled herself together and answered, "Yes, but those differences don't affect our ability to intermarry and raise children."

Antoinette was quiet for a moment. Then she said, "That's true. But what about queer parents raising queer children?"

"LGBTQ pups, just like the human equivalent, come from all kinds of parents. Just like heterosexual little ones come from any parents. If that wasn't the case, there would be no LGBTQ children at all. They would have never come into existence. And, perhaps it's time to ask yourself this: do you want basilisk babies that are created in one stringent image? Because that could take centuries of trial and error to bring about. Or do you want to wait the three to ten years it may take to have children at all?"

The duchess was quiet. Then she said softly, "I

want to hold my basi. I want to hold him or her and know that they're mine." She turned her head and said, "Merle Judah, send us any of your wolves, in your pack or from any other, who will be gracious enough to contribute their DNA. We are grateful."

Sonya lowered herself into her chair and gripped her shaking knees with both hands. As the talk turned to preparations for swabbing and other less volatile matters, Sonya heard Tilthos Charles murmur in her mind, *Well done*."

* * *

When Maxine came to Sonya's office, the new one she'd been allocated for the duration of the DNA testing, she found her mate waiting impatiently for her.

It was not an unpleasant impatience, but one filled with the smell of arousal. Sonya had both fans in her office going, but there were no windows for the scent to be blown out of. She sat behind her desk and her lips were parted. Maxine glimpsed her shoes sitting on the shelf behind her. Quickly, Maxine shut the door and locked it. In a whisper, she asked, "What's got you all hot and bothered this afternoon?"

Sonya watched with mounting lust as Maxine unzipped her skirt. Then she let the fabric drop to the floor. She wore nothing beneath. Yummy.

"What if I hadn't been the one to walk in here?" Maxine asked as she crossed to her mate and put both hands on the warm skin of her waist.

"Then I wouldn't have let you in. Remember, you knocked and asked if I was here."

Maxine laughed. "And if I'd just barged in?"

"That's not your style, dear."

Maxine's cock was half erect by now, pulling free of the tuck Maxine had performed that morning to hide it from the world. Now it gave another twitch and she laughed softly. She loved hearing her pet name for her beloved on Sonya's lips. "How would you like to do this?"

"Quickly. Unfortunately." Sonya pulled off her blouse and tossed it onto the chair. Her bra was comely, and made of lace.

Maxine cupped Sonya's breast with one hand. Then she unzipped her dress pants and let them pool around her ankles. She had to use two hands to pull down the underwear that helped keep her cock confined and she did so.

Sonya retreated until she was against the wall. Then she spread her legs in obvious invitation.

Maxine, aware of how truly short their time was, was inside her mate in less than a minute, not neglecting to wear a condom. They did not need a mess to clean up. She'd been amused to find out Sonya kept a small plastic baggie on her devoted to the little rubbers.

They began to move as one almost immediately, Sonya's urgency catching. It was so sweet, being buried in Sonya's heat, and Maxine lost herself to the in and out slide of her cock and the press of Sonya's nipples, slightly felt through her shirt and the lacy bra.

Sonya tossed her head and moaned almost inaudibly. She was so wet that Maxine, reaching for her clitoris, realized her mate didn't need that extra stimulus.

Then her orgasm began to build in her thighs and her belly and her balls and she shuddered, pushing in and pulling out faster and faster until...

Maxine held Sonya against her as she came.

Only as her climax passed did she understand that Sonya was finding her release as well.

After taking a few moments to catch their breath,

they began putting themselves to rights. Maxine lit two of the scented candles Sonya had already moved into the office. Both smelled of pine, one of Sonya's favorite aromas.

When she turned around to gauge her mate's progress, she found Sonya completely put together and just dabbing a touch of citrus perfume at the base of her throat. The scent of oranges and star fruit made Maxine's mouth water, and not because she was in love with the fruits local to Florida. That smell would forever remind her of her mate.

"What got into you?" she asked, teasing.

Sonya laughed; it sounded a touch self-conscious and Maxine added, "Not that I mind."

"It's just… sitting with all those men and those two females throwing their hormones around…" Sonya shook her head. "I don't think that's what they were really doing, but that was how it felt. I wanted to feel like I belonged to you instead of to their power game."

Maxine hugged her close, kissing her temple. "You're definitely mine, just as I'm yours."

Someone knocked on the door. It sounded urgent, especially when accompanied by a frantic voice saying, "Dr. Brown, Dr. Brown, quick!"

Sonya went to the door, patting her hair with light, quick movements. When she opened the door, she appeared completely composed. "What's wrong, Ms. Stewart?"

Maxine recognized the woman, couldn't remember where she'd seen her, and then remembered. This was the secretary for the entire med tech department.

A puff of air from the overhead vent startled Maxine and she jumped as it slid across her exposed penis. She turned away quickly and tucked the troublesome organ that was the cause of so much pleasure.

"The refrigeration unit," the secretary was saying. "There's a red light on it and it's not making any noise."

Sonya said, "Okay," as if this wasn't a serious matter.

Maxine asked, "Is it the fridge where the first DNA samples that arrived today are stored?"

"Exactly!" Ms. Stewart cried.

"I'll take care of it," Sonya soothed.

"But we don't have another refrigeration unit."

Sonya touched the secretary's arm. "I promise, it will be okay."

"Do you think it was sabotage?" asked another voice.

Maxine turned back around and saw the guard, a tracker who'd been posted there for the duration of the DNA gathering process. He only looked mildly concerned.

"I won't know until I examine it." Sonya turned back to Ms. Stewart. "Please, go tell Agent Corelli."

"He's not here," she answered, sounding a touch less frantic.

"All right. Leave him a message on his desk. I'll check the refrigeration unit." And she brushed gently past the other woman.

Maxine followed. When they were out of the human's earshot, although maybe the tracker, a werewolf, could still hear them, she asked quietly, "Why are you so calm?"

"Because we don't actually need the fridge for the samples. They weren't stored at cooler temperatures for their transport here. Why would they need it now?"

Maxine gaped. Then she asked, "Why do it?"

Sonya chuckled. "The lower temperatures are another line of defense against contamination, but it's really unnecessary. Still, I'll make sure it gets fixed. Even if the basilisks know it's unnecessary, they'll be worried about our competence."

They parted in front of Sonya's office. Maxine's phone chimed. It was a mild thing, that tinkling of electronic bells, and she almost ignored it. Then it came again. And again.

The tracker, the one who'd asked if it was sabotage, still stood in his place. Maxine decided to step into Sonya's office for a little privacy.

It was Michaela, all three times, and Maxine scanned the first message quickly.

Heidi says there's a black cloud of danger hanging over SearchLight, specifically over the Tampa campus, perhaps even more specifically over Sonya. It's "made up of many droplets that could be deadly to the pups and the mother." That's a direct quote.

Maxine's gut twisted. She read through the other two messages, which were repeats, and then she typed "received" and hit the Send button. She left the office and approached the tracker. Reminding herself that he wouldn't know Heidi from a hole in the wall, she forced herself calm.

"Agent?"

He nodded. "Agent Brown."

Damn trackers, knowing everyone's names as if they'd plucked them out of the target's head. Maxine took a breath. "Heidi is a powerful precog from my pack, the Fehrna pack." Damn, but she was nervous. She reminded herself that this tracker was a wolf, was younger than her more than likely, and put his pants on one leg at a time.

It didn't help that he was wearing a smug, pretending-to-be-patient look.

"She says there's a danger cloud hanging over this campus, specifically over my mate, Dr. Brown." Sonya had legally changed her name last Thursday.

He nodded, that look of patience not changing.

"I thought, with the recent attack on the refrigeration unit..." She stopped. Did she know it was an attack? Her heart knew it, she realized.

"It may have been a simple malfunction," he said.

"It wasn't."

"Are you a precog?"

She sighed. "No, but..." She saw she wasn't going to convince him. "Have you or other trackers received intelligence about any attacks?"

"Not yet," he said complacently. "But I'll take this under advisement. We are not in the business of ignoring precog feelings."

She went back into Sonya's office, retreating there. She doubted like hell if he was taking anything "under advisement."

Chapter Six

Maxine paced in the apartment she shared with Sonya. It had been their home for five months and it had never felt more like this was where they were supposed to be.

So, why was she pacing?

Because I'm furious. But exactly why I'm furious is an open question.

She stalked around the main room of the apartment in her socks, not wanting to inform the whole pack that she was agitated. She'd actually learned this trick from Sonya, who liked to pace when she felt out of sorts.

Sonya was supposed to be heading for the doctor's just about now, a human doctor who would see the pups as wholly human but could at least tell Sonya their sexes. Would they both be girls? Boys? Or one of each? Maxine found she longed for that last, but her heart simply fluttered every time she thought of having pups at all.

Still, she was angry. At Sonya. It was an uncomfortable feeling; she didn't like being mad at her mate. It was wrong to be so.

"No," she whispered, "emotions aren't wrong. They just are." That was something the counseling with Fehrna Susan had taught her. So, if anger wasn't wrong, why was she feeling it?

The answer eluded her.

She decided to call Sonya's office and find out if her mate was still there. Maybe they could puzzle this out together.

But her call went straight to Sonya's voicemail.

That wasn't like Sonya at all. She turned off her phone when she was in a meeting, but it was six-thirty.

Her appointment was at seven, part of a we-stay-late doctor's office that saw evening patients once a week. Sonya had been granted one of their coveted after-five spots.

She called Sonya's secretary, Ms. Stewart.

"Good evening, Agent Brown," Ms. Stewart said after Maxine introduced herself.

It occurred to Maxine to ask, "Why are you staying so late?" That had become Sonya's habit, but not Ms. Stewart's.

She chuckled. "I have tomorrow off and volunteered to stay, for time and a half of course, for a couple of extra hours tonight. I'll be leaving at seven."

"Is Sonya still there?"

"She is."

"Can you ring me through to Sonya's office?"

"Of c --" The secretary screamed and presumably dropped the phone because there was a loud bump. Then she screamed again.

There was a crunch. The connection went dead.

Maxine cursed. Then she called Fehrna Susan. The moment her alpha answered, Maxine said, "Something's wrong at SearchLight. Please assemble the pack. I'm headed over there, but I think Sonya's involved."

"You're sure she's still there?"

"Yes."

"All right. We'll meet you at the medical building. Assuming we'll be let in." She hung up.

Maxine headed for the door. Now, when she wasn't chewing it over, she realized why she was angry with her mate: she didn't want Sonya to spend so much time at work. And wasn't that a laugh, considering their last major argument, their only real argument, actually had been about *Maxine* spending too much time away from Sonya.

Her cell phone rang.

Without looking, she answered. "I'll be there in ten minutes, Alpha. I'm going to stay human. For now."

"Be there as soon as you can," Heidi said. "The cloud with many droplets shows the Rainbow Wolf's Head and is surrounded by a coiling and uncoiling snake."

Maxine processed that as she took the steps down to the first floor. The Rainbow Wolf's Head, all three words capitalized, was the symbol of the TruWolves. But what could the huge snake mean? And surely, the tracker she'd talked to would have mentioned the TruWolves if they were involved.

"Unless he didn't know about them," she muttered.

"What?" Heidi asked.

"Nothing. I guess…" Maxine burst out onto the street and beat feet for the SearchLight campus, which was five blocks away. She ran as fast as humanly possible, and maybe a little beyond, hoping people who saw her would just assume "quick" and not "preternatural." She remembered she was supposed to be saying something to Heidi and recollected her thoughts. "Please tell Fehrna Susan that I'm going in."

"I will. And be careful, Maxine. There are at least two of them, if not three or four."

* * *

It had been an incredibly long two weeks since all this shit began.

Sonya sighed. Thinking of the gathering of DNA samples as "shit" was *not* the best way to go about improving her mood. She should be excited. She was heading to a doctor's appointment to at last have a sonogram and know what the sexes of her two pups were.

Although could they be called pups when they'd never know the troubles or joys of shifting to lupine guise?

Her tired brain wanted to run with that debate, but she had to get going. She was expected at the doctor's at seven and it was six-thirty.

But, she couldn't quite leave the document she was looking at. It was a breakdown of the one dragon/werewolf child they'd seen so far, the one that gave the basilisks hope because one of its four forms had been a basilisk. Four guises, when most magical creatures barely managed two. At the time, Sonya had speculated that it was having so many different shapes that had killed the child. Now, however, something was bothering her about it. Something about the baby being only half werewolf, half dragon, and yet...

Her desk phone rang and she answered automatically, "Brown."

"Dr. Brown?" a familiar voice asked.

Sonya tried to figure out who it was, but she'd always been a visual person and trying to identify voices over the phone, unless she'd been on long acquaintance with them, was not her strong suit. "Yes, ma'am? How may I help you?"

"This is Antoinette."

"Oh!" Sonya felt herself blush. "I'm sorry. Is something wrong?"

"No, I just wanted to tell you..." She coughed. "This is difficult for me, going against generations of tradition, but I'm afraid without this knowledge..."

Sonya waited, her curiosity in full flower.

"You know a werewolf can be made to take its furry form after death?"

"Yes." Sonya was amazed about where this might be going. It seemed to be along the same lines she'd been thinking about, and Sonya wondered if basilisks, like some werewolves and some dragons, had telepathy. She was amazed all over again by how much the SearchLight community didn't know.

"Even half dragons and half werewolves can be turned after they're dead."

Which meant the form must already live within them. Why was Antoinette bringing this up? Sonya's pulse picked up. Was this duchess saying what she thought she was saying? That werewolves, even *half* werewolves...

Her door burst open. "Dr. Brown, I need your help. Right now."

It was the tracker, Agent Winters, who'd been assigned to watch over the med tech floor during the day.

Sonya held up a finger, asking him silently to wait.

He shook his head. "This is urgent."

Apparently, basilisks had one thing in common with dragons and werewolves: sensitive hearing. "I'll call back later." And the Duchess Antoinette was gone.

Sonya closed her eyes for a moment, knowing this further delay would probably piss off Agent Winters. But she needed to take a second or she was going to do something really stupid, like yell at a tracker.

When she had herself under control, she opened her eyes. "All right. How may I help you?"

"Dr. Brown, can I can I speak to you?" He seemed to realize, at last, that he'd interrupted something because he colored. But he offered no apology. Instead, he gestured toward the hallway.

Pain in the ass. Sonya rose, rounded her desk, and followed the tracker down to the room where the samples were kept.

"These are not to be tampered with," she said. "Each is labeled and each has been put into the computer."

"Which ones are the LGBTQ wolves?"

"There is no segregation here," she snapped.

He sighed. "Then I guess I'll just have to take everything." And he drew a thin billy club from a holster and struck her over the head with it.

She went down like a sack of flour even though she wasn't completely unconscious. The world seemed to be spinning and she threw up.

He hit her in the back, maybe with the same billy club, maybe just with his hand. It was probably only meant to make her stay down, but she felt her belly clench.

No, you don't, you bastard. You will not beat my babies out of me. She rolled away from him... and directly against someone else, who crouched and began binding her wrists. A third person seized her ankles and set about tying those as well.

She screamed.

"Too late for that," the one at her wrists said. He patted her cheek. "But --"

An alarm blared into life.

Agent Winters cursed. "Let's go. Pick her up."

She was hauled off the floor and tossed over a shoulder.

Her head was still reeling and she threw up again.

The one carrying her jostled her, hard, and complained, "Bitch puked on me."

"Keep going," Winters said.

She was carried up the stairs and out into the pouring rain.

They'll never get off campus, she thought. *Not on foot.* But that was when she was dumped into the backseat of a car.

Someone got in next to her and straightened her up so she was sitting on the seat with her wrists bound behind her back. She groaned.

Winters was looking at her as the car sped into the storm. "You'll still be doing the same work," he said soothingly. "Just for the right side."

What in the name of God did that mean?

He patted her arm, and she flinched.

Chapter Seven

Sonya had been insecurely bound to a chair. She couldn't get away while she was being watched, but she'd been affixed to the chair with bungee cords. Who the hell used bungees to make sure a victim didn't go anywhere?

Her analytical mind clicked on and answered, *Someone who doesn't expect you to run. Or thinks of you as extremely fragile. And since they took the trouble to catch you in the first place and will assume you don't want to stay, what does that leave?*

Sonya considered the relatively gentle way she'd been subdued, along with the solicitous way Winters had spoken to her. Her captors, or at least Winters, thought her weak and easily bruised. They wanted her alive for something. And they wanted her to think them, if not her benefactors, then at the very least kindly abductors.

She was confined in a small room that smelled of cleaning supplies. *I guess they didn't have a basement to store me in.* She had to smile, just a little, despite how much her head hurt. Back in the summer of last year, she'd gone down into a basement of a house in St. Petersburg, a small city/suburb outside of Tampa. She'd thought nothing of it at the time, but there were very few basements in Florida because of the low sea level and the shifting soil. How long must that basilisk renegade have searched for a basement where could keep her victims? And had she simply kept them in the house where she'd been living before she was discovered? That didn't seem likely, so a further question was, why had she dumped them all the way in Ybor City, which was in Tampa? To throw SearchLight off the trail?

By all the gods that are or ever were, why are you worrying about long-gone danger when you're right in the middle of it now?

Good question. Sonya checked her mental shields, which were depleted, and began the process of building them up. She raised them quickly, but they remained insufficient. She focused on strengthening them.

As soon as she began to concentrate, she found that her thoughts ran more smoothly and in a straight line. Something had surely been affecting them. And whether it had been the blow to her head or someone messing around in her mind didn't matter -- although the second possibility definitely gave her the creeps and made her furious at the same time. She harnessed her rage and used it as mortar as she slammed mental bricks into place.

The door to her prison opened, and she squinted as light poured in. It had been dim before, though she'd been able to make out the shadowy form of a desk. She squinted to lessen the trouble the light caused her, not caring if this made her seem more frightened or weaker or anything similar. Maybe if she could convince them she was helpless, they'd let their guard down.

Agent Winters, although surely he was just Winters now, having betrayed everything SearchLight stood for, stepped in.

Sonya tightened her control on her wandering thoughts. Being distracted was so unlike her that she was convinced someone was screwing with her mind. She frowned at Winters and waited to see what he wanted.

Another person entered the tiny room; now it was positively crowded.

Sonya was tempted to look away from them, to see her surroundings in more detail, but she held her focus. She knew this second person also. "You're one of Merle Judah's bodyguards," she said softly.

The werewolf looked guilty. "Yes, well --"

"Shut up," Winters said, but mildly. As if he didn't need to throw his weight around to get what he wanted.

He was maybe disappointed this time because the werewolf said, "But she knows who I am."

Winters sighed and spoke directly to Sonya. "Your mental shields are strong for a human."

She was possessed by an urge to wonder what kind of magical creature Winters was. This wasn't entirely useless speculation, and she chased it for about thirty seconds before she realized she was being manipulated. Again. She swore and glared at him. "What do you want?"

Merle Judah's ex-bodyguard took a swipe at her.

Sonya ducked reflexively and he laughed.

"Keep your hands off her," Winters snapped, seizing the werewolf's shoulder as if he could really restrain him.

Maybe he's something powerful. She grimaced but didn't say anything. She had a feeling, because all of Winters's attention was on the werewolf, that this was simply her mind going in the direction it had been previously led. Still, it was a viable question. "Are you a werewolf too?" Then she remembered how this self-same bodyguard had been talking about the TruWolves and she added, "You're members of the TruWolves, aren't you? Who's your new leader?"

Winters glanced at her without taking his hand off his companion. "You're quick as well as mentally gifted. Are you sure you're all human?" Then he smiled charmingly. "Forgive my inborn prejudice. I meant nothing by it. You're here to help keep the psychic wolves out of harm's way. Our future does not rely on cross-breeding and genetic experiments," He glanced at the door and then, lowering his voice, confided, "Our bosses don't actually agree with all of our values, but they agree with this much: psychic wolves do not belong in this insanity."

Sonya listened as he went into a full-on rant.

"Most of the snakes, excuse me, basilisks," he amended sarcastically, "want a genetic sample from all of the werewolves. The holier-than-thou snakes we are working with believe fully realized werewolves like me, psychic wolves, are dirt. They want to keep us out of the gene pool, which is fine with us because their experiments are bestiality. We're only working with this trio of basilisks because our short-term goals are the same: preventing psychic wolves from mixing with animals."

Sonya thought, *In this wolf's mind, I believe "animals" means dragons and non-psychic werewolves.* She nodded, and then asked, "Why do you call the basilisks your bosses, if you think they're snakes?"

"Even the humans' Christ child submitted himself to lesser beings in pursuit of a higher goal." He twitched. "Enough for now. One of the snakes is coming."

Sonya heard nothing. Even though she was convinced Winters was nucking futs, she thought someone probably was approaching because he looked abruptly nervous.

The door opened and someone who looked about Sonya's own age stepped in. She was olive-skinned like someone from Spain or Algeria. "I hope my allies are treating you well?"

She waved at the two werewolves and they stepped hastily out.

Crouching before Sonya, she made their faces level. "You will be working for the greater good, discovering why half dragons and werewolves die in infancy before they can manifest as basilisks."

"That's what I'm doing now," Sonya said carefully.

"Ah, but not quite. You're toying with their genetics, not cutting right to the chase, forcing them together for procreation."

"That's rape," Sonya blurted.

"It's standing stud," the unknown female answered. "Like horses. Natural intercourse is always preferred to in vitro fertilization."

"Except these are sentient beings."

Her captor straightened. "You're of that mind, are you? Well, after you see them through my eyes, you'll understand." And she laid a hand on Sonya's shoulder.

This time, Sonya felt her thoughts being twisted. She struggled to bring her shields up but they were knocked aside. She cried out, but this went ignored.

She witnessed the LGBTQ wolves having sex, being watched secretly and judged. Anal play was seen as a manifestation of their baseness. And when they did have sex the "normal" way, it was seen as their way of pretending to be "like basilisks and decent wolves."

Except all wolves were considered beasts. They changed into monsters that --

Sonya fought harder, managing to cry out, "You shift into monsters too."

"We are the original 'monsters,' the connection between dinosaurs and humans, the missing link that mates instinct, the best of it, with intelligence and morality."

Sonya watched the dragons laying their spawn in the sand and covering the eggs like alligators. She watched the forced sexual interaction between a dragon and werewolf she recognized. She'd performed autopsies on their remains.

"Why did the half dragon, half werewolf die?" she asked.

"Nothing conclusive."

"Half werewolves can't shift."

"Oh, but they can. Under the influence of drugs, anything is possible. And when they're older, they'll shift too if they're not told it's impossible." She sighed. "Maybe we did force their change too many times, but we were looking for the basilisk form that should have been there."

Sonya tried to hold her tongue, but a savage twist deep inside her head made her blurt, "There were four forms. The basilisk was just slower to develop. But it was very much there in the one left on my desk."

"As I said, forcing them into coitus is necessary." She stepped back, releasing her hold on Sonya's shoulder and her mind. "I was not personally involved in this groundbreaking experiment. However, the basilisk you killed shared her experiences mind to mind with me."

Holy crap, how powerful is a basilisk's telepathy?

"I can see by your face that you want to ask about our telepathy, and why we do not approve of werewolves with similar powers. It infuriates us that such beautiful talents should be relegated to the sexually deviant."

The female basilisk smiled, showing a hint of pointed teeth. "Food will be brought, although you won't be allowed to eat until you accept our way of thinking. Rest now. You've had a long, challenging day."

And Sonya was left alone.

For a while, she wasn't able to do anything but struggle not to sob. She'd been violated and she felt filthy. "God help me," she whispered.

After a little time had passed, she realized she was still confined by bungee cords and that she could free herself if she was patient. She whispered, "I can worry about being mentally raped later. Right now, I need to get out of here."

Chapter Eight

Maxine had been forced to wait for her pack, or at least Fehrna Susan, Michaela, and Heidi. Fehrna Susan and her mate because they were strong and fearless; Heidi because she, being the strongest precog they had, might actually be able to find Sonya.

SearchLight was looking too, of course, using whatever methods were at their disposal. And even though Maxine and her packmates had been encouraged not to seek Sonya's kidnappers, they weren't expressly forbidden. That was outside SearchLight's purview.

So, here they were, four werewolves in a minivan, and didn't that sound like the beginning of a bad joke? Three of them, all but Heidi, were in wolf guise. Their noses would help them find Sonya quicker once Heidi could pinpoint her location to within a few blocks.

Maxine's heart thundered in her chest and she knew one thing: if Sonya died, taking their pups with her, Maxine would be hard-pressed not to follow. She hadn't committed suicide when her first mate, Carrie, had taken her life, and what did it say that she wanted to now? That she loved Sonya more, or that she'd only had enough of living disappointments and grief?

Whichever it was, this truth remained: surviving after Sonya's death would be nearly impossible. She thought about staying in lupine guise for decades, as some grieving wolves did because the beast's feelings were simpler and a little easier to deal with.

Enough of this. I will find her alive and that's all there is to it. And if, somehow, her captors have made it so she loses the pups, I know she will have fought her hardest to keep them safe. And, moon goddess willing, they could have more.

But, oh, she wanted these pups to be all right. She wanted these twins, which had seemed like a blessing from the first, to thrive. Twins were such a rarity among werewolves that the idea of two, *two*, pups at once, was almost more than she could imagine.

She longed to see Sonya's beautiful face smiling at her, Sonya's eyes sparkling. She wanted this endless searching to be over.

And, warring with her fears was the knowledge that she would kill whoever had taken Sonya. Kill them without showing any mercy, no matter who they were or what their connections might be. They had forfeited everything when they decided not to leave Sonya alone.

She looked out the window and panted, aware that she looked very much like a huge dog enjoying a ride. She didn't care. She was watching to see if they were somewhere she recognized.

Hadn't they passed this street before? They had!

She turned her head, took a half step toward the front of the minivan, and growled low. Heidi flinched.

Fehrna Susan nipped Maxine's shoulder. Maxine swung toward her, ready to fight... and gave way when she saw the power of alpha in the other wolf's eyes. She ducked her head and then brushed a paw down her long, brown nose, asking forgiveness.

Heidi seemed to be circling and circling endlessly. But gradually, Maxine became aware that they were zeroing in on a bunch of buildings surrounded by Florida landscaping: grass and palms.

She peered out the window and recognized a local campus. A college campus. They were going to encounter humans. She shifted back to human began, hurriedly, to dress. Fehrna Susan and Michaela did the same.

"I think she's in that building with the mural of the mermaids on it," Heidi told them, "Fuck! There are two of those -- one on each end of the campus."

Maxine opened her mind, reaching with her telepathy. She probably should wait for SearchLight, but if she felt Sonya in pain or terror, all bets were off.

Behind her, through the open door of the van, she heard Fehrna Susan making the call, letting SearchLight know where their seeking had led.

"We'll wait," her alpha said. "As long as we can, anyway."

And that was when Michaela cried out and put her hands to her temples.

Maxine reached out in that distanceless and directionless way telepathy had. She sought her mate, any trace of her mate.

And felt Sonya's burning, all-encompassing rage. And, just beneath it, her shame and sense of emptiness. Something had happened to the twins. Maxine knew it as well as she knew her own name.

Following her mental sense, she began to run. And stopped, confused, when she couldn't find the path to take.

Michaela sprinted past her and Maxine went after the powerful empath. Fehrna Susan and Heidi, the latter armed with some sort of weapon, flanked her.

I'm coming, Sonya my dear. Just hang on. Just hang on.

* * *

"Will you eat?"

Sonya had been released from the bungee cords, and Winters, the one who'd freed her, had laughed ruefully and with surprising good humor when he realized she'd been about halfway through ridding herself of them. "You're not as weak as everyone thinks, are you?" he'd asked.

Now, he stood back with his hands at parade rest, watching with a small contemptuous smile on his face as the basilisk offered Sonya succulent-smelling fruit and aromatic meat.

Sonya hesitated. "You said I couldn't eat unless I joined you."

"True, but it occurred to me that you wouldn't be ready to trust us after just a little while. You need to walk among us, see what we're dealing with. Then you'll join us wholeheartedly and SearchLight won't come down on our heads because you'll gladly be here." The basilisk smiled slightly. "We'll probably get in trouble for destroying the samples and for grabbing you the way we did, but at least you won't be asking for rescue."

Sonya knew she was hungry; it was well past dinnertime and she didn't want to starve her pups. Still, she refused. What if the food was drugged? And she could not forget how casually this solicitous-sounding basilisk had shoved images into her mind. Not just images either, but ideas, which she had a feeling would be plaguing her for a long time.

Brainwashing is what it was, and brainwashing is not carried out by sane people, or people who truly want to be my friends.

The female basilisk said regretfully, "I am sorry I forced our views on you, but it was necessary. You have been raised to think of equality when what we teach is superiority."

Sonya decided to take some meat to shut her up. She chewed and quickly rebuilt her shields.

"I can demolish them in an instant. Why do you

bother erecting them? It costs you energy."

Sonya was careful to keep her mind blank as she constructed the walls that would only protect her for a few precious seconds, if even that long.

"I understand. You want the freedom to think ill of me without my overhearing. That is quite comprehensible."

Sonya took more food, fruit this time. "Thank you for feeding me," she said when she thought she could speak without giving anything away. "I sort of see where you're coming from, although I'd like to hear more about how you plan to keep the babies alive until they can turn into basilisks." She was genuinely curious about this and hoped it was evident in her voice and face.

"Well, for one thing, we're going to let things progress naturally instead of forcing changes with curare and hemlock. Those are poisons, as you may know, and they thus affect the human shape that is also within."

"So, you were not part of the initial attempt to force dragons and werewolves together?"

"I was not," she replied. "But even had I been, we were not aware of the poisonous effect on humans until recently."

There seemed to be an awful lot of gaps in the basilisk's information. Sonya asked, "Why are working with the TruWolves? I thought they were beneath you."

"It is a regrettable short-term alliance."

Sonya nodded as she looked past the female basilisk and saw that Winters was the only one who was armed. She didn't know what kind of weapon it was, with half of it hidden by his body, but she would make him her first target.

She returned her gaze quickly to the basilisk, not wanting to seem rude or distracted.

But she'd been caught, although the basilisk misunderstood. "Would you feel more comfortable if they weren't here?"

Yes and no. She needed a weapon or she'd never escape. This basilisk was acting kind, but Sonya knew basilisks were as strong as werewolves and just as fast. "No, it's all right." She stood, hoping it looked casual. She moved so she was closer to Winters but had her back to him.

And that was when Sonya struck. She whirled, moving with liquid grace and speed. Her brown belt in karate hadn't been gathering dust; she'd practiced twice a week before joining Fehrna Susan's pack and now three times a week with Heidi, with whom she'd become fast friends.

She took Winters completely by surprise. He barely had time to uncross his hands before she was on him, stealing his weapon. It was a psychic resonator, she saw, and she had time for only one thought before she turned it on him. The words came in the voice of Professor Boyle, the parapsychology professor from SearchLight Academy. "If you doubt such a weapon, it will always fail."

The other werewolf who'd been standing beside Winters knocked her a glancing blow across her side and she staggered, but this didn't affect her rage or aim. She blanketed the room with psychically driven fury.

It didn't matter that she was only human or that she didn't possess even a tenth of the basilisk's raw power. She had the advantage of surprise and the power of righteous anger. The anger came not only from her confinement but from the fear that the glancing blow she'd been dealt had hurt the pups because she could feel the ache in her ribs. She mowed all three of them down.

She didn't give a shit whether they were dead or just unconscious. Most likely, she didn't have enough energy to kill them.

She moved toward the door, hoping it was unlocked. And that was when she heard someone scream. It didn't last long.

She brought the weapon up against her right cheek, opened the door, and stepped out into the hallway.

And saw a miracle in the flesh: Maxine, in lupine guise, running toward her. Her mate's muzzle was dripping with blood.

Sonya smiled a little as she pressed her hand to her ribs. "I hope you got them all." She nodded at the room she'd just left. "These ones need to be guarded, they need to stand trial."

Maxine wagged her tail, probably to signify that she understood. Then she howled.

Soon, other wolves joined them, followed by SearchLight trackers with more psychic resonators. Sonya carefully put hers down on the tile where they could see it.

Apparently not caring if she was naked in front of the rest, Maxine turned to human. She wiped her face on her arm and then approached Sonya.

Not worried about the blood, at least not right now, Sonya went to her and fell into her arms. Safe. She was safe.

Chapter Nine

Fehrna Susan had insisted they go to the SearchLight-run hospital in Orlando. It had been a grueling journey, and Maxine knew Sonya was exhausted. She'd fallen asleep on the trip, snuggled against Maxine's furry side. Maxine had changed again, after showering, because Sonya asked her to, saying, "I feel safer with your fangs ready to rip any threat to shreds."

Fehrna Susan had done a preliminary examination before calling off of work for the rest of the day and ordering them to Orlando, where the SearchLight hospital staff could provide specialized care. She'd insisted on driving once she realized Sonya needed Maxine in her wolf likeness.

It was the middle of the night, so it didn't take as long to get to Orlando as it would have during rush hour when everyone and their brother seemed to be headed for Disney World, SeaWorld, or Universal Studios. Still, it was long enough for Sonya to get a nap in and to confess her fears to Maxine, that the glancing blow from the second werewolf guard had injured the pups.

Maxine battled her rage and fear, and also her sneaking suspicion that Sonya hadn't told her all that had happened.

They were still half an hour from the outskirts of Orlando when Fehrna Susan asked, "Sonya?"

Without raising her head from where she lay against Maxine's side, Sonya answered, "Hmm?"

"What did that basilisk bitch do to you?"

Maxine felt Sonya tense. "Nothing," she clearly lied. Then she swore. "Thanks for tricking me into…" She sighed. "Into nothing, I suppose, since I tried to lie, but I was not prepared for you to go there." She sighed again and sat up. "Look, both of you, it was a problem, but she's in custody. And I'll get to speak at her trial."

So they had been promised by the trackers who took the unconscious bodies under their protection. Maxine licked the side of Sonya's face delicately, not leaving a lot of slobber.

Sonya smiled weakly. "Okay. Fine. She forced images and ideas into my head. I have every right to be frightened and on edge."

Maxine wagged her tail and nuzzled Sonya's arm.

Sonya nodded. "I know you're with me." She glared at Fehrna Susan's back. "Okay?"

"You'll need to see a therapist. Someone outside the pack. Someone trained in psychic invasion."

Sonya grumbled but finally said, "I know. And it's not like I haven't done the counseling thing before. But I don't relish it, and I'm pissed that she fucked me up enough that I need a therapist."

Maxine considered shifting back to human so she could talk, but she glanced at Fehrna Susan, meeting her alpha's gaze briefly in the rearview mirror, and the other wolf shook her head slightly. So, Maxine nudged Sonya again and lay down so Sonya could rest against her once more.

Sonya did, burying her face in Maxine's fur momentarily. Then she sighed for the third time and turned her face so she could be heard. "It's going to be a while before I can trust anyone enough to let my shields down. At least Professor Boyle taught us how to keep them up reflexively instead of having to concentrate on them all the time."

"Tilthos Charles may be able to help you with your shields," Fehrna Susan suggested gently.

"Or Mark," Sonya added, naming the dragon who was her close friend in his own right. She nodded. "I can do this." She winced and rubbed at her ribs. "I can't tell if this is phantom pain or real."

"A sonogram will help," the alpha told her. "It will put your mind at ease."

"I don't want a CAT scan if I can avoid it. The radiation wouldn't be good for the pups."

"Agreed." Once they were in the hospital, things happened fast. Sonya was whisked into the sonogram room, Maxine was asked to change into human guise, and Fehrna Susan helped her make the transition by feeding her.

"Can't I be with her?" Maxine asked after she'd eaten a third hamburger. Shifting took a lot out of a wolf in terms of energy, and energy had to come from somewhere.

"After they've managed the first couple scans. They do have to do something about checking her ribs."

"Not a CAT scan?"

"No. There are telekinetics who are so attuned to the human body that they can feel if something's broken or deeply bruised. They feel the increased blood flow in that area and can almost see a break in their mind's eye."

Maxine knew she was sweating. "I want to be with her."

"Soon."

Maxine paced while Fehrna Susan sat quietly.

At last, fifteen minutes later according to the clock, although it seemed like much longer, Maxine and Fehrna Susan were allowed into the room where Sonya would have her sonogram.

"There was a little blood in my underwear,"

Sonya whispered as she squeezed Maxine's hand. "It wasn't much, and the telekinetic scan was negative for breaks. But I am bruised. Damn werewolf." Then she seemed to remember who she was talking to because she added, "Damn TruWolf."

Maxine relaxed just a little. She'd been afraid, she realized now, that Sonya's encounter with the TruWolves would bring up her old fears of werewolves. Maybe it had, but Sonya was obviously working to overcome any damage.

"All right," a soft-spoken nurse said as he approached the bed. "Be still as you can."

Sonya gripped Maxine's hand but didn't move otherwise.

After an interminable time, the nurse smiled. "Two healthy pups. Do you want to know their sexes?"

"Please," Sonya whispered, her grip easing.

"One of each. The male is a little larger, but nothing to write home about." He smiled. "And they're beautifully shifted."

Maxine gaped. 'They're…what?" She couldn't have heard him correctly.

He chuckled. "Shifted to wolf guise in the womb." He showed them the picture on monitor. "See? There's the male's tail and there's the female's. There are their muzzles."

"But… but werewolf pups that are half human, half anything, can't shift." This from Fehrna Susan.

The nurse chuckled again. "Have you ever performed a sonogram on a pregnant werewolf, doctor?"

The alpha shook her head. "I specialize in humans. And even though I've performed a few sonograms, it's not my area. Those were done under extreme circumstances." She laughed a little. "And as you know, werewolves don't like to be probed as a rule."

He nodded, his eyes twinkling. "I know. I also know werewolves have been told, for centuries, that they're unable to shift if they're only half wolf. They are perfectly capable of shifting, but their change is not called out by the moon, so they only shift when they are strong enough. You have a very healthy set of fraternal twins here."

Sonya asked, "Why don't they shift after birth?"

"We don't have all the answers. It may have something to do with the safety inside the mother's womb."

"You knew they could still change?" Maxine asked. "Why haven't you told the world?"

"Who would listen to a lowly sonogram tech?" He glanced at Sonya. "You don't seem surprised."

"I learned this a couple of hours ago," she admitted, grinning. "So, Maxine, can we now call one of them Fenris?"

"But..." Fehrna Susan wasn't ready to let this go apparently.

Well, and Maxine was with her!

"Why don't they shift with the first full moon?"

"That's something that's never been answered," he responded. "Maybe it's because they are only half and so not as susceptible to the moon's call. Maybe, once they're grown, they've grown up with the idea that they can't change so they never try."

Sonya laughed and the picture on the monitor jumped. "Don't worry. We'll raise our pups to believe anything is possible."

Maxine's knees buckled and she turned jerkily to plop onto the edge of the bed. "Is Sonya all right? She's not hurt?"

"Absolutely not."

"But the blood?"

"Spotting can happen. It just occurred at the wrong time, at a time that would frighten you."

Sonya groaned and rubbed her stomach.

Instantly terrified, Maxine cried, "What's wrong?"

"Nothing," the nurse answered for Sonya. "They just shifted back."

Maxine stared at the screen, seeing two tiny babies where the wolves had been.

Sonya had eased back into her pillows. "I'm hungry."

The nurse turned off the machine. "Then you should eat." He smiled gently and promised, "I'll get copies of the sonogram to you so you can keep the pictures."

* * *

About a month later, Sonya came home to the smell of shrimp frying. Her stomach growled and she strode into the kitchen. Maxine was at the stove, but she didn't seem to be cooking, just staring at the finished product.

Sonya walked behind her and hugged her close. "Hi. Thank you for cooking."

Maxine turned in the circle of her arms. "We need to talk."

"Uh-oh." Sonya smiled a little. "Did you decide Fenris is a good name after all?"

To her enormous relief, Maxine smiled. "I love you, dear." She guided Sonya into the living room and they sat on the couch. She took Sonya's hands. "You're working too much. Not too much for the health of the pups, but for our relationship's health."

Sonya opened her mouth. Shut it. "Oh, hell." She

laughed. She couldn't help herself. "I am taking on a lot, aren't I?"

"You are. I probably wouldn't have realized what it was unless I'd done exactly the same thing not six months ago."

"Not the same thing," Sonya said. "When you were running around taking care of the pack, it was harder for me because I didn't have anyone to talk to. I was all by myself most of the time, and I didn't have any friends in close proximity."

Maxine nodded. She looked chastened.

"Don't take my words for me being angry," Sonya said, kissing the back of her lover's right hand. Then she kissed the left. "Beloved, I stopped being angry at you a long time ago. I just wanted you to realize that it was different for me."

Maxine nodded. "I get it."

"Good. That being said, you're absolutely right. I need to spread the work around a little more. That's what my team is for. But work's been keeping my head away from what that basilisk did to me."

"Your therapist --"

"Is wonderful, and you've been understanding and amazing. But it's going to take me a while to get over it." She leaned forward and kissed Maxine. "I want to show you my progress."

They hadn't made love since Sonya was rescued. Mostly because of the bruising along her side but also because of that damned basilisk. Maxine's heart pounded harder. She could see the spark of lust in Sonya's eyes.

"Don't push yourself," she warned.

"I'm ready. Lovemaking first, shrimp after?"

They went to the bedroom and were both out of their clothes in a trice. Sonya was definitely starting to show; her breasts were lovely and round, her belly full and like a rising moon. Maxine went to her knees before her mate and kissed just above her navel. "You're so beautiful."

"So are you." Sonya urged her to her feet. "I want to be on top."

"Whatever my lady wants." Then she gasped when Sonya cupped her balls. "Keep doing that and you won't have a chance to get on top."

Sonya wrapped her gorgeous hand around Maxine's short, narrow length. Then she stroked. Just once.

Maxine was on the bed in moments and waiting. She touched herself, just a single time, to make sure her cock was covered in precum. Then she smiled at Sonya, who was doing the same, one finger deep inside her pussy.

Sonya mounted Maxine and settled atop her, moving until Maxine's cock was deep inside her. Then she raised herself up and lowered herself again.

The slickness and heat of her pussy was a dream. Maxine moaned. Then she remembered. "We didn't turn on any music."

Sonya laughed softly. "Oh well."

"But the pack --"

"Oh well," Sonya repeated. Then she smirked. "Can't you be quieter than usual?"

Maxine typically didn't make much noise. "What about you?" she teased.

"I'll try."

Maxine reached between them and ran the tip of her finger over Sonya's clit. "And now?"

Sonya came, hard, shuddering. But she kept her mouth shut.

She was so beautiful in the throes of her passion.

Maxine almost spilled right there.

When Sonya was breathing a little less raggedly, she began to move once more. It was glorious, the undulating of her hips and the bob of her breasts.

Need bloomed in Maxine's belly and tightened the muscles in her thighs. She groaned softly, mindful of the pack's sensitive hearing. Then she shouted in surprise when Sonya ran a fingernail over her right nipple, sending a shock of pleasure through her entire body.

"Shh." Sonya was laughing. "Shh."

Maxine came, and Sonya did likewise moments later.

Half an hour later, after they'd taken a joint shower and Maxine had brought Sonya to a third climax, they sat down to their shrimp.

"Fenris?" Sonya prodded.

Maxine snorted. "You're not going to let that go, are you?"

"You look like you've thought about it," Sonya countered.

"I have," Maxine admitted. "If I can name the female pup Riley, you can name her brother Fenris."

"Why Riley?"

"Because it came to me in a dream?" It actually had, but she'd decided to make that a joke.

"Why Riley?" she asked again.

"Because it means courageous and we'll be courageous parents, raising the first two half werewolves who'll be able to take their lupine guises."

"Just raising twins is courageous." Sonya kissed Maxine. "Riley it is."

Dedication

To my wonderful friend Lisa, with whom I have shared many excellent years. Thank you so much for making the publishing of this book a reality.

Emily Carrington

Emily Carrington is a multipublished author of male/male and transgender erotica. Seeking a world made of equality, she created SearchLight to live out her dreams. But even SearchLight has its problems, and Emily is looking forward to working all of these out with a host of characters from dragons and genies to psychic vampires.

Fantasy creatures not your thing? Emily has also created a contemporary romance world, called Sticks and Stones, where she explores being "different" in a small town.

Emily at Changeling: changelingpress.com/emily-carrington-a-207

Changeling Press E-Books

More Sci-Fi, Fantasy, Paranormal, and BDSM adventures available in e-book format for immediate download at ChangelingPress.com -- Werewolves, Vampires, Dragons, Shapeshifters and more -- Erotic Tales from the edge of your imagination.

What are E-Books?

E-books, or electronic books, are books designed to be read in digital format -- on your desktop or laptop computer, notebook, tablet, Smart Phone, or any electronic e-book reader.

Where can I get Changeling Press E-Books?

Changeling Press e-books are available at ChangelingPress.com, Amazon, Apple Books, Barnes & Noble, and Kobo/Walmart.

Changeling Press, LLC

ChangelingPress.com